SAVAGE SANCTUARY

CROWNE POINT
BOOK 5

MARY CATHERINE GEBHARD

UNGLUED BOOKS

Line editing by James Gallagher of Evident Ink
Proof Reading by Rumi

Savage Sanctuary
ISBN-13: 978-1-952808-07-4
An Unglued Books Publication
www.MaryGebhard.com

For the girls who wished the monster under the bed would eat them.

ONE

GEMMA

When I was a little girl, my friends used to dream of meeting their Prince Charming. I dreamed of meeting the guy who would ruin me. As we grew up, their dreams became less about pumpkins and glass slippers, and more about Lambos and Manolo Blahniks.

Mine never changed.

I knew a love like that couldn't exist, one not sprung from my dreams, but my nightmares.

Until I met him.

"Gemma." My friend Blaire waved a freshly manicured hand in my face. "Earth to Gemma. You've been zoned out, like, all night. Did you already take something?"

"It's rude not to share, Gemma," my other friend Kennedy pointed out.

"Says the girl who kept the year eleven test answers to herself," I said.

We were at the Underworld, the hottest club on the

East Coast, and also the one place in Crowne Point where no paparazzi could reach us. Our private booth was shaped like a horseshoe and the center of the table was filled with a bucket of ice, more Dom than we'd ever drink, and truffle fries. Beyond us, the dance floor undulated with bodies.

"Yeah! I bombed that test," Blaire said, indignant through a mouthful of fries she would later purge. "My dad had to buy a new wing so I didn't fucking fail."

"Did you sleep with Mr. Larsen?" Kennedy rounded on Blaire. "No? Then shut the fuck up."

"Dude, what?" I started laughing. "He was, like, seventy."

Kennedy chucked one of Blaire's fries at our heads. "He was a very young-looking fifty—oh my God, shut up, shut up! They're *here*."

"No way," Blaire said without looking up from her phone. "They're never here."

As she spoke, our gazes drifted up to the balcony through confetti falling like glitter. Their backs were to the club, and the magenta light from the dance floor illuminated them like shadows of hell. The four boys who owned this club, who ruled everything criminal in Crowne Point.

The Horsemen.

Blaire coughed on her fries. "Holy shit, all *four* of them?"

"What goes on up there?" Kennedy whispered.

"I heard they torture people, that's why the music is so loud," Blaire said.

My phone vibrated for the one hundredth time of the night.

"Is it seriously your mom again?" Blaire asked. "Since when does she give a shit?"

"Since our world imploded." I rolled my eyes. My

mother didn't used to be so...*involved*. We had a nice deal going. As long as I was who every girl wanted to be and who every boy wanted to fuck, she left me alone.

But then, in an instant, my brother dissolved a marriage my mother had been planning since I was thirteen. For Tansy Crowne, there was no greater achievement than marrying someone of status. Which meant all her time—and mine—was focused on finding that someone. For all her class and subversion, my mother had all but hired a skywriter: *Gemma Crowne Desperately in Need of Dick.*

"Do you really think they murder people?" Kennedy asked, drawing our attention back to the four boys lurking above us.

"They're just a bunch of burn-out druggie losers from the townie school—no offense, Gemma." Blaire swiped the powder beneath her nose and grimaced at me, the girl whose grandfather made her drop out of our boarding school to go to said townie school. "This whole town is so without culture they have to invent weird cults."

"I'm starting to come down," I groaned, rubbing my temples.

"I still have bars!" Blaire said. "And powder!"

"I have crystal—"

"No one wants your *meth*, Kennedy," Blaire said, cutting her off. "When your fucking teeth fall out, we're not gonna be nice about it."

My friends littered pills and lined up powder on the sparkly black table as a server approached with a drink.

"We didn't order anything," I said, waving him away. There was always some guy who thought buying *the* Gemma Crowne a twelve-dollar drink meant I'd want to hop in his pants.

When I reached to grab a xanny, the tray was placed in my path.

The tray was exactly like the rest, except that glittering rubies cut like pomegranates were sprinkled along the circumference. My phone vibrated again, two words bright on the screen.

You're late.

"Oh my God!" Kennedy exclaimed. "He's looking down."

"Who?" Blaire asked.

"The Reaper."

My gaze shifted again to the four shadows looming over the club. One had put his elbows on the railing, leaning just a little bit forward. He took a puff of something, probably weed—he hated cigarettes—eyes narrowing on me.

A bang louder than a gunshot sounded and more glitter fell from the ceiling.

I shot out of the leather couch. "I...gotta pee."

Glitter fell like sparkling rain while a slow, upbeat rhythm thrummed. I wove through faceless grinding bodies.

I didn't really have a plan.

Just had to move.

Postpone the inevitable, I guess.

I settled into a shadowy corner, my back to the club, but knew I was being watched. Because even the people who frequented the upper deck didn't know this club's true nature. Like the cameras placed strategically, recording their every move, to later be used as blackmail if necessary.

I eyed one in the black chandelier—

"The Reaper's girl down here without the Reaper?"

You don't grow up in Crowne Point without hearing the smoky rumors of what happened when the Horsemen claimed their girl.

But that wasn't me, and it never would be.

Something was different about this guy. Different from all the other guys holding whatever brand of whiskey was in vogue now, chatting up every girl who would listen, playing the numbers game.

He was older, maybe late forties, early fifties, with salt-and-pepper hair. He was smoking weed openly, and he didn't even glance up from his phone. Like calling me out as belonging to the Underworld's most notorious was just like saying *hey*.

I was also pretty sure the two men in charcoal-gray suits just off to the side were not here to party, but packing heat.

I stepped to him. "You afraid?"

He took a puff of his joint, still not looking up from his phone.

The man kept ignoring me, so I plucked the joint from his hand. He raised a hand as one of his guards took a step toward me. The guard stilled.

"I'm not here for you."

Who are you here for?

"Oh, but you could be." I took a deep draw of smoke into my lungs, relishing the hazy peace that soon followed.

There's something wrong with me.

Mentally.

Emotionally.

Soul deep.

A horrible hurricane hit Crowne Point a year after my father's death. I remember it as the only time my mother hugged me—us. She wrapped all of us together in a blanket down in the servants' quarters as the wind slammed against the wall.

My mother said things under her breath that night.

Things I'd never heard her utter before or since. About God. About her love, for *us*.

I remember not being afraid.

I was *excited*.

The chaos of the wind had fed something inside me. The morning after, I walked among the ruins. Wind had ripped off the black shingles of Crowne Hall and the facade was broken toothed. Branches lay scattered among the beach and blocked Main Street and I felt...peace.

Not just for the first time since my father's death—for the first time in my life.

Among the desolation and devastation, I took a big breath of the brackish after-storm air. The smell of something new, rebirth that comes only after something terrible.

I remember thinking then I wasn't normal. Everyone else had wrinkles in their brows, and I was smiling. I eventually found a facsimile of that peace...in pills. And one night, I tasted the real thing again—in *him*.

But it was so small, so brief, it had been like a drop of wine in the ocean.

Hot and Scary Older Guy, heretofore known as HSOG, slowly lifted his head, eyes locking with mine. "Didn't your mother teach you not to play with fire?"

"My mother taught me not to look under the bed for monsters. I guess that made me want to look more."

HSOG laughed, *hard*, and put his hands in his pockets. "Do you know who I am?"

I blew smoke in his face. "Someone scary?"

He laughed again. I got close to him, until I could taste the musky smoke on his lips—and was promptly yanked back and behind a wall of muscle.

Two out of the four Horsemen.

"This one is off limits," the first one spoke.

"She belongs to us," the second added.

Behind me spoke a third. "Unfortunately."

I'd recognize that low voice anywhere.

Grim Reyes.

The king of the Underworld and leader of the Horsemen. The man who didn't want my soul but held it hostage anyway—the Reaper.

TWO

GEMMA

"Off limits...I don't see a tattoo on her." HSOG's eyes glittered at me through a slit in the wall of muscle. "The Reaper really hasn't claimed this girl?"

"The Reaper has no girl," Grim said. "Will never have one."

He was too close. All he had to do was take a step and his breath would be on my neck.

"It's true." I beamed at the mystery guy. "You can kill me, fuck me, do both at the same time, nothing's gonna happen but a good time."

HSOG laughed, tilting his head with a smile. "That so?"

Grim moved closer to me, his heat soaking into my back. A hot, menacing shadow taunting me to turn around.

"Off fucking limits." Grim's voice took on a smoky quality, one I only ever heard when he was about to go off the edge. My gut tightened.

A flash of something like fury clouded HSOG's eyes. "Unmarked, unclaimed, not off limits. You'd do well to remember that."

And then he left.

"You forget who owns you?" Grim's lips barely grazed my ear and I jumped, immediately hating that I'd given him that response.

"You don't have any say in who I fuck," I gritted out, still refusing to turn around.

"I don't give a shit what you put in your cunt." Grim's voice got lower, smokier. "This is business."

My ears perked. *Business?* The two Horsemen in front of me turned around—Hemlock and Raze.

"Funny, she doesn't look dead," Lock mused, voice light.

If all Horsemen were named after the four of the Apocalypse, Hemlock, named after the beautiful but deadly flower, would have been Conquest—but he practiced a different kind than the myth. A cruel playboy with a deadly charm, too many had fallen into his trap.

There was a reason girls went wild over the Horsemen, even if they were all soulless.

"Only good reason I can think of for why she's missed two check-ins and is late to the third," Raze added.

Raze was easily War, but he could have been a K-pop idol—if not for the tattoos, and the whole *look at me the wrong way and I might fucking cut you* vibe. He had the luscious lips, the perfect dewy skin. Messy hair that fell over apathetic eyes.

I looked to the side. "I was busy."

Grim's unamused, cold laugh pressed against my back.

The last was missing—but I know he was around somewhere, watching. There was a reason he was called Wraith. He was only ever seen shortly before your death. Some said he didn't even exist. But that was a lie. Wraith served a very special, very cruel function within the Horsemen, and smart people feared him more than Grim.

Like the Horseman Wraith must wear on his back, he decimated lives and left nothing but waste behind. You'd have to be truly insane to take a contract from him.

Only Grim was named after the Horseman inked on his back.

"There isn't anything to tell you. Nothing to check in about. Have you heard the saying, this coulda been an email?"

"You don't get it, Rich Girl." A soft touch—Grim's palm —landed on my exposed shoulder, and I instantly regretted wearing a strapless dress. Traitorous goose bumps followed his hand.

Grim's fingertips traveled the expanse of my shoulder to my collarbone, until we were face-to-face. Thumbs slowly slid into place on either side of my neck. The air soft and heavy with our breathing.

Bored.

He looked so fucking bored.

That always twisted me up. Like I was nothing. The world looked at me like I was precious; Grim looked at me like I was dirt.

"I own you. I own the blood that beats outta your heart. I own the thoughts you think. I own those hot breaths you take when I get too close. The ones you think I don't notice."

I bit the inside of my cheek, hating that he noticed.

Hating that I gave him that.

His hand slid around my neck, to the nape.

"Or what?" I leaned in. "You gonna kill me?"

A slight smile.

A dangerous smile.

That gentle touch at the back of my neck turned vicious, bruising. His eyes dark, cold.

"I think you know *what*, Gemma."

He stepped back, wiping his hands on his jeans like I was dirty.

When you're indebted to the Horsemen, you sign your life away until the contract is fulfilled. Each contract was different, tailored to the person, but one thing remained the same: you did whatever they demanded, laws and morals be damned, until your term was up. If you didn't? Death was the least of your problems.

But five years ago I didn't get that choice.

I didn't sign shit. I didn't *choose* shit.

The Reaper decided he wanted me, so he took me.

Grim pulled my chin between his thumb and forefinger, forcing me to meet his black stare. "What's the deal, Rich Girl?"

I had every intention of pushing him off, but then that thing happened, that *Grim* thing. Where I couldn't breathe. All I saw was the gleam in his eyes, like he could see the skip in my heartbeat as if he'd thrown the stone that put it there.

"My life belongs to you...my death is yours to take."

THREE

GEMMA

Five years ago I fell underwater and never came up. I live in a place no one can imagine exists, all the while walking side by side with them as Gemma Crowne.

I live in the Underworld.

I live on borrowed time.

In my time being enslaved to the Reaper, I've done many dark deeds to pay off my dark debt. I made my sister think I slept with the love of her life, so I could get his journal and give it to Grim.

At the time I didn't know why Grim wanted it. Now I knew it was to blackmail a politician.

I've given them information on my grandfather, on Crowne family finances.

I've stolen from my friends' houses.

I've done so many things, I've lost count. Grim asked, I delivered. My soul was already shadowed, now it was oily and tainted. The dirty truth? None of these things fazed me in the slightest. I actually...*liked* doing it. It added sparks of color into my numb, gray life—

My double doors flew open, and along with them came a flurry of people and cameras. I shrieked, pulling my covers over my head, assuming there was some kind of *serious* lapse in security at Crowne Hall, when the unmistakably soft and sonorous voice of Tansy Crowne came.

"*Here* she is!" my mother said. "You were supposed be downstairs an hour ago—" She broke off, covering her lips with her always-nude manicured hand.

"Mom?" I peeled the covers past my nose. "What the hell?"

My mother waved an outstretched hand in my direction. A murder of aestheticians descended. They pulled me out of bed, tugged at my shirt, assessed my fingernails.

I winced as someone pulled my hair.

A camera flashed in my face and I shoved everyone away. "Get off!"

"Gemma *Antionette!*"

Antionette.

Like so many of her other hopes and dreams, I was the lucky Crowne who got to carry my mother's name.

I had just committed one of Tansy Crowne's unforgivable sins: uncontrolled displays of emotion. I quickly composed myself and when I spoke next my voice was level and clear.

"What's going on?"

She exhaled, rubbing the muscle between the wrinkle in her brow she'd long since Botoxed away. "*The heirloom exhibit.*"

Oh, right.

It was a little more than a month until Valentine's Day and this year Valentine's Day happened to also coincide with the two hundredth anniversary of the founding of Crowne Hall. To my mother, that meant parties on top of parties leading up to the main event. As if celebrating the moment our ancestors descended like a plague on this small town would make everyone forget about the very real present.

Thus entered the heirloom exhibit, where our family artifacts, antiques, and relics were displayed as "Treasures of Crowne Point."

"Gemma, are you unwell?"

Which was Crowne for *Are you high as balls right now, lady?*

"Of course not." I lifted my sheets off, feet colliding with soft white carpet, and followed the team of aestheticians to my vanity. "Just a little sleepy, is all."

The makeup artist held up two different shades of lipstick against my skin. The hairstylist lifted my hair, head tilting like she was trying to imagine the book she was reading. It was time for me to be the perfect porcelain doll for someone else to paint. While someone lifted my hand to check the polish, my eyes drifted over my vanity to the window.

On a clear day, you could see far enough down the beach to the Wharf, the abandoned carnival pier that the Horsemen had turned into their infamous club, Underworld. It was unusually dark and stormy, even for January, the beach shadowed under velvety clouds, the horizon engulfed in black.

Down on the blustering sand, vendors rushed to clear tables and decorations before the rain hit—a reminder that it was nearly time for *Gemma Crowne, America's Princess*, to make her first appearance since the dramatic cancellation of her more-than-decade-long engagement.

Heirlooms and priceless artifacts were being set up for public consumption, but the real artifact was me. I was to behave like a good little Crowne family trinket for potential buyers.

"Stop picking your lip." My mother slapped my hand. "Your lip gloss won't sit well."

I yanked my stinging hand away from my mouth, finding the sharp eyes of Tansy Crowne.

My mother replaced the hairdresser at my back, distorted in the mirror, head cut off at the neck, hands gripping the back of my chair. "There is a slew of eligible bachelors downstairs. Diplomats. Princes. Heirs..."

The Crowne family had once been the most powerful in the world. We were known for elaborate, insanely luxurious parties that even kings begged to attend. In order to keep our status, we married who we were told.

Then my sister abandoned us for her bodyguard, my brother fell in love with a servant, and my grandfather went to prison. My brother replaced him as CEO, and now Crowne Hall, once known for its draconian rules, was... modern. Servants who used to get punished for looking us in the eyes now got maternity leave and Christmas bonuses.

To say my mother was having a hard time adjusting to the new status quo was an understatement.

I stared at my reflection in the mirror as my mother droned on about the dying star of the family Crowne. This was the Gemma Crowne who sold magazines, the one they called America's Princess.

Famous Crowne blue eyes, a little more wintry and baby blue than my brother's. Rose gold hair that fell just below my chin. A perfect—and well-paid-for—button nose. Expertly arched brows, golden tan, freckles that were the bane of my mother's existence, always hidden behind makeup.

I stared so long my face blurred into nothing.

"I was already pregnant with my last child at your age. Head of a great house. Rubbing elbows with kings and dignitaries..."

I wanted to scream, but I had to stay still as my lip gloss was applied. Not like I *wanted* to be in this position.

"Not that one," my mother spoke, turning her attention to a woman holding a dress. "The Russo."

I slid into a soft pink gown that was both effortless and expensive. My mother assessed me like her polished silver. With a curt nod of approval, the flurry of people departed.

For a finishing touch, my mother handed me a pair of pale-pink flats embroidered with tiny seed pearls. Hand-made, almost two hundred years old, and dating back to the first Crowne girl to marry into wealth—a famous ballerina.

I slid my feet into the shoes, and my mom returned her attention to me. "Happily ever afters don't exist, Gemma—"

"I should look for opportunity," I said, ending the adage she'd been telling me since I'd been old enough to listen.

For as long as I could remember, I'd had my life planned for me. I had been betrothed from the moment I turned thirteen. I wasn't like my sister or my brother, I never made a fuss about it. Like the perfect daughter I was, I accepted it.

My ex-fiancé, Horace, had been more boring than wet bread, not the love of my life by any stretch, but he was safety. With him, my life had been on autopilot and I didn't have to worry about crashing. There was something inside me that I didn't understand. I didn't know how to control it, how to tame it. And now for the first time in my life, I had freedom to choose.

Freedom to crash.

FOUR

GEMMA

Under a ceiling dripping with Swarovski crystals designed to look like stars, I lingered among the glitterati, smiled for photos, swiveled and laughed with socialites. *Smile. Laugh. Pose.* No longer Gemma, but *Gemma Crowne, America's Princess.*

One by one, men approached. In the back of my mind I heard the nasally, rapid-fire drawl of the auctioneer: *Ding ding, step right up, America's Princess is for sale.* I gave them my Gemma Crowne smile, my head a mental Rolodex of information my mother had stocked.

He's from old money.

He's from new money.

He's broke—but royal—and looking to marry into money.

Sure, he's old, but he's too old to expect sex and his family line goes back to the Stuarts.

I was careful with my responses—crafted.

Every word I spoke a headline.

Every photo a potential to go viral.

I had perfected this. The ability to be present and disappear at the same time.

The storm outside had broken, no longer raining a sheet of metal. My mother had already commented on how it had fucked up the valet—not in so many words. To her horror, people would have to fetch their own cars. It was now softly drizzling. Far away lightning crashed into the black ocean waves.

My eyes drifted to some old and famous rug my mother had hung for display, and the two girls staring at it, pretending to care. Blaire's curly black hair was done up in diamonds. The hair that Kennedy colored weekly, and that gained her millions of followers, was dyed a soft pastel pink and straightened down to her waist. She'd toned down some of the e-girl look that made her famous, a piercing removed from her nostril, the pink in her hair made more acceptable by a headband.

They saw me and pushed their tongues into their cheeks, mimicking a blow job.

I laughed.

"Gemma?"

Oh. Right.

I blinked back into the dead eyes of some...tech mogul? I don't know. He was explaining crypto to me. Guess what he'd said wasn't supposed to be funny.

Oops.

"So...you were saying I should invest in Bitcoin, because it's more established or something?" I twirled the yellow diamond pendant at my throat. "Altcoins are too volatile for someone like me?"

"Uh-huh." His eyes dropped to it, to my neckline and

the subtle cleavage designed to catch attention without being obvious.

"Hmm...but what about staking? Or are you just, like, holding your coins?"

His eyes grew, coming back to mine.

Bad Gemma. Tansy Rule #1: Let them be smarter.

"Uh..." He rubbed the back of his neck. "I'm gonna get a drink."

I watched him walk away, still playing with the pendant. Noticing a lull in the meat market, Kennedy and Blaire beckoned me to them. Kennedy raised a small bag with candy-colored pills into the air, just as someone stepped before me, blocking them. Brown hair, green eyes—he was like every other man here with the same arrogant, self-important countenance.

"Gemma."

My name slid oily from his lips. I knew him as one of my brother's friends—or, I guess, ex-friend. Gray hadn't been seen with any of his old friends since finding his wife, Story.

This man was old-school. Which meant he had a reputation for harassing and assaulting women, but his bank account still had enough zeros in it. He'd always watched me unabashed and lecherous, but I'd been with Horace. He might not respect a woman, but he respected a man's claim to her.

"Geoff." I plastered on a smile.

"Gemma Crowne finally on the market."

I ignored the nausea in my gut and demurred. "Surprised you're still on said market."

Barf.

He grinned at my compliment. "I've waited a long time to try such famous pussy."

I let my smile drop. "Oh dear, my mother is calling for me—"

He grabbed my arm as I tried to leave.

The smile on his face hadn't moved, but now his eyes dripped something mean. "You know, I'd be doing you a favor fucking you. Isn't that what all this is for?" With his free hand, he gestured at the party. "Whore you out so your name means something again?"

That hurricane feeling slid into my veins. America's Princess is supposed to play dumb at blatant disrespect, bat her eyelashes if a man held his hand up to hit her.

It was getting harder to play the role.

I laughed. "I think you have severely overestimated your dick's social capital."

Sharp pain spiraled out from where his fingers pushed white into my skin.

"Don't be a bitch," he hissed.

"Geoff!" Kennedy appeared, behind her Blaire. "I didn't know you were coming." Geoff let me go, but not before giving an extra-sharp squeeze.

"I haven't seen you since you totaled the first daughter's car," Blaire added. "I thought you were shipped off to some black ops island." Blaire and Kennedy discreetly stepped between Geoff and me, peppering him with questions.

Bruises had started to form where he'd gripped, purple spots snaking up my arm like a delicate lace sleeve.

The girls eyed my arm out of the corner of their eyes. They didn't ask what happened—they wouldn't. He was old-school, after all.

"And was that your Koenigsegg wrapped in fucking pink glitter?" Kennedy asked. Blaire and Kennedy moved closer together, forming a glittery, haute couture wall.

"Yeah," he said. "Lost a bet."

As my friends talked to Geoff about simple, plastic things like covering a four-million-dollar car in glitter, I took the opportunity to slip away.

No one was outside, the sky still too black and swollen. Wet wind whipped my hair, and the lingering storm made the tea lights sway on their strings. My mother always insisted on using real candles in imported French votives, which meant the fire had long since been snuffed. All that remained were shadows with edges that shivered like some virile, organic thing.

I walked until waves crashed on the sand. Water kissed the tips of my satin flats before sliding back to the sea. I lit a cigarette, staring at the black void.

With his back to me, he ripped off his soaking black shirt. The Reaper's emblem, inky and black, shining from the salty ocean water, rippled across his shoulder blades and dripped down his muscles.

A horse.

A skull.

A scythe.

A warning to me—a warning to anyone who saw it. You don't see a Horseman's emblem and live to tell the tale.

He spun, eyes ravenous.

I rubbed my temples. Not now. Not this memory. Salty sea drenched the ends of my dress, staining the pink silk.

The first and last time I ever kissed Grim was a night like this, the night I tried to kill myself. He dragged me from the ocean, and I woke to him giving me CPR. Water dripped from his inky-black hair, down his full lips. There was a look in his eyes that didn't make sense. We didn't know each other. We'd met *once*—barely.

He didn't take me to the hospital or call for help. He fucked me. On the wet sand. Moments after ripping me from the waves. With the cold ocean dragging at our ankles, salt stinging cuts on my skin.

I would never forget the wildness in his eyes. The fever in his touch. He fucked me like he was mad—like he wanted to heal me, so he could then steal back the life he breathed into me.

I think people might say it was wrong, because I was vulnerable. Weak. That wasn't wrong but...it wasn't *right* either. He didn't heal me. I didn't suddenly walk away all happy and shit, like his perfect dick had healed my broken soul.

Maybe that was why it happened. Why he'd shown up with the tattoo. Why my soul became so twisted in his. Because he did breathe life into me, for a few hours on that beach.

I still didn't know why or how he'd found me that night. Why he wouldn't let go...what he *wanted*. I wasn't foolish enough to believe he loved me or even *liked* me.

My cigarette whispered fingerlings of smoke into the air. I watched it tango with the clouds in the sky when I heard the muted brush of sand beneath shoes. I turned around, expecting one of the girls, and instead met a man. He was just under six feet, with snow-white hair.

I had no second to react before he wrapped his hands around my throat. My cigarette fell burning to the sand.

I held his wrists, my mouth parting, and soon all thoughts faded as his thumbs pressed deeper into my throat. My body relaxed.

This wasn't a bad day to die.

My mom might find my body, and I'd give her some trauma. That thought would have made me laugh if my throat wasn't being crushed.

Suddenly he stopped choking me, eyes wide and frozen.

A wet, surprised-sounding gurgle slipped from his lips, followed by a cough of blood. I closed my eyes against the wet spray.

Ew.

His whole body went slack, and he fell to the ground.

In his place a shadow of a person stood, knife in hand.

Dripping blood.

Grim.

FIVE

GEMMA

"Who was he, Gemma?" Grim asked, staring at the foggy ocean waves. His voice betrayed no emotion, but the muscle in his neck flexed, making the tattoos there jump threateningly.

"Who?"

"The guy I just killed." Grim's mouth was set in a flat line, pearly black eyes staring out at the ocean.

I glanced down at the body lying gracelessly in the sand. In the night, blood stained the achromatic sand black. Specks of blood stained my heirloom flats, red seeping into the two-hundred-year-old silk.

I looked back to Grim. "How would I know?"

I knew better than to ask or even question how Grim had gotten inside Crowne Hall, a place more heavily guarded than the White House. He was always like carbon monoxide, sliding in without detection until it was too late.

"Wanna try that answer again?" Behind him, feathery

black clouds swallowed the white moon, snuffing what little light we had. He turned to me, the slightest hint of irritation on his lips.

Oh, so he doesn't want to play the game he *started?*

Whatever.

"You can always let them kill me." I shrugged. "You're not supposed to be saving me, *Reaper.*"

I saw a flash of some emotion in his eyes, briefly, before Grim bent down, ripping the shoes off my feet. He pulled my leg up and I teetered, forced to hop on one foot and grab his shoulder. But when he ripped the other shoe off, I fell to my ass.

Grim threw my shoes into the ocean. The pink satin bobbed up and down with the black current, until the pearly tips disappeared beneath the ink.

Silence settled. Grim wasn't someone who talked to fill in the silence. He didn't feel discomfort, he created it. It made the moments when he spoke so fucking addicting.

My gaze shifted to the thick veins and sinewy muscles on his forearm, to the tattoo of a skeleton hand holding a dead rose.

A wicker branch peeking out of the sleeve of his bicep.

My family's seal on his wrist.

All with a single, haphazard line drawn through them.

Tattoos—*contracts.* Horsemen didn't take contracts lightly, because their reputation, their livelihood, their very existence, depended on them. When a line was drawn through the tattoo, the contract was complete.

My eyes wandered back to his chest, where beneath soft black fabric scratch marks lay etched on his left pectoral. His one unmarked tattoo, his one unfinished debt—*me.*

Lines that bound us and said my soul belonged to his forever. A tattoo he'd gotten because of me.

For me.

In *spite* of me.

"Do the rest of your Horsemen know you're here?" I stood back up, brushing sand off my dress, and laughed when he looked to the side. "Uh-oh. Guess I'm not the only one breaking rules. Bad things happen when they're not around to watch—"

He gripped my chin, bruising. "Piss off another monster and I'm letting it drag you under the bed."

"No, you won't." I angled my chin into his grip, smiling. "You want to be the one dragging me under too badly."

His eyes dropped to my mouth, in the dark depths some kind of emotion burning that was too real for the game we played.

Danger, some small part me whispered.

Instinctively, I took a step back when Grim grabbed me, cutting off my train of thought, and tore one sleeve of my dress down, stretching the gown until it hung limp on my bicep. His lips crashed against my neck, sucking hard, making his own marks where the man's thumbs had been.

He was entirely unaffected. As if I was a chore. As if stopping monsters from getting me was the same as vacuuming.

I swallowed my gasp, trying to appear as bored as him, but with each swipe of his tongue my legs turned to jelly.

Then as quickly as he started, he stopped. His eyes pulsed, lips wet.

"Where were you, Gemma?" he asked, emotionless.

I took a deep, stuttering breath, feeling like the salty night breeze could topple me if not for his grip on my bicep.

But I knew the answer he wanted.

"With a boy," I rasped. "I don't remember his name. Someone from the party."

He didn't release me right away, tracing his knuckles from my neck down to my elbow. He paused when he reached the marks Geoff had left. For a single moment, shorter than it took a drop of rain to hit the ocean, Grim's mask dropped.

There was more than anger in his eyes. It was fury—*possession*—and it curled around my gut like a wire. As quickly as it came, it left, and Grim stepped away.

He nodded toward the house at my back. "Go."

And just like that, we fell into our game. Tomorrow we would pretend none of this happened. I would go back to being Gemma Crowne, and he would be the reaper who owned my soul.

SIX

GRIM

It wasn't my and Gemma's first dead body—our love story was littered with them.

Gemma hadn't left the beach, her body a silhouette against the moonlit sky. Despite ordering her to leave, she stayed to watch me dispose of the body. My shoulder blades were still tense from that small act of defiance.

The Crowne party continued as shadows danced against the drapes. I eyed the blood still crusted on my hands.

Contrary to the Horseman on my back, this was not my job.

I don't do this.

Wraith was the one who made and disposed of bodies. But if I called on Wraith, I'd have to tell him everything. So I'd done what I always did with Gemma's monsters—fed them to the sea.

My phone vibrated—the Horsemen.

Fuck.

I picked up the call. "What?"

"Where the fuck are you?" Lock asked.

My gaze traveled beyond the mansion's inky-black shingles to the beach, where Gemma was starting to move.

"Busy," I said.

"White Privilege Barbie is becoming a fucking problem," Raze said. "You seen her?"

I eyed Gemma's shadow. "Nah."

"This is why I should have put a tracker in her," Wraith growled. "This is bullshit."

"She—" I started, only to be cut off by a *tap, tap, tap.*

A frat-boy-looking motherfucker with green eyes fogged my window with his mouth. Behind him, a pink sports car glittered on the cobblestone driveway.

"Bro." Frat Boy tapped my window again. Behind the tempered-glass window, his voice softened as if underwater.

I muted the phone and rolled the window down just enough to see green eyes, red with weed.

Frat Boy laid his arm on my hood. "You're blocking me—"

I snaked my hand through the sliver of space in the window, grasping his collar and slamming him against the glass. A thin trail of blood smeared a line down the window as he fell to the ground.

I got out of my car.

"Starting to hear a lot of rumors around this, man," Lock continued. "People saying we're weak, that we don't enforce contracts."

"Dude," Raze added on the call. "Sometimes I think she *wants* us to kill her."

I nearly laughed.

If they only fucking knew.

I stepped on either side of him, staring down. "You should really learn to keep your hands to yourself."

"Word on the street is that she's off limits," Raze continued. "They're saying she's the fucking Reaper's girl."

I nearly laughed at that. Gemma *Crowne* would never give up her sparkly, perfect life.

Not that I'd let her if she tried.

"They say we're killing people who mess with her," Lock cut in.

I unmuted. "They also think we do weird sex stuff in the dungeon together."

I bent over the asshole, bored. The cobblestone was wet with leftover rain, the reflection of my car's headlights smeared and blinding. Blood poured in the slits between his fingers as he held his nose. "*I'm sorry,*" he said, voice quiet and muffled.

Good.

He'd touched what wasn't his.

"We can't keep this contract. When you took her ink on your chest, you said it would be worth it."

I've only told one lie to my brothers, five years ago, the day I took Gemma's contract. They didn't know what really happened on that beach, or the promise I'd made to Gemma.

They didn't know she never asked for this. They didn't know I forced it on her—forced all of us into this. They definitely didn't know Gemma's response to being forced into this was to make a game out of making monsters mad, of forcing me to choose to save her or let her die.

Every body became another secret, another lie to tell.

"It's been five years," Raze added. "This contract is fucking *us*."

The asshole at my feet continued to slither backward,

crying and begging. I paused, finding Gemma's silhouette again.

The first time I met Gemma was back in high school, in a nearly abandoned storage room that I used to smoke. She didn't know I was there. The door opened and slammed shut just as I was about to light a joint, and then the tears started. I froze with the lighter in my hand, listening. When I saw her one-of-a-kind pink Vans, I knew it was Gemma Crowne.

I don't know why I'd stayed. At first I was pissed I couldn't smoke. But the longer I leaned on the other side, listening to her cry with the lights off, the less angry I was. Through the slats in the books, I watched her rip apart her manicure, picking off hot-pink flakes like she was on a mission.

I didn't plan to let her know I was there. Gemma Crowne was pretty much the last person I wanted to know.

Then I leaned too hard and a book fell.

"Who the fuck is there?" she'd sniffed.

I heard her shuffling to stand, so I came around. Gemma froze when she saw me, still on her knees. *Shit.* That memory was burned, tattooed, etched in all my neurons.

She was so vulnerable.

So broken.

So fucking beautiful.

What happened next was what always happened with us.

Instinct.

I smeared the black mascara under her eyes, marring the freckles on her red cheeks.

She fucking angled her chin toward me, defiant.

"You can't tell anyone about this," she'd said, voice huskier from the tears.

I could have kissed her then.

"This has to end," Wraith said, bringing me back to the present.

There was a reason I haven't fucked Gemma since the first time. I knew once I started, I wouldn't be able to stop. I'd never let her go.

I was fucking weak for her.

I've always been weak for her. The dirty, ugly truth was tattooed on my chest. I sold drugs, but I didn't fuck with them, because I already had one addiction fucking up my life.

Gemma Crowne.

"Agreed." I clicked off, focusing on the man bleeding at my feet.

One bullet, through the temple. Another body added to my Gemma Crowne collection.

SEVEN

GEMMA

I felt like my sister, Abigail, sneaking back into Crowne Hall. She was always the one coming home at all times of night. It was hours after the party ended. I'd stayed outside, stuck, watching the body disappear into the water.

Now I paused before a floor-length mirror, some gilded monstrosity my family had had for centuries. In my bloody dress, I felt like some ravaged princess of an older time.

Gemma Crowne, forever marked by the Reaper.

"Gemma?"

For a moment I froze at my mother's soft voice. She'd see the blood on my clothes. She'd *know*. But then I saw her glassy eyes, her droopy shoulders, and the way she clutched the wingback for support. She wasn't going to notice a railroad spike coming from my eye.

"You disappeared from the party," my mother said. "Where did you go?"

My gaze traveled to a floor-to-ceiling window. Outside,

stars suffocated under the storm, and I touched the bruises disguised as hickeys.

Where were you, Gemma?

"I was with a boy," I said. "I don't know, someone from the party."

My mom gestured for me again, and I went to her, wrapping my arm in her silk-clad one.

"What time is it?" she murmured.

"Late."

We walked to her wing, and I slid out of my ruined dress, tossing it in the trash so she wouldn't question it tomorrow. I put on a pair of her silk pajamas and sidled up into bed with her.

"Who was it?"

My mother's eyes were glassy, her face soft. Tansy Crowne was not known for chatting. She was hard. Elegant. But this was a side I knew well. A side I think *only* I knew.

I didn't have to wonder what my mother had taken tonight. She loved her benzos just as much as I did.

Like mother, like daughter, right?

"Hmm?"

"The boy." She patted my hand. "Who was he?"

"Oh, uh..." I thought to the boy who'd haunted me for years, a shadow at my back for a decade. The night replayed like a puppet show in my mind. Me, Grim, the body between us. "No one worth mentioning."

The first death between Grim and me was a mistake.

I was always taught never to give away my location, but I was in a club in the meatpacking district, something I'd been paid to promote, and *everyone* knew where I was that night. I'd done so many drugs, the memory was all a watercolor. The mirror dripped pearls into the quilted red satin walls. I'd bent over the sink, doing another line, when suddenly a shadow appeared behind me like smoke, engulfing the room.

Engulfing me.

He could have been anyone. I was eleven the first time I read something about my body in print. Thirteen when it started becoming a daily thing online. Fifteen when it started turning sexual. Eighteen when I found my first real death threat.

There are *so* many people who want to kill me.

I remember the way his hands felt on my neck.

I remember him telling me how he was going to kill me. Down to the last little detail, like he'd imagined my eyes popping out hundreds of times before.

But then he was off me, and Grim stood in his place.

When I could finally breathe again, it was...it was like the lights turned on. Gray vanished into Technicolor.

I've done every mind-bending drug from shrooms to Molly to LSD, but nothing flipped me open like that.

I didn't remember what happened to the body or Grim. I pushed through the nightclub, into the streets. The rain-water was a goddamn baptism. The neon reflecting red in the puddles on the asphalt vibrated and burned.

I almost died and *finally* came alive.

For...like, a day.

And then everything went gray again. The volume turned down. The keys slowed. I couldn't remember why the color in the puddle affected me so much. Or even really the color of it. After that, I'd post my location every now and then. It felt a little bit like driving without a seat belt. If something happened, it was still an accident.

"I worry about you, Gemma," my mother said, her sleep-soft voice cutting into the memory. "Who will take care of you? You have no husband. No prospects."

Part of me wanted to tell my mother I could take care of myself. That it wasn't 1821. Instead, I stayed quiet, because I knew it didn't matter.

"Mom…" I caressed a stray silk thread on the pillow, picking it. "How much did you take tonight?"

"Oh, just a little melatonin." She sighed and patted the pillow beside her sleepily, eyes closing.

"You'll never leave me, right?" my mom asked through closed eyes.

"Of course not."

"Because you're my perfect little girl." She gripped my wrist. "I knew you would be the day I found out I was pregnant." I rolled back, staring at the ceiling, my mother's hand still tight on my wrist.

A few moments later, my mom's soft snores demarcated she'd fallen asleep.

I got out of bed and walked to her bathroom, checking the little orange bottle lying haphazardly on its side. Only four pills were missing, plus a bottle of wine.

I grabbed the antique 24K gold wastebasket on my way out. Years ago, my mother tried to kill herself. It was after my father died in a car crash. Death wasn't something she planned, but she definitely wasn't trying to live. She would have died had I not found her and forced her to throw up a month's worth of pills and alcohol.

As I placed the basket on the floor beside her, I caught my image in a floor-length mirror. My hair tangled. Bags under my eyes. It felt like I'd stepped into quicksand five years ago, and now it's starting to reach my torso.

The bruises on my arms and neck were darker. Fresher. I ghosted my touch across the purple spots. Maybe Mom thought if something had happened tonight, it was still an accident.

I shook that off and slid back into bed.

We never talked about that day, but for a year I sneaked into her room and hid her pills. At night I would come to her room and find her knocked out on whatever was left.

Then I got engaged. It was like a switch flipped in my mom, and suddenly she was normal again. For years my mother was focused on me—my reputation, my wedding, my life, but after Grayson blew up our family...

I glanced at my mother, her mouth hanging open as she slept.

I stayed up, watching the sparkling stars fade into inky black, snuffed under the clouds. I didn't remember falling asleep, but then the caw of seagulls woke me up. It was still early in the morning, the sky iron blue with lingering night.

"You're awake."

I jumped at my mother's voice.

My mother sat on a chaise longue beneath her window, two fingers to her temple. I pulled the blankets off me and went to her, touching her shoulder. She went stiff at my touch.

They say every sibling was raised by different parents. The mother who raised me never stopped hoping for my dad to love her again. When he died, a vacuum formed in its absence. The gnawing hope changed her, made her unable to love anything.

Without another word, my mother stood up and left me alone in her bedroom.

The next week passed uneventfully. There were no parties, my brother and his wife were out of town, and my mother ignored me.

I didn't hear from Grim until Thursday morning, in text.

One hour.

I sighed. As Lock and Raze had pointed out, I'd already missed the last two check-ins. I knew if I pushed back too much, I'd regret it.

So I found myself walking along an empty beach toward the Wharf, blowing candy-flavored smoke from my vape into the air. It had snowed a little, and the flakes dusted the beach like powdered sugar—

"Ow, shit." I rubbed my wrist, where a red mark in the shape of my vape had burned the skin.

I shook my head. Fucking rookie shit.

Less than an hour later I approached the rusted Ferris wheel that marked the Wharf. This was my favorite part of Crowne Beach.

The sand always felt softer.

The fog sweeter.

Like something was going to slip out from the thin white tendrils and steal me away forever.

Grim waited at the pier, leaning on a nearly rotted wood railing. Fog swirled at his feet, the Ferris wheel at his back. He didn't react when I approached.

"You know the drill," he said.

"It's outside. And it's *winter*."

Grim looked up from his phone, eyes hard.

He didn't say anything.

He didn't have to.

I tore off my shirt, unbuttoned my pants. I stayed like that, naked save for my La Perla, clothes in hand.

Grim's eyes traveled down my body. Slow. Lazy. Leaving a trail of fire as they went.

These "check-ins" were categorically different from when the rest of the Horsemen were around. Those were bureaucratic, like a banker following up on a credit check.

But these?

"The rest." His voice was cold with an apathy that matched his gaze.

Rolling my eyes, I unclasped the bra at my front and shimmied out of my underwear. The winter wind blew across my skin, frosty and bitter.

Grim stared without shame.

The Horsemen were not gentlemen.

I wouldn't expect them to be.

Grim did a slow circle around me, his inspection cold and clinical. "Lift up your arm."

I did as I was told.

For most, a debt meant they asked something of the Horsemen—revenge, wealth—boring shit like that. My contract was not so simple. Grim saved me, and in return he owned my life.

He grasped my wrist, looking at the fresh burn. "What is this?"

"You think I tried to kill myself with my vape?" I glared at him. "I burned my wrist."

His grip remained tight on my wrist, eyes hard on mine, as if trying to spot the lie.

The day after Grim saved me, he appeared with his tattoo freshly wrapped on his chest. The red ink was too bright. I didn't realize until after it was because of the blood.

That was how it all started.

Grim never said that I had a contract now, or I had to do *this* to get *that*. No, that moment was more primal. The tattoo a fucking statement.

I slid back into my life easily, and it was because of that ease that I never really fought back. Months would go by without me ever seeing him, but it was almost like he could sense when the ocean was starting to look tempting.

Grim dropped my wrist.

I quickly threw on my clothes.

I wouldn't fool myself into thinking he cared. To Grim, and to everyone else in the world, I was merchandise, useless when broken.

Living was my punishment, and the Reaper was going to make damn sure I was punished.

EIGHT

GEMMA

A cool gush of salty winter air woke me up. My shimmering muslin curtains fluttered in the breeze. The balcony door was open, and the musky smell of cannabis drifted on the air.

He'd been here.

I quickly sat up and opened my nightstand.

Empty.

Fuck.

For years I'd had no problem getting drugs. Now no one would sell to me. If I did manage to get something, Grim would slide into my room and steal it.

I pushed my satin duvet off my body and went out to my balcony. It was iron cold outside, the air sharp and biting. Gauzy curtains whispered against my skin, and the faint hint of light illumined the horizon a gray purple.

A black streak of ash marred my balcony, the only evidence Grim had been there.

I stared down to the night-darkened beach, imagining my footprints in the sand, disappearing into the glimmering black waters.

It's a beautiful day to die.

I smeared the ash with my finger, the pad turning black. Grim didn't scare me. I was scared of myself.

I don't know why I went into the ocean that day. I don't know what was stopping me from walking back into it. Why do I want the salty water to fill up my lungs until I breathe nothing but burning, bitter cold? Why do I want to die?

But there was no *why*. It was just a feeling—a colorless, dark urge.

Still in my pajamas, I grabbed a puffy overcoat and went down to the beach. For one week in the summer, these beaches would be flooded with swans. Known as the Swan Swell, it was an anomaly unique to Crowne Point. Now, the swans had mostly migrated, but there was always one swan that remained.

"Hey, buddy."

I sat on the sand, breaking off a piece of croissant I'd snagged from the kitchen to give him.

I called him my suicide swan. He—or she? How did you even tell?—was always there when I was fucked up. Swans were notorious assholes, but not this guy. This guy was always separate from the pack. I think it had something to do with its fucked-up wing.

The swan honked and took the offered piece of flaky pastry.

I pressed my cheek against my knee, watching the sun rise over the ocean, the sound of the waves crashing like shattered glass.

Nothing was ever in my control. Who I was, my personality, my likes and dislikes, were all chosen by the world.

Love was controlled by my mother, and if I didn't obey and act perfectly, I wasn't loved.

Even my death wasn't my choice. Grim inked my life on his chest, forcing me to live, stripping me of my last shred of control.

I stayed on the beach until the sun rose high into midmorning, then gave my swan the last piece of croissant. By the time I got back to the house, a flurry of people were hanging portraits and unwrapping antique china. Down the hall, more workers rushed in and out of my mother's favorite room.

Shit.

The Sunroom Revival was today.

Not more than two seconds later, my mother appeared. "Where have you been?" She didn't give me a chance to respond, dragging me off to the side. "We start in an hour. A prince who, by some miracle, expressed interest in you is coming."

Princes stopped being cute when I was seven. Outside of Disney, they weren't so charming. Pedophiles, rapists, fetishes that border on torture, all hidden by a shiny crown.

No, thanks.

I rubbed the back of my neck. "I forgot."

She looked at me like I'd grown two heads. "Sometimes I think you're as bad as your sister. Do you even want this, Gemma?"

I paused.

Do I want this?

I'd never really been allowed to ask myself that question.

As if sensing my hesitation, my mother asked, "What could be more important?"

Wasn't this what I wanted? To marry someone who

would put me back on the cover of magazines? To be Gemma Crowne, and have that *mean* something again.

To have *control*.

"To be a queen, you need a king, Gemma," my mother said. "Otherwise you're just a little girl playing dress-up."

Hours later the sunset painted the sky in oranges and reds. I waited for my hair to set, makeup already done, and scrolled.

It didn't take long to find someone talking shit about me. They loved to tag me. Someone had posted a zoomed-in version of two photos, side by side, for comparison. The second photo was a still from some video, distorted. *Gemma: before and after*, the caption read.

I glanced at the mirror.

Did I look like that?

I shook my head and read the comments.

She was hot before she started fucking with her face.

I saw Gemma Crowne in person and it made me realize she's so empty. She's just a character giving a performance.

Gemma was so much less annoying when she was engaged to Horace.

I used to stab safety pins in my leg to avoid scars. I stopped when even that started to blemish.

Now I guess I used this to cut. Social media.

"Finished!"

My girl, Olivia—or rather, she wasn't *my* girl anymore. That was another thing Grayson had ended. We used to have personal maids and valets, but now no one person was responsible for a Crowne. Still, Olivia had been by my side the longest.

She stepped back, turning her attention to a dress hanging against my window. It was white, with black trim on the bodice and delicate black bows on the skirt. She held it out for me to step into.

The dress was fitted and flowed outward from my waist. It landed just above my ankles, the chiffon skirt giving an airy, effortless beauty.

Olivia held out black gloves, and I slid my arms into them, just above my elbow. The outfit was Parisian, with a little New York, like something out of *Breakfast at Tiffany's*.

Today's event was to celebrate the Sunroom Revival. In reality, it was an excuse to write off renovations my mother wanted.

The sunroom was second only to the hedge maze in my mother's eyes. It overlooked three miles of gardens, wintry skies, and the iron Atlantic Ocean. My mother spent the majority of her days here drinking tea and eating biscuits. Now she spoke with an older woman, gesturing out the window toward the garden.

Men old enough to be my grandfather flirted with me. Women who would dance on my grave came up with overly saccharine smiles. I think I talked. Laughed.

My eyes wandered across the orchestrated glamour. The harmonious *plink* of silver spoons on porcelain teacups, faces frozen with Botox and polite laughter that didn't reach the eyes.

"Oh my God, Gemma? It's been *ages*."

I recognized the voice before I turned to meet her overly spray-tanned face—Trinity. We had gone to boarding school together. She had an uncanny ability to be present at any event that was leaked to the press.

"Oh my God, *Trin*. I had no idea you'd be here."

We butterfly hugged.

"It was a last-minute thing," she said.

"Isn't it always?"

Silence settled. I stared out to the circular room, wishing this bitch would take a hint.

"Have you had a chance to speak with the prince yet?" Trinity asked.

"The prince?" I asked, and then a second later remembered what my mom had said. "Uh, no, I don't even know what he looks like."

My gaze drifted back to the room, bouncing from man to man, all in well-tailored suits and all with the same bloviated, arrogant, and self-important countenance.

"He's over there." She pointed toward the periphery of the sunroom, near a window overlooking the beach. "The only one not wearing a suit. Tall."

I followed her finger to a man with salt-and-pepper hair, black jeans and sneakers, and a T-shirt.

I sucked in a breath.

I don't give a shit what you put in your cunt. This is business.

That was the prince? The hot, scary older man from the club was also the same man my mother was doing cartwheels over to get me to marry?

He raised his glass to me with a smirk when he caught me staring.

"Oh my God," she whispered. "Do you know him too?"

"Not quite." I tilted my head to the side, arms folded, my champagne flute cold against my bicep. "What do you know about him?"

I was expecting inbreeding—Charles II of Spain. Instead I got forbidden, mysterious, and dangerous.

"Um...not much, actually. He's from some small European province."

The prince had turned back to his conversation, but I continued to study him.

The guys I'd seen packing heat at the club made sense now—bodyguards. But how and why was he connected to Grim?

"Do you want to take a selfie?" Trinity asked. "The lighting here is great."

I'd rather deep-throat your dad's dick.

"Oh my God, yes."

Trinity snapped the selfie. When she finished, I looked back toward the prince.

"I'll tag you!" she said.

Shoot me. "Can't wait!"

I'd been under Grim's thumb for five years—had been entwined for even longer—but I still didn't know much more than the average person. What could he want with a prince?

I landed before the prince, and as I did, he raised a hand. Those around us dissipated.

He arched a brow. "Dangerous to be seen talking to you."

"Oh yeah?"

"Rumor is you're a curse. Bodies tend to drop around you. Because once you see the Reaper's girl, the Reaper soon follows."

My smile faltered.

"Well, it's a good thing I'm not the Reaper's girl." I took a sip of my champagne.

"I think we're going in circles." He laughed. "So, what's the not-Reaper's girl doing talking to me?"

"Depends," I said. "Why is a prince talking to the king of the Underworld?"

NINE

GEMMA

"King, huh?" Something inscrutable flickered in his eyes, as if he knew something I didn't. Before I could press, he continued. "Couldn't I be your white knight?" He stepped closer, forcing me to take a step back, until I was flush against the window. "Rescuing you from captivity."

I looked over his shoulder, at the party. Everyone was now too busy fawning over the gift bags my mother had procured. For once, no eyes were on me.

"My white knight?" I arched a brow at HSOG—*the prince*.

Maybe in a fairy tale. Where princes were noble, where someone like me was virtuous. But this was not a fairy tale, and this prince's eyes had too much darkness to be my savior.

"What's an innocent girl like you doing indebted to the Horsemen, anyway?" he asked.

"If you're hoping I'm an innocent girl, you're going to be very disappointed."

He took a drink, smiling into his glass. "That so?"

I shrugged like *maybe.* "For a prince, you sure know a lot about the Underworld."

"It's a world not dissimilar from this." He gestured around us.

"How so?"

"There are rules to follow and consequences for breaking them, like never touch someone who is claimed."

I was taught at a young age to never be too eager. If I asked a question, it could never belie my ignorance. But Grim knew everything about me. He knew my deepest, darkest secrets, and I know nothing about his world beyond rumor. This was the most I'd learned about Grim's world in the years I'd known him. So I did the unthinkable—I let myself be curious.

"What does that mean?" I asked. "Claimed?"

Prince HSOG's blue eyes glimmered, as if he could see the war between propriety and curiosity raging in my head.

"A claim is the only thing respected more than a debt. That's why they mark the claimed with a tattoo. So everyone knows."

Unmarked. Unclaimed.

The words he'd spoken when we first met suddenly took on a new meaning.

"Until she has a tattoo, she's up for grabs. Once she's marked, even the wrong look can be considered a declaration of war, but—"He leaned in like he was about to let me in on some big conspiracy. "—it goes both ways. The Reaper's girl —or anyone who is publicly claimed—has a target on her head. They'll want to hurt her, just to hurt him."

"What people?"

He shrugged. "Rival factions. Petty criminals trying to climb the ladder. You name it, anyone trying to grasp a semblance of power."

My eyes narrowed. "Who *are* you?"

He smiled in response, teeth white and sharp. "So, you never did answer me. What are you doing talking to a guy like me?"

With that, he closed the line of questioning. Things like the Underworld didn't exist anymore, our world was *tea*. It was like the sound turned back on. Soft, plastic laughter, the clinking of tea glasses, a sharp gasp as someone listened to juicy gossip.

What am I doing talking to him? Well, I'd wanted to know about his connection to Grim. But outside of that...

"I guess I'm here for you." He arched a brow, and I explained. "My mother told me to seduce you in order to stop bringing shame to our family."

He laughed.

"So then if I did this, your mother would approve?" He snaked his hand around my hip, grasping so tight I nearly gasped.

"Very much so."

He stepped closer until I could taste spicy cigar smoke on his breath. "And if I kissed you?"

"She would be ecstatic."

"I'll keep that in mind." He leaned forward and I sucked in a breath. This was so *not* proper. Maybe he would kiss me. Maybe I would let him. Get my mom off my back and piss off Grim.

Two birds and all that.

Then, all at once, he stepped back. I followed his stare and found his guards at the door, gesturing for him.

"Until next time, Gemma."

I watched him leave. That tiny bit of excitement—of *relief*—from this world drained out of me. I felt wooden. Stuck.

My mother was still by the window, showing a new batch of victims her famous garden. I took the opportunity to slink out unnoticed.

Reaper's girl.

If I became the Reaper's girl, I'd have more targets on my head than I could count. If I became the Reaper's girl... my life wouldn't belong to me. My life would be entangled with his.

I don't know why the idea sent hot, tingling shivers down my spine.

I could never be claimed. I couldn't be Gemma Crowne *and* the Reaper's girl.

When I got to my wing, my friends were already there. Blaire lay on my ivory couch, scrolling on her phone with one heel still on her foot, the other dropped unceremoniously to the floor.

Kennedy did lines on the coffee table next to her.

This wasn't unusual. They often sneaked in here to get high. Hearing me, they turned their heads in unison.

"You started without me," I said, and dropped down next to them to do a line. "Rude."

We stayed like that until the sun had long since disappeared into black night, trading in our gowns for plush, oversize sweats.

"I need to get fucked," Blaire said, sounding bored. She was on the floor now, her head propped against my couch at an awkward angle. "I only have, like, two days left before my period."

"So?" Kennedy asked.

"So I don't want some fucking psycho to tell a blog how he got his red wings with me," Blaire snapped.

"Jesus Christ, are you sure you haven't started it already?" Kennedy muttered.

As they bickered, I stared out my balcony's French doors. A sliver of the stone railing was visible through the glass. I rubbed my fingers together, feeling the ghost of Grim's ash from earlier this morning.

"Let's go," I said, standing up.

"Where?" Kennedy asked.

I know I shouldn't want to go there. I should stay as far away from Grim as possible. And yet...

"The Underworld."

Just a short while later, we arrived. In my silver-pink Hervé Léger, with my tits pushed up and rose gold hair to match my rose gold dress and stilettos, for a few minutes I felt at home. No quicksand, just time to be Queen Gemma.

Everyone thought of druggies as greasy, *Requiem for a Dream* addicts who steal your wallet. Not only was that, well, *crazy rude*, but it was a straight-up lie. Everyone I know is on something. From the Goody Two-shoes assholes at my old school who took addy to up their test scores, to my friends looking to party, to my own fucking mother.

It was a world of glitterati who are dead without an extra pill or two, where someone would pop a pill with one hand and donate to a senator who spent all his time funding anti-drug laws with the other.

And *that* was the world Grim Reyes ruled.

"I feel like I've already fucked every guy here." Blaire sighed. "And no one made me want to go back for seconds."

"That guy in the black turtleneck just exited," Kennedy offered. "He's worth, like, a couple billion."

"I'm looking to get fucked tonight, so unless his dick is as big as his portfolio, no thanks."

"Why don't you go stand in line?" Kennedy said. "Maybe they'll call you up."

Blaire's mouth parted. "I know you didn't just call me a groupie."

Everyone wanted to fuck a Horsemen, so many that there was always a line at the bottom of the stairs, just hoping one of them glanced in their direction and waved them up.

"The stairs are never guarded," Kennedy pointed out. "Anyone can walk up them."

Blaire glared at her. "Then you go do it."

She wrapped her "definitely not filled or anything" lips around a neon-pink straw, staying silent.

My eyes traveled to the balcony, where one lone shadow stood, his back to the club.

Grim.

He'd been there since we arrived, never turning around. I stared at his back, and a feeling—an *urge*—took over. My mother called it a pathological need for attention, but it was also darker than that. Primeval. Something that had existed in my soul before I'd had a body.

I climbed onto the table and started to dance.

"We're live!" Kennedy said, angling her phone toward me.

I bent over, blowing a kiss to the camera. My friends cheered me on as I twirled, doing my best not to pull an Abigail and show the world my...everything. This dress wasn't designed for dancing. It was designed to sit still and look hot.

I did another twirl, all those years my mother forced me

to play ballerina really paying off. As I finished the twirl, my gaze traveled back up to the balcony.

Grim was watching.

I stumbled, nearly falling off the table.

He bent over the railing and crooked his finger. *Come hither.* I waved, then transformed my wave into the middle finger, before blowing him a kiss.

His lip twitched slightly.

When I went back to dancing, the air changed. I could imagine his hot stare on my neck, and I was no longer dancing for whatever thousands of strangers watched Kennedy's live. I was dancing for him. The night we shared rushed over me. How I felt then, able to let loose completely, be free.

My dancing transformed, no longer about what would go viral but about those few hours on the beach, the hot, whispered words that had slid into my veins.

Good girl.

I'll kill anyone who touches you.

I had bent over, grasping my ankles, when sharp *whoops* and cheers sounded from my friends. I snapped back to the present with whiplash. I wasn't on the beach, I was *here*.

I froze on the table, suddenly feeling exposed.

What the fuck?

Seriously, what the actual fuck was wrong with me? Against my better judgment, I looked back to the balcony. He was gone.

I quickly climbed off the table.

"It already has, like, a hundred thousand likes," Kennedy said, showing me the video. "Don't worry. I angled it away when you bent over—people are pissed, though."

"Don't forget to tag everyone," Blaire said. Kennedy waved her away, like, *Duh.* Kennedy tried to show me something from the live, a comment from some rich playboy actor.

I stared at the empty balcony, the shadows moving like smoke.

"Uh, great." I ran a hand through my hair, damp with sweat. "That's great. Look, show me later. I need...water."

"We have water?" Blaire held up one of the many complimentary Fiji waters that came with a private booth and bottle service.

I didn't respond, weaving my way through the club, toward the back. Far enough away from the main floor, in the shadows where I'd first met Prince HSOG, I watched my friends. Kennedy had climbed on the table, dancing as Blaire filmed.

I rubbed my chest, heart pounding.

What is happening to me?

"What were you doing?"

My heart stuttered and skipped at Grim's voice, but I refused to turn. I could *feel* him next to me. Feel the heat of his shoulder next to mine. Smell his unmistakable and irresistible scent, one that belonged only to Grim—dark and earthy, like his soul. It felt like protection. Hear his steady, even breathing. I could practically see the way he dragged his thumb across his jaw.

The heat in his stare.

"Uh..." I swallowed. "Dancing."

"Someone must have told you it looks good," he said, and stood in front of me, forcing me to acknowledge him. An inky, wavy lock of hair fell haphazard across one eye. A warmth in them that made my gut twist.

He leaned forward, lips at my neck, like he had a secret. "It doesn't."

I shoved him off, finally turning to face him. "I already

have a hundred thousand likes. It hasn't even been two minutes. So someone thinks it looks good."

He clicked his tongue. "I don't know, I remember someone commanding a lot of attention at a school dance."

My mind flashed back to ten years ago, to the only school dance I'd ever gone to. The rare time Abby and I weren't at each other's throats. Trauma bonded through the shitty school our grandfather forced on us. We'd gotten drunk in my room and decided, *fuck it.*

It was supposed to be a joke, a way for us to laugh at townies. My mother put me in dance as soon as I could walk. I didn't dance for fun; it was just another facet of my carefully orchestrated persona. Gemma Crowne can waltz *and* shake it like Britney.

But then a stupid, silly song from our childhood came on and Abby dragged me to the dance floor. Abby was always the best at rebelling. My heart thrummed at the memory. It was one of the only good ones I'd had as a kid.

"Oh my God!" I said. "I was fifteen."

Grim's lip twitched. "You almost took out a rib."

The beat of the club pounded in my blood as what he'd said, what he'd *meant*, washed over me. Grim had watched me, even back then.

"So this is how you want me to dance?" I threw my arms in the air, dancing like I was with Abby again. "To look like a fool?"

I shook my arms and head, spinning and twirling and not giving a shit if my dance was cringe or had good angles. For a moment I actually was fifteen again. Then the song changed, and reality slapped me in the face. I stopped abruptly, feeling all at once stupid and vulnerable. Like my skin had been stripped to only raw nerves.

Except, Grim didn't look at me like I was a joke.

His stare was lethal.

Hungry.

"I'm all sweaty and gross now. Happy?" I pushed past him to get space between him and that look in his eyes when he gripped my wrist, dragging me back.

Against *him*.

My back to his chest. Flush.

"Wha—"

He captured my hair, moving it to the other side and exposing my neck.

He slid one hand down the side of me, my curves, and we moved. In the dark of the club, where no one was watching, he moved us together. It was more than a dance. It was a memory inside a promise.

Of when he'd moved inside me on that beach.

"You can't touch me like this," I breathed.

The Horsemen don't trade in sex.

The Horsemen *never* touch their contracts, let alone fuck them.

Whatever was happening between Grim and me was off the books. Tomorrow we would pretend none of this happened.

His open palm slid over my belly, stopping just above my pussy, holding me closer against him. His cock grew hard on my ass. I sucked in a breath I knew he could feel.

As if to prove me wrong, he dragged me closer. Moved me. Commanded me.

"I like you sweaty, Gemma," he rasped against my neck. "Dirty. Ugly. Messy."

I closed my eyes, sinking into him—but he was gone.

TEN

GRIM

I leaned over the railing, watching the club below. Gemma was getting too drunk. She swayed, laughing too hard and leaning on her friends. My eyes dropped to her lips, bitten and red. She always chewed them when she was high.

"Please tell me I didn't see you dancing with Gemma Crowne."

Shit.

I glanced at Lock from the corner of my eye. He stood next to me, brows drawn, jaw tight. Lock was the tallest of us, and we were all pretty fucking tall—except Wraith, whose short stature worked for his line of work. Lock was also the most empathetic of us. Where we were all like too much scar tissue, hardened and callous, Lock still had some humanity left. Could be why he got so much ass.

I rubbed my jaw. "Didn't know I was being watched."

"She's America's Princess. Her life is splashed across

magazines. She thrives under a microscope, and our survival depends on the shadows."

I turned away from Gemma falling drunk into her private booth, and leaned against the railing, eyes on Lock. The piercings in his lip and brow glinted in the club light. On the surface there wasn't much that connected Lock, Raze, Wraith, and me. Not our taste in music or women, not the type of clothes we bought or the media we consumed.

But, like me, he had the misfortune of being born in Crowne Point. Crowne Point was the wealthiest city in America, which meant it was also the most corrupt. Growing up as a poor kid with no family meant you were either a charity case or something to exploit—usually both.

I'd known Lock longer than my other brothers. Before we were inked, just two kids playing with broken toy trucks while our parents got high in the next room. Which was probably why he saw through me the best.

"You never should have taken her contract," Lock continued. "Then you took her brother's."

"You think I don't fucking know that?" I growled.

I knew I wasn't pissed that he was calling me out. I was pissed that he was right. Loyalty, trust, ride or die—these were things we didn't have growing up. You didn't become like us by having a perfect childhood.

So we became the family we didn't have. We built an empire on blood and blackmail. What I did with Gemma undermined everything the Horsemen and I stood for.

I should have let her die that day. I definitely shouldn't have let it last this long.

"In five years she hasn't done one fucking thing we've asked of her without whining," he said.

"And?"

"And if she were anyone else, if this were any other situation, she'd be dead. I know I don't need to tell you this, but—"

"So then why are you still talking?"

"But," Lock emphasized. "Every minute you spend with her puts all of us at risk. Almost a decade of work, man. For what? A dance that meant nothing?"

ELEVEN

GEMMA

Something smacked into my face, and I woke with a jolt. My temples throbbed with a hangover. The sun had melted into a snowy white sky. It was too bright. I vaguely remembered coming home, doing more lines with the girls, but after that the night blurred. Now, Blaire and Kennedy were in bed with me.

I shoved Kennedy's hand off my face and sat up, leaning against my quilted headrest. In the mirror opposite my bed, I saw myself clearly. Mascara streaked. Hair unkempt and unbrushed. Lips swollen from sleep.

Messy.

I like you sweaty, Gemma. Dirty. Ugly. Messy.

Last night came rushing back in a wave of heat.

Grim knew things about me. Fucked-up things. Things I liked. Things I didn't tell people. Things that would very much ruin my image.

Things I *craved*.

Sometimes when he looked at me, I could see him crave them too. I could feel those cravings twist my gut into knots, our shared addiction we never talk about.

I rubbed the mascara from under my eyes, trying to forget the night. There was always *something* there, something I didn't want to admit.

Not love. Not butterflies. Some twisted, sinister need deep inside me.

But I was Gemma Crowne, America's Princess. My life's map was drawn before I ever talked to him. He was Grim, a criminal from the wrong side of the tracks. We were never meant to be anything but this—one soul enslaved to another—because the day we finally gave in to our temptation was the moment he became my reaper.

Feeling suffocated, I shoved the heavy satin duvet off my body and got out of bed. Kennedy rolled into the spot I'd been in. I needed air, so instead of having breakfast delivered to the room like I usually did, I threw on a pair of oversize sweats and went downstairs.

My mother insisted on a full breakfast made every morning—even though we rarely ate together, let alone even touched breakfast. Flaky, golden croissants made with imported French butter, truffle poached eggs with caviar sprinkles, fruit from all over the world, and at least three types of freshly squeezed juice.

I was expecting the dining room to be empty, but my brother, Grayson, and his wife and daughter, Story and Sonnet, were seated and eating.

I immediately spun around on my heel to avoid them.

"Gemma?" Story said to my back.

Fuck.

"You're back," I said, sitting down and grabbing the breakfast I had every morning: hot lemon water with chia seeds. *America's Princess* doesn't stay a size zero by eating croissants.

Grayson played with Sonnet. "We got in last night—" He broke off when he saw me.

I gave him a face. "What?"

"Late night?" Grayson shared a look with Story—concern. I pretended I didn't see it. "Are you okay?" he continued, voice soft.

Gentle.

I wanted to break it.

"Weird how everyone forgets the past," I said. "You used to go out more than me. You were Playboy Gray—in fact, I distinctly remember you using your now-wife as a bargaining chip in a poker match." Displeasure warped Grayson's face, and he glanced at Sonnet—as if a fucking one-year-old could understand me. A little bit of the old Gray, the one before his wife, appeared. The guy who used to come home with bloody knuckles and a nose permanently crooked from too many hits.

I leaned back in my chair, smiling.

"Hey, it happened," Story said, trying to defuse the conversation. "But we had something important to ask you, remember?" She gave Grayson a pointed look.

The tension in his shoulders released on an exhale. "We wanted to ask you a question."

I took a drink of my lemon water, waiting.

"Will you be Sonnet's godmother?"

I choked on the water.

Godmother?

Story handed me Sonnet before I could respond.

A small, tiny thing. Too tiny.

I studied her scrunched face. "I don't think—"

"You're the reason this baby is alive."

"Grim is the reason," I said without thinking.

A weird, sticky tension filled the room. Almost a year ago, my grandfather went mad, Story was about to give birth, and we had nowhere to go. And almost a year ago, Grim showed up. He delivered my brother's child on the sand. He saved us.

Maybe Grim came when I called because he felt the same twisted ache I do.

More likely it was because by saving the future Crowne heir, he had the entire Crowne family fully under his grasp.

"Are you still involved with him?" Grayson asked, voice low.

"Involved?" I feigned ignorance, forcing myself to stare at Sonnet. She made one of those adorable baby faces, so new to the world she couldn't fathom a future where she wasn't this wide-eyed, happy creature.

"What are you doing, Gemma?" His voice thinned in exasperation. "He kills people. He's fucking bad news."

"What are *you* doing?" I countered. "Because you got some happily ever after, you think this family is, like, not fucked up anymore?"

I don't know when it happened, but the Crowne family once known for its dysfunction and hate had overwhelmingly become...functional. Fucking loving.

Except here I was—very much *not* functional, and now trusted with holding on to the tiniest Crowne.

I was lost.

Lost among my siblings and this new, wholesome, and normal family. I was always the perfect American princess to the outside world, but my family knew I was fucked up on the inside. The one with the pill problem. The mean girl.

It didn't matter, though, because we were all messed up.

Grayson was an asshole, a playboy.

Abigail was an attention seeker, she ruined everything she touched.

Now Grayson was a loving father and husband. Abigail was a mother and wife with a thriving business. And me? I was the fucking same. I still wore sunglasses inside to hide what I did the night before.

A lump stuck in my throat. I swallowed, trying to clear it. I could see it in my brother's eyes, in the way his brow furrowed as he watched me hold his daughter. I could see the concern in Story's eyes as she dragged her bottom lip between her teeth.

They were worried.

Fuck them.

"Here." I shoved Sonnet back into Story's arms.

"Gemma!" Story called after me. "Wait!"

"Let her go..." My brother's voice trailed into quiet as I left the room.

When I got upstairs, Blaire and Kennedy were just waking up. Kennedy had snuggled into Blaire at some point. I sat on my chaise, picking off my nail polish.

Godmother?

Pick.

"I stole a pair of your underwear," Blaire said. "Period came early. They're mine now."

"How long have you been awake?" Kennedy asked as Blaire shoved her off.

Pick.

"I don't want to remember yesterday, today, or tomorrow," I said.

"Damn, okay," Kennedy said. "Let's get fucked up."

TWELVE

GEMMA

Hours later we found ourselves in Kennedy's bathroom as a party raged below. With the door shut, the sounds of the party were muffled as if beneath a pillow. The constant thumping of EDM was muted, like a heartbeat hidden in the floorboards.

Thump. Thump. Thump.

Kennedy's home—or rather her *parents'* home—was like every other mansion in upstate New York. Gothic brick architecture, sprawling gardens, and bosky beaches. Kennedy lived about an hour from Crowne Point, and much less when you took my family's helicopter, but for my wants, it felt like I was an entire continent away.

No Underworld.

No shifting family dynamics.

Just...this.

"I'm telling you," Kennedy said to Blaire, lifting herself

onto the white marble sink. "Bumping makes a huge difference."

"I'm telling *you*," Blaire countered. "Your nose is gonna fall off. Ya gonna look like a moldy-ass jack-o'-lantern."

Kennedy's foot was in the sink, her shimmering and sheer lilac dress trailing to the floor. Blaire sat on the toilet, scrolling on her phone as she took a hit off her vape, rolling her eyes at Kennedy.

What would America think if they knew their favorite sweethearts didn't trade gossip in the bathroom, but drugs?

Kennedy and Blaire went back to arguing their points on the bumping versus ingesting debate. I stared at my face in her antique, feminine mirror. The longer I looked, the more distorted I became. I took a hit off Blaire's vape, obscuring my reflection in smoke, and the beehive inside my chest, the thing that urged me to end it all, quieted a little.

I'd been friends with Kennedy and Blaire for over a decade, but they didn't *know* me. They sold my secrets to tabloids. They talked shit behind my back. They would drop me in a heartbeat if I wasn't Gemma Crowne.

I know that, and I was okay with it, because real friendship was a Hollywood lie.

I was using them too.

My mom had done some focus group shit, and people really loved it when I supported other women. They didn't give a shit if I actually meant it, or if the women I promoted were good people. They just liked the buzzwords.

You see, I wasn't really a person. I was just…an entity. So Gemma Crowne had to have a squad, because Gemma Crowne was girl power—rah!

Kennedy put some of the powder on her finger, lifting it to Blaire. "Just try it—"

"I can't fucking listen to this anymore!" Blaire lifted her

head from her phone. "You realize bumping benzos does nothing, right? Like, they're *supposed* to be digested. All you're doing is fucking up your nose. Chew them if you want to get higher."

Kennedy's brow furrowed. "But—"

"Do you get any special perks?" Blaire asked, turning her attention to me and cutting off Kennedy.

Blaire was one of those girls who was friends with everyone. You had to be wary of the bitches who were friends with everyone. You couldn't *be* friends with everyone. That chick who has everyone's back? Yeah, she was watching no one's.

But most girls really thought she was their friend, and that was a huge fucking network.

I sank into Kennedy's claw-foot tub, one leg dangling over the edge. "Perks?" I blew musky, hazy smoke through the glittering cut-crystal chandelier, until the glimmer died in the smoke.

"Like, when you become god queen," Kennedy said.

"God*mother*," Blaire corrected.

Kennedy used me because being friends with Gemma Crowne helped promote her makeup line. She sold more of my secrets than anyone, but she had a demographic I'd never reach on my own: the poor. Kennedy hadn't been poor since she was a baby and her mother married the heir to a supermarket chain, but she sold herself as a rags-to-riches girl, and the world bought it.

She made me appear relatable—said my mother.

Kennedy made a face. "Whatever. My godmother always sent me these weird preachy books on my birthday. Like, thanks, but who asked you, bitch?"

"That's what she's supposed to do," Blaire said. "She's a *god*mother. She guides you in your faith."

Everyone paused, then laughed.

Me *guiding* my niece? What would I guide her in? Her first trip? *Be sure to check your shrooms for mold, little Sonnet. You're not supposed to get nauseated when you trip. If you do, you're eatin' mold, kid.*

Or maybe I could teach her how to self-harm without anyone knowing. Safety pins—a stab from a safety pin looked just like a freckle.

"I'm pretty sure if they die you have to raise it," Blaire said.

I jerked back. "What?"

"The kid. If the parents die, you have to raise it."

I made a face. What the *fuck* was my brother thinking?

Kennedy started telling a story about her godmother and how she was pretty sure she was one of her father's affair partners. I eyed the benzos Kennedy was still trying to get Blaire to try. How many would I need to take to die? I opened my phone to ask, and in response, Google gave me the fucking suicide hotline.

Hey, bitch, have you considered therapy?

Thanks, Google, but I was clearly trying to spend some quality time with my demons.

"What would you do if you knew it was your last night on earth?" I asked, focusing on the chandelier's sparkle. "Like, if you were going to die today?"

Kennedy swiped at her nose. "I don't know, like, do I have cancer or something? Oh my God, Gemma—" Her smile dropped, mouth open. "Do you have that thing, that—that—I don't—know—how—to—pronounce—" She pressed a hand to the diamond pendant at her chest, hyperventilating. "Is that why you made us all do that stupid ice challenge?"

"That was, like, twenty years ago." I slid farther down

into the tub, one leg out, heel dangling. "I don't have ALS, Kennedy."

"The fuck, Ken?" Blaire stared at her, mouth open.

"You know benzos make me emotional!"

Sometimes it felt like I had a friend inside my head who was constantly giving me the *worst* advice. When I woke up and the world was gray and I just wanted to know how to fix it, that friend has their hand raised *so high*, just *waiting* for me to call on them.

Have you considered killing yourself? the friend suggested.

And I was like, *Does anyone else want to offer a suggestion? Like anything. Seriously.*

And everyone shrugged.

I stood up. "Let's go back."

"Okay, but first, break the tie. Powder or bar?" Kennedy pointed at the crushed-up xanny on her left, and the bars on her right.

"Neither," I said.

"Neither?" they said in unison, eyes popping out of their heads.

"I want both."

It burned my nostrils, and I knew it wouldn't enhance the high, but fuck it, was I supposed to waste it?

I swiped the powder on my philtrum with my middle finger, adjusting my foundation. Good as new.

"This is why you're the fucking queen!"

We linked arms and returned to the party. Inside Kennedy's house was nothing like the stately facade. Lilac lights strobed in time with the thumping of a beat. On the table a crystal bowl glowing with a rainbow LED light from the base held a plethora of mystery pills.

When your parents spent the majority of their time in another continent, you could do whatever you wanted.

"Oh my God, why is *she* here?" Blaire asked.

Kennedy and Blaire turned their attention to some girl I recognized from boarding school.

"I thought she was in rehab," Kennedy said, tilting her head in confusion.

"She's literally flirting with Sebastian right in front of my fucking face," Blaire said.

"Why do you care?" Kennedy asked. "You said you ended the situationship because Seb was, like, the not-hot version of Patrick Bateman."

These were my closest friends.

My *best* friends.

I'd laughed and cried with them. I'd held their hair back while they vomited the night's alcohol and pills. I'd put my finger down their throats to make *sure* they vomited.

And when I looked at them, I saw markets and quid pro quo. All three of us were in a twisted parasitic relationship, surviving and thriving off each other.

That's just the way friendship is.

My eyes wandered from people dancing, to those taking selfies, to the group skinny-dipping, landing on another group gambling for pink slips and whatever the hell else they had.

The memories we looked back on, the photos we enjoyed the most, were the blurry ones, the ugly ones, the ones we accidentally took. Those filled with laughter, or sorrow and mistakes.

My life was populated with perfection.

Nothing to look back on but ivory and cold pictures.

I wanted to run out into the ocean. Ruin it. Ruin the pretty hand-sewn crystal beading on my dress. Ruin the makeup someone spent over an hour on. Crush the diamonds on my neck. Everything.

"It's the principle of the thing, Kennedy—"

"I'm gonna go for a smoke," I said, not waiting for them to respond.

Outside, a gush of salty winter air whispered across my cheek, followed by the sound of the waves shattering like sugar candy on the sand. The cold felt good on my over-heated skin.

Marshmallows replaced the thorny blood inside my body. Minutes expanded into forever. It was like I was underwater, staring at my world reflected back at me. Slow. Peaceful.

That lovely, fuzzy haze filled my veins like the cotton-tails that grew in our home in Italy. The look, not the feel. They were always so scratchy...

The benzos hit.

It was okay. Everything was okay.

Finally.

I lit my cigarette and kicked off my shoes, dipping my toes in the icy sea. The red cigarette tip burned bright in the night.

I knew he was behind me before I heard the soft crunch of sand. Maybe it was the musky smell of cannabis drifting on the night breeze that seemed to follow him wherever he went. More likely, it was that inexplicable thing that tied us together.

"You're not supposed to be here, Reaper." I tapped my cigarette, ash falling like stardust to the sand.

Horror movies would have you believe monsters can't wait to eat little girls. They lay in wait to deflower virgins, rip apart our insides, and drag us to their hell.

As an adult, I'd learned monsters weren't tempted by such banalities.

Hell was a privilege.

Real monsters wanted your soul.

I went to take another puff, when Grim stepped into view and gripped my hand. The cigarette was suspended, a sliver from my lips.

His voice came low and smoky in the dark. "You taste better when you don't smoke."

THIRTEEN

GEMMA

Grim hooked one finger into the cleavage of my dress, dragging me to him. "I really hate when you wear this shit."

I smiled. "So take it off me."

His gaze sharpened, but then his head tilted slightly, his lips lifting, and a softness overcame his features that made the wire in my gut tighten.

"The fuck did you take this time?" He wasn't angry. He sounded...a little humored, and a lot hungry.

I scrunched my face into a frown. "I didn't take anything."

I was tall, taller than all the girls at my old school, but with Grim, I still had to crane my neck to see into his eyes. Grim had such beautiful eyes. They were always hidden under his hair or a hoodie, but up close...they were dark, glittering, mesmerizing—

"You only look at me like this when you're fucked up."

He laughed. I liked his laugh. Like everything about Grim, it was rough. Vicious. Secret. And only for me.

He pulled his bottom lip between his teeth and dipped his head to catch my gaze, a black lock of hair falling over one eye.

He looked boyish.

Predatory.

Deadly.

All at once.

"That's not true," I breathed.

The waves crashed on the beach, a visceral, jagged reminder of the only day Grim had ever looked at me with anything other than nothing.

The reason I couldn't *stop* looking at him.

"Who sold to you?" he asked.

I opened my eyes, not realizing I'd closed them, finding Grim's glare.

"Why?" I bit my smile. "Gonna kill them too?"

Grim's face was iron. "Yes." He tugged me closer, pulling at the pink material of my dress until it stretched. Until I was pressed hard against his chest.

My breath hitched at his cock throbbing hard on my stomach.

I slid my hands into his hair. "*You* could sell to me again."

I couldn't stop touching him. The soft stubble of his cheek. The angle of his jaw. My stomach was warm, and I wanted him. His soft, his hard, his breath on my lips and flesh.

Somewhere in my brain, I know this is the drugs. I know I'll regret this, but I liked it too much to stop.

"A better boy wouldn't take advantage of me in this state," I breathed.

He pulled me harder against his cock on a dark laugh. "I'm not a better boy."

Some sliver of the sober part of me said to pull back. You couldn't be fuck buddies with the guy you were indebted to, with the man who owned your life.

But this close to him I could see the half-moon scar on his bottom lip.

"Prove it."

I had a second for my heartbeat to skyrocket at the heat in his eyes, before his hand was between my thighs.

He hissed, eyes black, when he realized I wasn't wearing panties.

His hand completely enveloped my pussy. And I suddenly couldn't think of anything else but Grim touching me, his hand chilled from the winter air against my hot flesh.

I barely inhaled and his eyes dropped to my mouth, muscle twerking with the clench of his jaw. I couldn't breathe. I couldn't think. My heart hammering.

The air felt leaden with his stare.

His free hand gripped my hip, as if trying to hold himself back. It was because of that dichotomy I was so spun out—that wire inside me hot and vibrating and about to snap. The picture of him in my head was like a mirage. Every time I got close, it vanished between my fingers. I wanted him on me. In me. To just *feel* what he was doing to me.

My mouth parted, heart skipping in my chest, waiting for him to just *do it* and cross the line we'd drawn years ago.

I arched, trying to get him inside me, but his hand stayed firm and unmoving. I felt deliciously trapped and at his mercy. That hot, throbbing part of my soul came loose.

The part that wanted to drop to my knees and do anything for him, *let* him do anything for me.

His palm curled ever so slightly tighter against my pussy, like he could read the filthy, desperate pleas in my mind.

"When I have you again, you'll be sober," he said, parting me with his thumb and lightly touching the aching center of me. "Remember every cutting, jagged edge."

Then he stepped back, the night air cold between my thighs.

I knew I should pull the skirt of my dress down, move—*something*. I stayed frozen. His eyes dropped between my thighs, smoldering like the cigarette at my feet. Then he turned without another word, disappearing down the beach.

FOURTEEN

GRIM

A short hour later, I climbed into Gemma's room. She would be out for a while, so it was as good a time as any to check in. I bent down, pressing a little black button hidden inside the doorjamb's weather strip, and tried not to think about how close I came to crossing the line.

How much I fucking wanted to.

How *wet* she was on my hand. The silent plea in her eyes, her body and mind yielding so easily for me. Gemma's obedience was a drug I would kill myself with. Happily. In life she was a spoiled, entitled brat, but with me?

Fuck.

I shook my head as a cherry-red light blinked. Still armed. It was a secret dual-locking system that only I knew about—Gemma always left her fucking room unlocked. The moment her door opened, an alarm went off, alerting only me.

There were three things I focused on with Gemma

Crowne: secure from outsiders, accessible to me, invisible to her.

I walked past the red light and into her room, reading it like a diary. The book she was reading was face down, the bookmark deeper inside than the last time I'd been here. I lifted it up to see the title. Gemma Crowne pretended to read whatever book Reese Witherspoon picked out that month.

Madame Bovary.

This she was reading for real. Gemma liked dark and broken; old books that spoke of timeless pain.

I dusted my finger along the white powder on the vanity, remnants of cocaine.

Didn't matter how many fuckers I threatened in this town, Gemma always found a way to get drugs.

Next to the powder, shiny pink flecks of nail polish caught the light. I stilled.

Something had made her sad.

Gemma liked to pretend she was perfect and happy, but there were tells. I pictured her ripping apart her manicure, that stony, walled look in her eyes.

I opened and closed my fists, tried to reason with the blood rushing through me, with the spikes in my veins screaming that she may have shed tears for someone other than me.

Those were my fucking tears.

I took one last look at the nail polish—*who the fuck made her sad?*—then moved on. It was a few hours before the night maid service. Her bedsheets were wrinkled, and a distinctly not-blonde hair lay on the pillow.

I swallowed, possession sliding like a knife down my throat.

Did someone sleep here?

The hair glowed a soft purple lilac in the moonlight.

One of her friends.

I pulled open her nightstand, the usual place for drugs. Empty. I went to the dryer vent. The dust pattern matched how I left it. The camera I'd placed undisturbed. No new ones.

Opened the smoke detector, checking for bugs. I checked the router for unfamiliar devices or Bluetooth signals. All good.

Her closet consisted of rows of sleek, shiny dressers, a wall of backlit shoes, an island with jewelry glowing through a glass top, and two chaise longues. Her dresses were always a finger width apart, pink the dominant color. I paused on the skintight dress she'd worn to the club, the memory of how it hugged her body shooting straight to my cock.

Fuck.

This was a Princess Gemma outfit. I liked Princess Gemma, because I loved fucking up her perfect pink exterior. Still, as I walked toward her shoes, I imagined her in black. That fantasy really fucked me up.

A color as powerful and darkly feminine as she pretended she wasn't.

Shoes were the same, jewelry the same. There was nothing hidden in the first dresser. I pushed around scarves, still nothing.

I went to the second dresser. Her underwear was neatly arranged and color coordinated in its velvet-lined shelf. I pushed them aside and found a ziplock bag of loose pills.

Bingo.

I shoved them into my pocket, ready to shut the drawer, and paused. Gemma always had exactly ninety-seven pairs of panties in rotation. I counted ninety-six—

she'd worn nothing tonight, and her laundry was done daily.

Where the fuck did it go?

That fucked sense of possession slid into my veins and I pulled out my cock. I wanted to mark her like a goddamn animal. Anyone who came near her would know.

Unmarked, unclaimed, not off limits.

I fisted my cock, stroking it over her perfectly aligned rows of panties.

I'd long since accepted that Gemma Crowne was more than a passing fixation. She was inside me, burrowed so deep in my marrow that even trying to get her out would render me lifeless.

But this wasn't how this went. I didn't fucking jack off into her clothes like a psycho in some early-2000s movie. I came in, I checked things, and I left.

But the idea that someone was here, *someone* had touched what belonged to me, twisted me up. That off-limits, forbidden fantasy where Gemma Crowne wore my mark has me fucked in the head.

I gripped the wall above me as an anchor.

Her colorful panties blurred with each stroke. The real Gemma Crowne was messy, dirty. That night on the beach I hadn't just seen it, I'd *felt* it. The room dissolved and I was back there, back between Gemma's thighs as she begged me to fulfill her fucked-up fantasies. Back when I consumed her illicit ecstasy, her sighs, her perfect, tight pussy.

Her skin dimpled beneath my fingers when I gripped her hips.

Her legs found my back, pushing me deeper.

I gripped harder, stroked faster, a strangled, involuntary groan leaving my lips.

Fuck.

I hadn't fucked anyone since her.

It had been five years, I was basically a monk.

I'd tried, but nothing compared to her. Gemma said the dirtiest fucking shit when she got going. I only saw her pristine princess act slip away once, but now she was stuck inside me. Every goddamn time I came, I heard her husky voice telling me to make her cry.

I grabbed a pair of her panties to smother my come.

Seconds passed in what felt like minutes. My head hung heavy, the arm anchored to the wall strained. She'd opened up for me on the beach—*only for me*—and goddamn if that wasn't the most addicting drug.

Because, for a moment, I felt something.

I took a deep breath, a deadly truth passing through my thoughts.

This dark, vicious need is growing beyond something I can control.

I stuffed myself back into my jeans, prepared to toss the panties when I got back, when that same need curled in my gut. I placed them on top of her neatly organized ones. Messy. Fucked up with me.

Then left.

FIFTEEN

GRIM

The sun had risen into morning when I got back to the Wharf. I immediately clocked something was amiss. A sleek black Rolls-Royce was in the middle of the regularly empty parking lot. The driver inside didn't turn to look as I walked past him.

Whatever high I had from seeing Gemma vanished.

The club was quiet with daytime. I already knew who would be waiting before I saw his back, salt-and-pepper hair illuminated under the bright overhead lights. My three brothers stood in front of him, arms folded. Upon hearing the door open, their eyes lifted over his head, to me.

"Why the fuck are you here?" I said.

He turned around, a smile spearing his lips that didn't meet his eyes. "The man of the hour."

I shared another look with my brothers. It was the second time in less than a month Vander Archeron had paid us a visit. The most he showed up was once every six months, if that.

Unmarked, unclaimed, not off limits.

He left that night without another word, so I never found out why he was talking to Gemma Crowne. What he wanted.

"What the fuck do you want?" I repeated.

He rubbed the side of his neck. "Just checking in."

I bit my molars, jaw tweaking. "Checking in."

He smiled, and this time it did reach his eyes. "You any closer to closing the Crowne girl's contract?"

I shifted. "I'll close it when I close it."

He laughed, reaching inside the breast of his jacket. "Sure you're not getting business mixed with pleasure?"

He pulled out a small, square photograph. It appeared to be taken far away, probably with a drone, but what you could see was clear: me with Gemma Crowne, on the beach yesterday.

Closer than we should be.

Shit.

Tension buzzed in the room. Lock pushed his tongue into the back of his teeth, and Raze clenched his jaw, nostrils flared. Wraith...well, he didn't seem mad or surprised, but it was impossible to know for sure with him.

"I was checking in on a contract," I said, voice even. "Isn't that what you're doing?"

Silence settled, then he shoved the photo back into his pocket. "Sure. How is everyone else doing? Your sister— Sabrina, right? She's doing good?"

Something unhinged fell across Lock's features. He took a step forward when Raze grabbed his elbow.

Vander laughed again. "I've given you five years to figure this out. Might be about time I choose for you."

With those parting words, he left. The metal door slammed shut behind him, briefly illuminating the club in white before being snuffed out.

"So..." Lock started. "You're lying to us now?"

If I didn't know better, I'd think Lock sounded worried.

I was always the one in control. Raze's anger got him into trouble. I couldn't count the number of times we'd had to clean up some mess because Lock had no control over where he stuck his dick. And Wraith? Wraith was like trying to keep a pet jaguar—the minute it was free, it would maul your face off.

"Are you fucking her?" Lock asked.

"No."

"Good. You can't fuck her."

I laughed, caustic. "I know you're not about to tell me where I can put my dick."

"Are you planning on fucking her?" Lock continued, undeterred.

I thought to what I'd left on Gemma's dresser. My come leaking and staining her pretty, perfect things.

Whenever I closed my eyes, I could still feel her perfect, soft cunt. Could still picture that pouty princess act slip into perfect surrender as she stretched for my cock. One night on the beach wasn't nearly enough.

There's still so much I need to do to her.

Finally, I answered. "No."

Raze exhaled, rubbing a hand across his face. "It feels a lot like five years ago."

A sludgy, foreign sensation filled my gut—*guilt*.

There were a lot of rumors surrounding the *why* of us. We were born into some top-secret, illuminati-style crime syndicate. We were a sex cult. We were the muscle of some shadowy power.

The truth was, we were just as indebted as whomever was inked on our skin. But five years ago, we were almost out.

I rubbed my neck. "What are you saying?"

"We were almost out. No, we fucking *were* out. Then you took her contract. I'm not doing another five years of this." He shoved his hand toward the door Vander had just left through.

"And you think I want that?" I said.

"I don't know," he said. "This is the second time in a month he's shown up. *Are* you any closer to closing her contract?"

Silence stretched again, thick and sticky.

"It's *us*," Raze said. "We know you, man. We know that you're acting differently with her. You treat her differently."

I rubbed my jaw. Not able to deny it, but not exactly going to confirm.

"You can't see her anymore," Lock said.

I stopped rubbing my jaw, hand frozen.

"Dude, you know I'm right," he continued. "Until we can figure out a way to get you out of her contract, you stay away. We don't need to give that asshole more ammo. We can handle any interactions. Don't let a fucked-up socialite be the reason ten years goes up in flames."

He *was* right. I should have stayed away years ago. There were already too many secrets I'd been keeping from my brothers because of her.

Too many times I'd gone to her and lied to them.

If there was ever a time when Gemma and I could have been something, it died the day we took our ink.

"Yeah," I said. "I'll keep my distance."

SIXTEEN

GEMMA

When I have you again, you'll be sober.

When, not if, Grim said. A promise.

It had been over two weeks since I last saw Grim, and two weeks ago, I'd found my underwear. Used. I knew immediately it was Grim. I had picked them up to throw them away when, like a fucking psycho, I kept them.

I blame it on the drugs.

Now, it was sunny outside and warm, too warm for January, which meant the cold would come soon and harsh. We were due for a snowstorm, anyway. Kennedy, Blaire, and I lay out by my heated pool, smoking Kennedy's newest hand-rolled joint, while near the garden, yet another anniversary party was being set up.

I shouldn't even be thinking about him, wondering where he was. Because that was our relationship. Grim would disappear for stretches and then only reappear to demand something of me, or take it.

So I could never fully forget him.

I shouldn't even be thinking about him, wondering where he was. Because that was our relationship. Grim would disappear for stretches and then only reappear to demand something of me, or take it.

So I could never fully forget him.

There were rules the Horsemen stuck to, a code. They never fraternized with their contracted, and they only met to discuss the terms of the contract.

I guess I got a little thrill knowing he broke them for me.

But those rules were there for protection—*my* protection. Every time he broke them, it eroded that safety net.

Lust fogged my mind. It felt like I was in a steam room. As my friends talked about random shit, I thought wrong, dirty thoughts. Like wondering if Grim had ever done something like that in my room before. Picturing his thick and tattooed cock—

"Gemma?" Kennedy said.

"What?" I blinked out of the fantasy.

I couldn't think straight.

Obsessed. That's what I am.

"Are we ever going to talk about Geoff?" Kennedy asked, half dipping her toes in the heated infinity pool that bled seamlessly into the horizon.

"What about him?" Blaire asked, taking the joint from Kennedy.

"He's a *missing* person," Kennedy said.

"Right, but what's there to talk about?"

"He's missing?" I asked. "Since when?"

Kennedy shrugged. "Your mom's party, I think."

I ghosted my touch along my arm, along bruises that had long since faded, remembering the look in Grim's eyes.

"It was leaked to one of the Crowne stan accounts."

Stan accounts: people who dedicated their entire lives to either worshipping us or tearing us down—sometimes both.

"He's probably on a bender. Remember last year when he stole his stepdad's yacht to France and tried to join the foreign legion?"

"Yeah..." I stared off, feeling hot. Sticky.

Some part of me knew I should be alarmed. My life was quickly changing, warping into something I couldn't recognize. Maybe that was why I had such a visceral reaction to being a godmother. It was another thing highlighting the chasm between my two selves that was quickly growing too wide to cross.

I grabbed my towel, covering up my naked chest, staring out at the ocean.

"Gemma, you're blocking my sun," Kennedy moaned.

"Good," Blaire snapped. "You're not even wearing sunscreen."

"It's winter."

"And? The sun still exists in winter."

"I swear to *God*, Blaire," Kennedy said, "if you go on another one of your skincare rants."

"At least Gemma put sunscreen on her boobs," Blaire said, gesturing to me. "Your tits are gonna look like raisins."

"Remind me to record this and tag all the stans who think you're body positive," Kennedy muttered.

It was already four. The sun falling in the sky. That stiff, hot feeling in the air when the sun has already hung around for too long.

"Shit." Kennedy sat up. "We should probably start getting ready."

"For?" I asked.

They stared at me. "The sponsored event in New York? You know, that new tech brand paying us to party."

Oh, right.

There was no reason for me not to go. I *should* be going. I'd have to pay a huge fee for breaking contract, not to mention it was great press.

So I don't know why the lie left my lips. "Oh, right. There was some contract issue." I slipped my sunglasses on, hoping they wouldn't question me. "Can't go anymore."

"Fucking lame," Blaire said. "Can we still use the helicopter?"

"Wait," Kennedy interrupted. "Are you still going to the tea tomorrow?"

I'd completely forgotten about it. It was like every other event in my world, somehow both perilously important and utterly banal. It wasn't like I was missing something once-in-a-lifetime, but the thing is, the more you miss in this world, the less you matter. I'd always understood that rule, but lately it was getting harder to follow it.

"I'm not sure," I said honestly.

They shared a look, *what the fuck is wrong with her?* written on their faces.

After agreeing to let them use the Crowne family heli-copter, they left. I watched them disappear, wondering if this was what insanity was: knowing what I was supposed to do, and doing the wrong thing anyway.

I know he's bad for me. I know I shouldn't be near him.

And yet.

A few hours later, when I was supposed to be *America's Princess,* I instead found myself at the Underworld.

My attraction to Grim, to this *place,* wasn't logical. It was the antithesis of what I should be. I promised my mom

—*myself*—I would find another Horace, I would somehow find a way to make *Crowne* acceptable again.

I traveled up the glowing stairs, the steps changing colors beneath my feet from pink, to purple, to blue. My fingers glided across the silky gold railing, and I looked down at the partiers below me, their bodies moving in snakelike unison with the beat. I'd tried to wear something nondescript. Not my usual platforms and mini. Opting for a skirt, an oversize tee, and hat. Because Gemma Crowne had every reason to be on that club floor, but no reason to be on these stairs.

Our eyes locked the second my foot hit the floor.

His black eyes were a nightmare.

Savage.

Deadly.

And it fed me.

The balcony was packed. Grim sat on a black velvet couch, arms spread wide on the top. Women danced, but no one touched him. Bodies blurred around him and he was frozen in time, a god passing time with mortals.

I didn't know how it was possible that just eye contact had the room dissolving. Our souls vibrating.

He raised a hand. The room emptied.

Even after everyone had gone down the stairs behind me, I stood there. The beat of the club pulsated between us.

Grim wasn't like anyone I'd met. He dripped sex and confidence like smoke. Every time I was in his presence, I got sucked in. I think he might be the only person I'd ever met who actually *knew* who he was, and that was so goddamn intoxicating, because I have no idea who I am.

I'd only ever slept with him once, and it was enough to fucking hypnotize me for life. Trying to figure him out drove me *insane*.

I'd never seen him with a girl but I *know* he's fucking. He *had* to be. So I just had to wonder. Who was warming Grim's bed?

He crooked a finger.

Without thought I walked over and climbed on top of him, thighs spread on either side of him. His hands found my thighs easily, with a familiar possession that made my gut flip.

I looked for the other Horsemen. "Are they here too?"

A slow shake of his head angled his jaw left, the deep purple light sharpening his jaw. His hands slid up my thighs, to my waist.

"Someone I know went missing," I said, leaning into the touch.

"That so?"

His eyes flared. One of his hands slid from my waist, back to the arch of my spine, dragging me closer. His dark, earthy scent sent my thoughts scrambling.

"Did you do it?" I started grinding into him. Addicted to that deep, dragging darkness in his stare, pulling on my chest like a fishhook.

He pulled my head closer, lips at my neck. "I don't like it when people touch my things."

My heart slammed against my chest. Something hot and pulsating dripped down my stomach, pooling hot and throbbing between my legs.

Grim pulled back, but was still close, our noses almost touching, then, wordlessly, he shifted me so I was pressed flat against his denim-covered cock. Hard. Throbbing. A shuddery breath racked through his body. He wanted this. I could *feel* it.

He stared where my thighs spread.

I was wearing the same panties he'd ruined—now

cleaned. Was that why the muscle jerked in his jaw? Did he recognize them?

I hoped so.

All he'd have to do was move my underwear aside, and I *wanted* him to, but he just stared, jaw clenched. I was mesmerized by him, by this dark liquor between us that we couldn't stop drinking.

Grim kept his soul behind a twenty-foot-thick concrete wall. He once told me his insides were radioactive, an inky glowing well of poison that corroded whatever and whomever they touched.

Many years ago, before Grim became my reaper, in a dimly lit spare high school room, he whispered a confession to me.

I'm poison, Gemma. Stay away.

"I'm poison too," I said.

His eyes flashed up, inky like always, but for a moment they glowed.

And I latched on to that.

My thighs slid farther open. His hands slid to my ass, pushing my skirt up to my hips. He tugged at my thong, pulling it tight enough to spread me.

His lips found my throat as I gasped.

This was the only language we ever spoke fluently.

I once read an explanation of suicide that said it was like someone jumping out of a burning building. They didn't jump because they wanted to die, but because they feared the fire.

I ground myself onto Grim's denim-covered cock as that explanation ran circles in my head. He gripped my hips, pushing me even deeper.

We were like two people stuck in a building. Refusing to jump or ask for help. Lying in the fire until it consumed us. But it wasn't the fire that drew us together, it was the smell of the smoke and ashes. The promise of ruin, and peace that follows.

I wondered if that was why he couldn't let me go. If he felt the same irrational, self-destructive, and fucking deadly need.

I know that's why I can't.

"Don't hold out for me, Gemma," he said against my skin, moving with me. "I'm already dead and gone."

Something stupid and insane overcame me, driven by the hungry, pained way he stared at me, or maybe the way his hands dragged down my back as if trying to pull me into his soul.

"There hasn't been anyone since you," I whispered. "Not since that night on...on the beach."

I wished I could swallow it back into my mouth.

He knotted his hand in my hair, yanking my head back to find my eyes. Like he wanted to see if I was telling the truth.

A moment later he groaned. "Don't tell me that." The jagged, pained sound slid into my bones.

He grabbed me by the hips and flipped me onto the soft velvet couch. The music thrummed through the fabric, vibrating against my back. One leg between mine, an arm above my head, I was caged.

"No one's taken care of you?" he asked.

This moment was different from any we'd shared. There was an urgency, a hunger in him. His head was bent, hair falling across his eyes, but beneath the locks I could see the gleam.

Feral. Predatory.

I shook my head.

"Poor girl." His free hand skated across my pussy, a soft

restraint in his touch that did not match the savage gleam in his eyes. I nearly jolted when he found the soft, bare skin he'd exposed.

"No one's made you come?" He stroked the backs of his knuckles along my pussy. Soft. Light. Too in control.

"You must be so strung out." As he spoke, one knuckle parted me.

My mouth dropped, but I said nothing. I could only nod frantically, like some possessed thing. I *was* strung out. I *was* losing it. And the too light way he touched me wasn't helping.

He stilled. "Why?"

I know he knew why. He wanted to hear it from me. But I couldn't. I couldn't give in to that. I couldn't tell him it was because he fucking ruined me. Because just the thought of someone else touching me made me want to dry heave. Because it was like everything about me was waiting for him.

I bit my lip. His eyes dropped to it. He lowered the distance between us, so close I could once again taste the whiskey. Grim's kiss was forever burned inside me. Punishing, insatiable. I closed my eyes.

This is it. After five years of nothing, we'll finally kiss.

All at once he pushed off me, putting distance between us, sitting on the edge of the couch.

"*Fuck*," he hissed, dragging his hands through his hair. Head in one hand, he craned his neck to look at me, eyes dropping to where my skirt was still pushed up. He shook his head. "God fucking dammit."

He looked oddly, surprisingly human.

"You need to go," he said.

The demand wasn't coated in the cruel venom he usually stabbed me with. His whole body was tense, and it sounded more like he was asking me to go, begging me to go. So that was why I didn't argue. Why I didn't pout.

I just stood up and pushed my skirt back down.

Eventually I called my car and made it home as the sun was rising above the sparkling, iron ocean. I made my way through the cavernous insides of my home in a daze.

What the fuck did I just do?

I'd always had these dark, uncontrollable thoughts. These stark and vivid scenes that just flew into my brain. When I was still in school, I used to stare at the windows, and they'd explode. The glass would fly at me, slicing open my skin.

And then my friends would say something and the windows were magically whole again.

I'd died, but was still there.

Being with Grim was like that, too, in a way.

So I guess what I was saying was, there was a part of me that didn't just want to know how far down the rabbit hole goes. I wanted the darkness to swallow me—

I stopped short.

Lock was on my bed, his shoes on and feet crossed.

"What the fuck?"

I should have known something was off right away, because when I got to my wing, my guards were gone. I was too in my head, though. I felt like I was on the Titanic, my perfect world slowly colliding with the darkness, and there was nothing I could do to stop it.

As I spoke, I caught a glimpse of a second shadow on my balcony—Wraith—and then I saw a third body at my desk, looking out the window—Raze.

Three Horsemen were in my bedroom.

Raze slowly turned around, facing me. "You're home late, Barbie."

SEVENTEEN

GEMMA

In all my years indebted to the Horsemen, I had only ever dealt with Grim. Rarely, his brothers would provide backup, but never alone.

Never like this, showing up in my fucking world.

I went to Lock and shoved his boots off my duvet. "Excuse you. This is imported."

Something like a smile tugged at the corner of his thick red lips. As quickly as I saw it come, he wiped it off.

"You can't just come into my home, my world. What if someone saw you?"

Lock stood off my bed. He was towering. Too imposing. "Now you care if someone sees you?"

"What the hell does that mean?"

"Where were you tonight, princess?"

The night rushed over me. Grim's touch searing my skin. The ravenous gleam in his eyes when he'd asked me to leave.

I shrugged. "Out."

I don't know why I lied. It's not like Grim wouldn't tell them, or they couldn't see on the billions of cameras they had.

But it felt special...secret.

Lock and Raze shared a look.

"You sure about that, Barbie?" Raze stepped away from my window, closer to me. His features were a mixture of bored and angry, like my existence was nothing save an active irritant.

I barely saw his cold eyes beneath his silky, wavy hair—black and white, split equally down the middle of his part. I knew he didn't dye it; it was that bright white naturally on the one side. There was a story there, one he didn't share.

Next to Wraith, Raze had the most tattoos.

I folded my arms. "Why do you care?"

The muscles in his jaw flexed, making the tattoos on his neck snake. "You're getting too comfortable."

"I assure you I'm not fucking comfortable right now—"

"You're forgetting your place," Raze continued, cutting me off. "You don't call us, you wait for our fucking call. You don't show up places without an invite. *You* belong to *us*."

They *had* seen...but that still didn't explain why they were here. Lock and Raze took a step toward me and instinctively I stepped back—into something hard.

"You know what happens when a dog disobeys?" His voice was like rocks, jagged and rough. Lower, somehow, than Grim's. The heat of it made the hair at my neck rise. "They get a leash."

Wraith.

My heartbeat froze, just stopped completely in my chest, before nose-diving into my gut.

I didn't consider myself very fearful. I wouldn't say I

was courageous, just...numb. Jaded, I guess. When you'd seen the shit I had, lived the life I had, you stopped caring.

But *Wraith?*

Yeah, he still made me shiver.

I stepped off with a jolt, putting space between me and him, and the other two.

At first, everything about Wraith screamed normal boy in his twenties. From the nondescript black hoodie and jeans to his dark sneakers. In high school, girls were all over his ass. He had that silky, curly hair you just wanted to run your fingers through.

His hoodie fell over his face, shadowing him. In the night, where you were most often likely to see him, that hoodie obscured his truth. He almost looked normal, until he stepped into the light. Then you knew why they called him Wraith.

Wraith was the only Horsemen with tattoos that covered half his face, a terrifying mask of black ink.

"Does Grim know about this—"

Wraith cut me off. "You don't worry about him; he's none of your concern."

My massive wing felt small, shrinking under them and their implications.

This isn't how it's supposed to be.

We had a fucking deal.

Stay out of my world. Stay out *of my world.*

Fuck. This.

I pushed through the wall of men. Lock grabbed my arm and shoved me against the wall. "Where are you going looking all determined?"

I stared up into Lock's blue eyes.

No use in lying.

"To see Grim."

He pushed his tongue into his cheek, looking me up and down. Finally, after what felt like forever, he said, "Nah, you're not. You're gonna stay right here."

I yanked my arm free. "Like fuck I am."

He slammed his hand against the wall as I tried to leave. "You don't go anywhere without one of us. You don't piss without us. If for some reason we're not with you, be back at your house before nightfall."

I think I did a double take. "Excuse me? A curfew?"

"I'm guessing that's something your spoiled ass has never had." He craned his neck to stare at my ass.

I turned away because, no, I'd never had a fucking curfew.

"If one of us texts, text back."

"And if I break these rules?" I stepped to him. "I already know the worst thing you can do to me, and I don't care."

He grabbed me by my hip bones, bruising. "You have *no idea* the things we can do to you."

I sucked in a breath.

He smiled, then let me go and walked back to my bed. Raze leaned against the wall, pulling out his phone.

They were settled in. Comfortable. Like they were planning to *stay*.

"So, it's late," I said. "You've made your point. I'm thoroughly terrified. I'll be a good little girl now."

Wraith sat down on my settee, his scary mad dog vibes totally at odds with the cream velvet.

I blinked. "You're not seriously thinking you can *sleep* here." Silence met me. "Grim knows about this?" I tested.

"All that fancy boarding school learning and they didn't teach you basic vocabulary?" Lock asked. "As far as you're concerned, Grim is dead. But don't worry, we'll be there for you, princess. Every day."

EIGHTEEN

GEMMA

The Horsemen left my room, but their shadows frosted the glass on my double door. I was trapped in my own fucking room. It didn't make any sense. I stared at their three unmoving shadows, trying to put pieces of the puzzle together, but there are too many gaps in the board.

I don't remember falling asleep. I woke up in the same position, a crick in my neck from having slept sitting up all night. The shadows at the door were gone. Rubbing my neck, I went out to my living room—

"There you are, sweetie." My mom stood in the living room, arms folded.

Sweetie?

Normally, my mother's kindness would elicit a bone-chilling dread. Today, I barely registered it past the fear screaming in my bones that she would see the Horsemen. She would know what I was hiding.

She would *know*.

I looked around my living room.

It was empty, no sign of the Horsemen.

Maybe it was a fluke. Just another Horseman scare tactic, but nervous tension still slid through me, wired and jittery.

Satisfied there were no illicit men in my room, I was able to fully focus on my mother. She was still in her pajamas despite it being light out. I rubbed my lips together. Tansy Crowne didn't stay in her pajamas past 5:00 a.m., even if the entire goddamn globe was on fire.

"What's going on?" I asked.

Not leaving her perch on the wall, my mom tossed something on my couch—*tossed*—the woman who believed walking too quickly was tantamount to spitting on the pope.

I leaned forward to see what it was: a magazine.

I snatched the glossy thing up. There was a photo of me in a tiara from my last birthday, when my hair was still long, before Abby took scissors to it. I was smiling at someone off camera. A bold, black serif headline overlay the photo.

AMERICA'S CRIME PRINCESS

The Crowne family is no stranger to scandal. With the most recent unearthing of Beryl Crowne's illegal practices, the world thought the Crowne family had turned over a new leaf. But could America's Princess also be tied into something criminal?

I hadn't had a panic attack in a few years, not since I'd started chewing benzos like Tums, but I felt one coming on.

I quickly flipped to the story, trying not to think of the three bodies that had shadowed my room all night. They had a photo of me smiling next to some Wall Street guy that, I guess, was arrested for fraud. I didn't remember him, like I didn't remember the hundreds of people I shook hands with.

Nothing about Grim or the Horsemen.

My heart calmed—a little.

This wasn't the first lie someone had told about me. Secretly a Scientologist. Member of the Illuminati. Married to this prince or that heir in some secret wedding.

It was just the first time they were almost right.

"It's not true," I said. "You know this kind of story blows over."

"There's more."

Frowning, I kept reading. On the last page was a horrible candid photo of me beside a red wooden cottage with white trim.

My stomach dropped. I knew that building.

There were things my mother and I didn't talk about, things we pretended never happened. The year her perfect, eldest daughter overdosed and was sent to a chic rehab in Sweden? Definitely one of those things.

Gemma Crowne is known for perfection. The perfect nude lip. The perfect pink mani. But if America's Princess hides a pill addiction—what else is she hiding?

I set the magazine down, winded. "How did they get this?"

My mother said nothing. She should be angry. My pristine crown was tarnished, so she should be giving me a smile while saying something diabolical. Instead, she just...leaned against the wall.

Her eyes were glassy, her posture soft.

Oh.

She came over, stroked my hair, and then left without another word. That was *so much* worse than if she'd called me a failure. It was like she was giving up.

Guilt tore shreds into my stomach.

Maybe that was why I went, to prove to my mother I could be what she needed.

Prove I wasn't an addict.

Prove I wasn't slowly sinking into shadow.

I was America's Princess.

Hours later, the bags under my eyes expertly color corrected, I stared at the orange-and-gold door of the teahouse, trying to tell myself to go inside. The people within were probably foaming at their expertly filled mouths. For the first time, Gemma Crowne's shiny, spotless persona had a crack in it.

Stalling, I took out my phone. My notifications had blown up.

She's pathetic.

Honestly, it's not even the drugs—addiction is a disease, right? It's the fact that she's been lying and pretending to be so fucking perfect.

The whole Crowne family is fucked up. You saw what they did to their grandfather—

"Hey, princess."

I startled at the voice, quickly shoving my phone back in my clutch.

He can't be here.

None of them can. This was the most exclusive tearoom in Crowne Point. As if to defy my inner voice, a heavy, muscled, and leather-clad arm landed on my shoulder.

"You can't be here," I whispered.

Lock spun me to face him and grabbed my chin, dragging my eyes to his icy-blue ones—a mean, deceptive blue, the color of thin ice right before you fell through and drowned.

"People will see you," I said.

See *me,* see all the dark secrets I'd managed to hide, the soul-deep bruises I'd covered.

Lock leaned forward, his head shadowing us. "Aw, afraid your friends won't like me?"

His inky-black hair fell haphazard over sharp brows and sharper blue eyes. The stenciled bloody hemlock on his neck flexed with his muscles and veins.

I swallowed, refusing to let him see my uncertainty and fear. "They wouldn't even let you in the fucking bathroom."

"Why don't you let me handle that?" Lock grinned slow, easy, and leonine, then stepped back. "After you, princess."

NINETEEN

GEMMA

The conversation dulled when I entered, linen suits and bodies clad in floral turning.

I was used to being the center of attention, but I'd weathered enough scandal to know the difference between awe and bloodlust. They stared and whispered, lips hidden clandestinely beneath teacups.

Everyone was staring at me—because of course they were. Gemma Crowne—*perfect* Gemma Crowne, America's Princess, the one who was always so good at showing how much better she was—brought a criminal to the tea party.

A sweet, floral smell wafted from the clusters of purple and blue wisteria dripping down the walls and ceiling. I stared out at the circular tearoom and let nothing on. Posing and smiling was as involuntary as breathing now, thanks to Tansy Crowne.

Lock laughed. "The fuck even is this, princess?"

"You wouldn't understand," I said, looking over my shoulder.

Sure it was a tea party, but not really. It was where we came to show off how wonderful we were. How perfect we were. How much better we were than everyone around us.

I turned forward.

If you focused, you could see where the wisteria roots were digging into the wall, starting to uproot the plaster. What a perfect flower choice. Like everything in my world, it hid a destructive truth through a beautiful facade.

The familiar waltz of civility continued on outside of the ten-foot bubble Lock's presence created. If my world was great at anything, it was at ignoring the elephant in the room.

But I saw the way they looked at me.

She's losing it.

Oh, poor girl, probably never got over her ex dumping her.

I needed them to love me, but I *hated* them.

And that dichotomy was ripping me in two.

I didn't know the shadowy beginnings of the Horsemen, how or why the boys I knew became *Horsemen*. There were all kinds of stories floating around Crowne Point, most of them tinged with supernatural horror.

Some people actually believed they sold their souls to the devil.

So a normal person would be scared.

A normal person wouldn't elbow the Horseman at her back. "No one will talk to me with you lurking like a six-foot shadow."

"So this is what you want, princess?" Lock asked. "To be sold to men who don't deserve you?"

"Depends." I spun to Lock. "Are you planning on scaring away every person who looks at me?"

"You can do better than these guys, princess. A fucking corpse could do better than these guys."

I stifled my laugh in my teacup. Not a second later, I frowned.

What is this?

I stood on my tiptoes to glare into his eyes. "Why are you being nice to me?"

He bent down, black hair shadowing his icy-blue eyes, tugging the silver piercing in his bottom lip with his teeth.

"Princess," Lock said. "You've got a visitor."

I blinked as he leaned back against the wall, a slight smile on his lips.

I turned around, finding that one man had finally made his way to me: Nathan Cartwright. Nathan had gone to the same boarding school as me before I transferred to Crowne Point High, but a few years before, so we'd not really hung in the same circles.

Nathan was a boring social climber.

In any other scenario, I wouldn't have given him a second look, but my mother's glassy eyes were still stuck in my mind.

"Did I just see Gemma Crowne laugh?" he asked, eyeing Lock at my back.

"Uh..." I arched a brow. "I laugh."

"You're usually pretty uptight at these things."

Was this motherfucker really trying to *neg* me?

I stayed silent, and Nathan continued. "Anyway, I wasn't sure I'd see you here today, what with the news." There was something tucked under his arm.

"News?" I asked, playing dumb.

The drink in Nathan's hand shook as he stared at Lock at my back.

"Have you not seen?" Nathan pulled out a magazine from under his arm—*the* magazine.

There it is.

Even the Horsemen couldn't deter the temptation to shove my shame in my face.

I eyed the glossy paper.

"What an interesting thing to bring to tea," I said at last, then lifted my eyes to his slowly. "You must have been as bored as I am with the company." *Choke, bitch.*

What the fuck am I doing here?

All my life I was prepared for one thing: to marry, and then my brother gave me a choice.

My mom seemed to think I could just show up and choose any one of these men, because that was what we did—we married. I used to think that too. But I was starting to realize the problem. Given the choice? Well, I wouldn't choose to be with any of these fuckers. Nathan. Horace. They were all the same.

So where did that leave me?

Because I still wanted to be Gemma Crowne, I wanted it to *mean* something, and who was Gemma Crowne without her crown?

"You were always so out of reach in boarding school," Nathan continued. "The top of the pack, the queen fucking bee. Not so much anymore, huh?"

I exhaled, preparing my *perfect* Gemma Crowne response, when a scream stopped me in my tracks.

It happened so fast, I didn't register anything until it was already over. I heard the *crack* first. Saw how Nathan's unctuous, smug smile collapsed in agony. Lock had reached over my shoulder, holding Nathan's hand in a vise grip.

That was the crack.

That was why tears wobbled on his lids.

Lock had broken his fucking fingers.

Lock pulled Nathan close by his now broken hand—as if they were old friends. "Scream out again, die. Call the cops, die. Tell your friends, die. Do anything but leave through that fuckin' ugly orange door, die. Nod so I know you're listening."

Nathan nodded, tears running down his face.

Lock laughed and released his hand.

My mouth dropped. Nathan's middle three fingers were bent and crumpled at odd angles.

"Good boy." Lock patted him on his shoulder. "Now go."

Nathan shot me a wide-eyed look, cradling his broken fingers, and left.

I released the breath I didn't realize I was holding.

"Are you fucking insane? Someone could have seen." I looked around, heartbeat like a hummingbird flapping against my rib cage. Even though paparazzi weren't allowed inside, that didn't stop phones.

Lock leaned against the wall, rubbing his jaw, bored.

"Why did you do that?" I asked. "You can't just...break the fucking fingers of a guy who *talks* to me. If you're trying to destroy my life—"

Lock stepped to me so fast my tea sloshed over the side, staining the fine silk of my sleeves caramel. He towered over me, shadowing us.

"You really think everything is about you, huh?"

I scoffed. "If that wasn't about me, then what the absolute fuck? Why are you here? Why did you break his fingers?"

Lock bent lower, neck craning with the effort. "Maybe I

didn't like the way he was talking to you." His words were tainted with sarcasm, bitter and acerbic.

I rolled my eyes, and he leaned back on the wall. Arms folded, with one leg crossed over the other, crushing the purple wisteria at his back, he continued. "You've been cosplaying Reaper's girl—"

I cut him off. "I have not."

"If you want to pretend to be the Reaper's girl," he continued, undeterred, "you should know what it means to wear that title."

TWENTY

GEMMA

Lock drove me home after tea. To my surprise and delight, he didn't follow me inside. Once again, I tried to lie to myself that it was just a fluke, until all three reappeared just a few hours later.

Now I sat in bed, staring at their three shadows. I'd since changed into a comfortable white nightshirt that said:

I FEEL GREAT.

PLEASE DIE.

And tried not to think about what Lock had said, instead scouring the internet for anything about me, Nathan, and Lock. There was nothing—well, nothing beyond the savage glee that Gemma Crowne was addicted to pills.

This was the worst press I'd received in...well, ever. Abigail always took the brunt of shitty tabloids. People said there was no such thing as bad press. Tansy Crowne said if you couldn't control the press, you didn't deserve to be in it.

I glanced back at the Horsemen's bodies shadowing my frosted double doors.

You should know what it means to wear that title.

I thought back to what HSOG had said. If I was marked, even the wrong look can be considered a declaration of war.

That shouldn't give me goose bumps, but it was a twisted fantasy I couldn't help but want to drown in.

"Don't you have people to enslave?" I yelled through the door. "You know, lives to destroy. Better things to do than babysit me?"

Silence.

I groaned, falling against my bed. That was how it had been for hours. It was almost twelve and any nightlife was just beginning. I wondered about Grim. Wondered if he was at the club, wondered if he was still sad, and why.

I wasn't supposed to be thinking about him. To *still* be thinking about him.

The space he occupied inside me grew and grew. He was smoke. I couldn't see him. I couldn't touch him. But he was there inside me, taking over. Until I couldn't breathe or move from it.

I was so goddamn *weak.*

Looking for a distraction, I pulled out my phone, to the last photo "I" posted. It was this morning, some scheduled post with a photo I'd taken over a year ago. I was in a bikini, because of course I was. I stared so long at the photo my face became unrecognizable. This Gemma was happy, whole—and never existed.

How could I compete with a version of myself that was so perfect everyone loved her?

Everything would be so much easier if I was just gone.

I will never be the Gemma Crowne in those photos.

All it would take is—

I chucked my phone at my mirror, hoping it would shatter to pieces. My phone slammed against the corner, and only a small, triangular piece of the glass fractured and fell to the ground.

Awesome.

A moment later, my doors flew open. Raze and Lock looked left and right, guns drawn. I had a half second to marvel at that—*no way were they worried about me, right?*—when my brother's voice sounded from behind them.

"What the fuck is going on here?"

Raze and Lock blocked my complete view. Behind them, I saw the outline of Wraith's feet perched on my coffee table. My brother stared at that, at Wraith sprawled out on my couch, before finding Raze and Lock, their weapons drawn.

After a half second, where they scanned every corner of my room, Raze and Lock put away their weapons, turning to my brother.

"What does it look like?" There was a suggestive tease in Lock's voice. My brother glared at Lock, before looking to me.

"Are you okay?" he asked.

Raze and Lock stepped together, closing the window where he could see me.

"She's great," Raze said.

"All right," Gray said, restraint roughening his voice. "Get the fuck out of my house."

Lock stepped to him. "Or what? Gonna call the police? Tell them about the deal *you* took with the devil?"

Guilt clawed my stomach. *I* was the reason Gray had anything to do with them. I could have found another way to save Story, one that didn't involve tying us to the Underworld.

A dark, fucked-up part of me whispered that it wouldn't have mattered.

I would have always called Grim.

Most people cowered at the mere sight of the Horsemen, but Grayson folded his arms, looking put out.

"I don't give a shit what you have on me, or what you'll do. She's my sister. Get. The. Fuck. Out."

"What about that pretty little wife?" Raze asked. "Care what happens to her?"

I saw the switch in Gray. The brief flash of fire in his eyes, before an iron coldness took over. He stepped to Raze, until their chests were nearly touching.

Grayson would kill them.

I ran and stepped between them, placing a hand on both their chests.

"It's fine," I said, gently pushing my brother farther away. "I'm fine."

He glared at them for what felt like too long, then stepped back.

"Are you in trouble?" he asked.

I thought about that. *Am* I in trouble? Yeah, probably. Probably been in trouble longer than the Horsemen were causing it.

I shrugged. "It's nothing. I needed drugs."

His brow furrowed, but his muscles noticeably relaxed. "What the fuck, Gemma? I saw the magazine—"

"I'm *fine*," I said, cutting him off.

Grayson's eyes narrowed on mine for too long. It wasn't like my pill problem was news to Grayson, but the questions in his eyes mirrored the press. *How bad is it really? How long? Should I have seen—*

"Can you please stop acting like you suddenly give a shit?" I snapped. "Save that for Story."

He opened and closed his mouth, looking like I'd slapped him. He shot one final glare to the Horsemen, then left without another word.

It was cruel, but it worked.

I stared at the empty space he left, feeling naked and vulnerable.

I spun around. They'd all sat back down, and Lock's black boots marked up the imported glass of my coffee table. My lungs vibrated, my gut squirmed. My world had tipped over, spinning on its axes.

"I've been trying to figure out why you're all here. I'm not so special—"

"We could have told you that," Lock said.

"So," I continued. "I've been thinking, maybe you just don't want Grim near me. I wonder why." Their feet were on my table, my friends had seen me with them, my brother was *worried*, and this was *not* the fucking deal.

They were silent, but a tension threaded their muscles.

I was poking places I shouldn't. And yet...

"I wonder what could possibly have you all spooked," I pressed. "Maybe you're afraid of *Grim* being with *me*—"

"You're an ungrateful, selfish, spoiled brat." Wraith was up faster than I could blink, scary tattooed eyes glaring in mine. I wasn't afraid, too stunned by what he'd said.

"Ungrateful—"

"You've spent the last five years making our lives hell for a contract you tricked Grim into taking."

All the air left me.

I stared at him, brain short-circuiting. By the time I spoke, my throat was dry and scratchy. "What did you say?"

"You think we can't see through you, see through this,

but we can. Unfortunately, we've known you our entire fucking lives, Gemma."

I smiled at him. "And what is it you see, Wraith?"

"A spoiled little brat ripping off her dolls' heads because she's scared no one loves her."

My lips parted, but no words came. It felt like my chest had been hollowed out.

If Wraith felt any satisfaction on getting a reaction, he didn't show it. He sat back down, pulling out his phone as if I wasn't there. I stared at them a moment longer, then went back to my bedroom and slammed the doors shut, maybe too hard.

I fell back against them, hands still holding the knob behind my back, trying to steady my breathing.

Tricked. They'd thought *I'd* somehow managed to trick *him.*

If anyone had tricked *anyone*, it was fucking Grim.

Tricked.

I walked over to my balcony, looking down two stories to the sand. I'd never had to sneak out of my room before, but... I leaned over, spotting a possible exit. If Grim could figure a way to sneak into my room, why couldn't I find a way to sneak out?

I glanced back at the doorway, to the three shadows.

Why would he lie to the Horsemen?

What does that mean?

Is it some kind of game?

It has to be some kind of game.

That restless, hurricane energy innervated my blood. I let that feeling carry me over the balcony, nearly slipping on the stone, before landing with a thud on the sand. It carried me all the way down the beach, to a packed club, through a packed dance floor, past the women lining up at the stairs, and to the *off-limits* second floor.

I'd played the Horsemen's good little slave for five years because we had an unspoken agreement: stay the fuck out of my world.

I gathered curious looks as I went. After the world just learned about her drug problem, *Gemma Crowne* was in a nightclub, wearing an oversize T-shirt, without any fucking shoes. All I needed was to shave my head.

If I had a plan, any semblance of it disappeared the moment I hit the top floor.

Grim was there, on a couch with two women, kissing them.

Huh. I guess this is what it feels like to be so mad you want to kill.

So first he all but promises to fuck me, then ignores me and installs guards, keeps me prisoner for no fucking reason, lies to everyone about *why*, and he was just...*kissing someone?*

I didn't feel jealousy, people felt jealous of *me*—so what was this hot twisting knife in my gut?

Grim must have known I was here, must have been told the minute I came into the club. There was no way I was getting upstairs without him knowing.

But he didn't open his eyes, didn't stop kissing.

Grim and I had kissed only that one time on the beach. There was something profoundly bullshit about the fact that he wouldn't kiss me, but he'd shove his tongue down some random girl.

Maybe that was why I found myself at his feet.

Why I bent over and slapped him.

TWENTY-ONE

GEMMA

Conversation stopped. Heads turned to stare. You didn't talk to the Horsemen without prior permission, let alone *slap* the head.

I didn't give a shit. What was he gonna do, kill me?

"Are you fucking kidding me?" *You're out here kissing some random chick.* "I've got three assholes ruining my life."

Grim dragged his hand across the spot I slapped on his jaw, a small smile playing on his lips. Slowly his eyes found mine. A dangerous humor ignited the dark depths. Like a shark in the water thinking my cage was so cute, as if it could protect me.

"And that's my problem, why?"

A shiver ran up my spine.

I swallowed. "It's clearly your doing."

I was tall. Taller than all the girls at my school. I towered at a cool five-ten. But with Grim, I had to crane my neck to see into his eyes.

"You—"

He gripped my chin, cutting me off. I sucked in a breath as he dragged his thumb across my bottom lip, pulling it down to see my teeth.

"Go home, Gemma."

He released me and fell back into the couch. Spiky hot liquid filled my chest. Indignation? Maybe. Or maybe it was the girls who immediately draped themselves over him.

I inhaled, finding calm. Practicing that bullshit breathing my therapist used to make me do.

Breathe one...two...three—

Fuck this.

"How much do they know about what happened that night?" I asked.

He stilled before slowly finding my eyes. "Enough."

I laughed. "*Enough.* All right. Do they know you fucked me? Do they know you're still touching me? What about the bodies—"

Before I knew it, he was in front of me, his mass shoving me farther and farther back until I nearly tripped.

"Do you like your world?" he gritted. "Do you like your pretty things and the stupid shit you think is power? Then go home, stop digging."

"I have more important things to deal with right now than your fucking Horsemen."

He laughed. "I'm sure you do, Rich Girl." A slight smirk pulled his gaze narrower, like he could see through me to things I hadn't even noticed about myself.

"Oh, and what's that supposed to mean?"

"You got real important shit, huh? What rich loser you gonna marry? What party you gonna throw? What bitch you gotta backstab this week? Yeah, real. Important. Shit."

He emphasized each word by stepping closer, until I was forced back against the balcony's private bar.

Grim looked me up and down, then scoffed and stepped off, as if he'd discovered some huge, damning insight about me.

"As opposed to you?" I asked. "Your life is so goddamn meaningful? All the drugs you sell, all the people you kill, you're really making an impact, Grim."

Grim pressed his thumb between his lips, bottom teeth biting the flesh in an *annoyingly* distracting way. He didn't say a word, eyes roaming up and down my body.

And I felt like a thing.

I got hungry because of it, no...*famished*. Achy and hot and twisted. All because of those dark eyes, sharpening on me like I was just another shiny damned soul for Grim Reyes to collect.

Of course, I didn't let him know.

I was Gemma fucking Crowne, he'd have to rip that bloody from my teeth.

"You should have left me in the ocean."

"You don't get to barter with death. Tough shit."

"Everyone knows you saved me, but nobody knows I didn't want you to. That I didn't want this contract. Isn't that kind of against the rules?" Still caged, I leaned closer, lips nearly touching. "Why are you keeping such a big secret, Grim? Do you care about me?"

He leaned closer, until I could practically taste his heady, earthy scent. His eyes dropped to my lips, and the air between us solidified into something about to snap. My back bit into the counter as his lips almost touched mine, goose bumps igniting a hot, shivering trail down my spine.

"You wanna know why I saved you? You wanna know why I lied? Why I'm still lying?" The heat of his breath brushed my lips with each word. "Every day you live is another day you suffer."

Icy cold drenched my insides.

He stepped off. "So I'm gonna keep you, Rich Girl. But don't read too much into it."

He found his way back to the couch and resumed making out, jaw flexing with the effort. Grim eyed me through the kiss, while the other woman started to rub his cock.

A cool sort of certainty replaced the fire in my veins.

Fine.

I walked to the other side of the room, hoisting myself up on a stool. I took a cue from my sister, Abby, and opened my legs wide, revealing that I wore no panties to the entire floor.

Almost instantly he sat up, rigid, shaking the girls off him.

I shrugged back into the bar, spreading my legs wider. He ground his jaw, the muscle twitching, as if realizing my ploy.

For a moment it looked like he might actually kill everyone.

He stood up and in two quick strides yanked me off the stool. He gripped my bicep, pulling me closer. I thought he was gonna tear into me, yell at me, rip me apart.

But then he was inside me.

One finger, two, sliding in and out of me in a punishing thrust. That careful line we toed obliterated in an instant. There was something in his stare that defied his savage thrusts. A longing ache peeked through like sunlight in winter. I drowned in it, in the promise his eyes carried, a burden his lips would never release.

His eyes only broke from mine when a whimper slipped from my lips, dropping to my mouth.

Kiss me.

But even as he hit every perfect spot, he still wouldn't fucking kiss me. The only thing keeping me from falling to a puddle was his grip on my bicep, holding me up as he fucked me with his fingers.

This was the first time in years that he'd touched me, and I knew in the starving, immutable part of my soul I couldn't wait another five.

The rough pad of his thumb rubbed my clit in delirious friction. I closed my eyes, falling into the moment. His fingers in my cunt, stretching and deep. The ache in his eyes seared into my brain. His unhinged breath falling fast and hot against my cheek.

It wasn't enough.

I needed all of him.

I arched into it, into him filling me up in a way I'd craved.

I was going to come. Come while a bunch of strangers watched.

"Open your eyes," Grim commanded. "Look at me when I let you come."

My eyes flew open.

"Good girl," Grim said, voice oddly warm through his growl. A new kind of pleasure twisted and dripped hot into my bones. The kind that came only from Grim's praise. That throbbing, hot wire in my gut snapped. My head fell to his chest as fireworks exploded through my blood.

The last thing I saw before I came was the hungry, crooked grin curving Grim's lips.

Grim's hand found the back of my neck and held me

against his chest, thumb rubbing circles in my skin. I steadied my breathing, focusing on the concentric motion.

Grim took forever removing his fingers from inside me. *Too* slow. Like he wanted me to feel his absence. Somehow *that* was more intimate than what had just happened seconds ago.

He tilted my chin up with sticky fingers, forcing me to meet his gaze, and I found myself standing up on tiptoes.

Our lips nearly touched when he said, "She's had enough for tonight."

I was still so lost in him. Stuck in the daze of Grim's praise, of him touching me in the way I'd craved for years. So I didn't notice the change, didn't see the mask fall back into place. Didn't register what he'd said until someone grabbed my elbow.

Security.

Grim stepped off and returned to the couch, not bothering to look back. The security guard gripped my elbow, trying to push me toward the stairs. I wrestled with every emotion. *Shame, humiliation—desire.*

I yanked my arm free as Grim reached the couch, and yelled, "This was the last time."

He paused, looking over his shoulder so I could see his smirk.

"I'm not fucking joking," I said.

He dragged the two fingers he'd just used to fuck me across his bottom lip, as if thinking hard. "Whatever you say, Rich Girl."

TWENTY-TWO

GEMMA

I didn't bother sneaking back in through the window. A small sliver of satisfaction hit me at the surprise on the Horsemen's faces when I walked through my front door. Before they could say anything, I went to my bedroom and slammed the door.

I fell to my bed, not bothering to pull back the sheets, replaying the night over and over again in my head, wishing I had some kind of drug to numb my inner thoughts.

Why did I let him touch me?

Why can't I stop thinking about the way his fingers felt?

The hungry, possessive look in his eyes when I came?

Like he'd been waiting for it.

My thighs ached with it. Even though I'd come, I wasn't satisfied. If anything, the orgasm released something I'd caged deep inside me. I was more out of control. More desperate. I scissored my legs and rolled onto my stomach, groaning as I slammed my head into the silk pillowcase.

I didn't like the goose bumps peppering my arms, the way my gut still twisted in knots.

Good girl.

Pathetic.

Black night faded into gray morning. I stared at the ceiling until it blurred. I was so sick of this. Sick of being on Grim's puppet strings. But I wasn't really the damsel in distress type. I was more the "light myself on fire to burn your house down" kind of person.

So I would set Grim's world on fire until it was nothing but ash. So he'd know exactly how I felt in this moment, and all the moments that led to this.

What did a Horseman really care about? What couldn't they stand to lose? I sat up on my elbows, looking to the shadows at my door.

It was time Grim lost something for once.

How would he feel if I fucked one of his brothers?

If I tried to fuck Wraith, pretty sure he'd kill me first.

If I went for Raze, he'd tell me to fuck off.

Lock...I assessed the six-foot-tall figure shadowing my door. Well, he'll put his cock in anything that moves.

So as the sun rose, lighting my room up in golds and yellows and whites, I planned. I went to my closet and picked out a lacy, pale-pink Cadolle guêpière. I slid into the top, laces open at the back, with matching lace panties.

"Lock?" I called through the door.

He opened the door, his unruly black hair falling over pale-gold skin and blue eyes. A joint poked out of his pierced lips.

He arched a pierced black brow at my state of undress. "Princess."

"I can't call my girl, because, well, you're here." I turned around, giving him my back, where the corset was undone. "Can you help me with the laces?"

His calloused hands rubbed against my flesh, gripping the laces.

It's working.

And when Grim finds out, he'll be—

Before I could finish my thought, Lock tightened them so I couldn't fucking breathe. He stabbed his joint into the wall above me.

"Think you're safe? Think I won't fuck you because I know you're fucking my brother?" I had a half second to register what he said before he gripped my hair, ripping me back so I had a view of his sharp jaw.

"You look like you love it rough, princess." His lips were hot against my ear. "I won't fuck you because you're so goddamn beneath me."

He shoved me off him and I stumbled, grabbing my vanity for stability.

Fucking Grim?

Grim won't even fucking kiss me.

I spun around and he snapped a picture of me with his phone. "Not beneath my spank bank, though. Nice tits, princess."

Lock turned to leave.

"Did he ever tell you about the night of our contract?" I said to his back. "It's an interesting story, but he doesn't always get it right."

He stilled for a half moment, then shut the door after him.

Time for the real trick.

It wasn't like I didn't expect this. It was no secret the Horsemen were into kinky, fucked-up shit. Shit most girls would balk at, yet still had girls lining up around the block to be their willing victims.

But you didn't rule the Underworld by thinking with your cock. They were cold, calculated, ruthless.

They didn't care about my ten-thousand-dollar tits or my perfect glowing skin. The ass I spent at least an hour a day on meant nothing to them. All the pieces of me, the parts I bought, chiseled, and erased so that I could be perfect—so that I could be *powerful*—had no effect on them.

I was a contract. A line that still needed to be drawn.

When that line was finally drawn, I would become something worse. I would become irrelevant.

I slid out of my clothes, held my phone up to find the right angle of my breasts, and posted it.

The photo was shared only to my close friends, a list of one: Grim's not-so-secret burner account.

But as far as he knew, I'd sent it to everyone.

I'd known Grim for over a decade. He might have me on his little puppet strings, but I knew how to make him dance too.

I put on a pair of soft cashmere pants, and waited.

I waited hours, watching the guard outside my door change. Lock had left, and by the shape of the shadow, the new one was Wraith. Sun was setting burnt orange on the horizon. I hadn't left my room all day, hadn't eaten anything, was ignoring the notifications on my phone.

He would come.

Before the faint smell of cannabis drifted through my window, before the balcony opened, I knew he was there.

That thing that connected us popped and sizzled, my skin suddenly too tight.

Then came his voice, rough like sandpaper on my skin. "Busy today?"

I stood off the bed, facing him.

"Maybe." I stepped to him. "Why didn't you come through the door? You know, say hello to your friends."

His attention traveled above my shoulder and to the door, some inscrutable emotion shadowing his eyes, before settling back on me.

Feral.

He shoved me to the bed in one rough push. The dying light shrouded him in thick shadow. I couldn't see his face, just the outline of him. Broad, strong shoulders swallowing all the space in the room.

He was like a monster out of an old horror movie.

My gut flipped. My breath caught.

He slammed his hands into the mattress on either side of me. Caging. A second stretched into forever, his shadowed features coming into clarity. Cheekbones like razor blades beneath his glare. Lips like bruised rose petals.

He sank deeper into me, swallowing any space, lips nearly touching.

He's going to kiss me.

At the last moment he diverted, pressing his face into the side of my neck. He took a deep, unrestrained inhale. The power and need of it caused my insides to fizzle and carbonate.

A ridiculous, needy thought slipped into my mind.

Now. He'll do it now.

"Reckless girl," he said, face still pressed against my neck, hand sliding beneath the waist of my pants. "You think I won't kill everyone who follows you? End the life of anyone who sees what's *mine*?"

The word *mine* disappeared into a sound not quite human. I knew I should tell him to stop, but instead I arched, making it easier for him to drag my pants off my body. He peeled away the cashmere with slow and torturous deliberation, landing on his knees between my thighs, pants discarded.

His thumbs dug into my thighs, pushing them so far apart the thin, thready muscles in my groin screamed. I was wet—embarrassingly so—dripping between the soft skin of my inner thighs.

Time stood still, held captive by his bruising thumbs, the starvation in his eyes.

"I can post whatever I want," I breathed, trying to regain some control.

Grim dragged his knuckles along the crease of my thigh, just barely grazing my pussy, gaze flashing to mine. For an instant I didn't think. I *felt* the intent in his eyes. He was going to make me regret that.

I couldn't fucking wait.

"I don't belong to you," I said, yet my voice came out breathy. "I'm not yours."

Grim slid a finger inside me, dragging it back out too quickly.

"Ah, Rich Girl..." He held his finger in the air, glistening with me, and arched a brow. "I don't give a shit who you think you belong to. I still own you in every way that counts."

There was no going back.

Good, some dark part of me whispered.

I waited for him to fulfill the promise blazing in his eyes. Seconds dragged on to what felt like forever, Grim unmoving between my legs, grip tantalizingly close to where I needed it. His stare fixed on the center of me, hungry.

Then his eyes tore from my pussy, locking with mine. "Touch yourself."

TWENTY-THREE

GEMMA

Touch myself?

Disappointment flashed briefly through me before I smothered it with a pillow. I wanted *him* to touch me.

Well, I knew what he wanted—what everyone always wanted. I slid my hand slowly down the curve of my hip, over my lace panties. I started to moan, to arch—

Grim tightened his grip on my thighs to the point of pain. I gasped.

"Stop that shit," he said, eyes lifting to mine. Cold. Bored. "If I wanted fake, I'd turn on some porn, Rich Girl." His grip loosened, thumb soothing the spot. "Do what you do when you're alone. When no one is watching you."

Fear stole my breath.

Dripped cold and icy down my spine.

For a few seconds I was frozen. Stuck between obeying and pushing him off me. What he wanted was too intimate. I couldn't control that—control *his* reaction to me.

I tried to push him off. "Fuck this—"

"Gemma." His grip tightened, but it was the tone of his voice that had me looking back at him. It wasn't cold, it was coaxing. Almost...warm. But there was a firmness in the tone that brooked no argument.

I swallowed. I was perfect Gemma Crowne, and perfect Gemma was perfect in *all* ways. Horace didn't want *me*, he wanted the fantasy of me. The girl who moaned and told him he had a big cock, who always got off right when he did, and who never asked him to do anything differently.

So I said the truth.

The thing I was afraid of.

"You'll get bored."

A slight smirk twitched his lips.

"Bored?" He pressed a hot, open-mouthed kiss to the crease of my thigh. "Never." His words disappeared into a growl, vibrating against my skin, twisting into my gut and dripping hot between my thighs.

He stood up and, for a split second, my heart dropped into my gut.

He's going to leave.

He doesn't want this—

Grim was on top of me, taking up all the space and pressing me into the mattress. My head caged by his elbows, his face so close to mine, his stare inescapable.

"Touch yourself, Gemma," he commanded again.

If I thought it was vulnerable before, it was agonizing now. He wasn't looking between my thighs, he was watching *me*, stripping away all my layers.

My breathing was shaky as I slid my hand back down my body. I did as I was told, touching myself like no one was watching. Warmth melted inside my skin like butter, and goose bumps peppered my flesh. A knot started to form in my gut, begging to be undone.

It's too quiet.

No man wants that.

Little voices poked at me, and I nearly opened my mouth to moan, but the look in Grim's eyes stopped me—burning coals. As if I was the hottest thing, like he was getting off on this as much as me—*more* than me.

It made the knot grow tighter.

With Horace—with any guy, really—I could always hide because they didn't *want* the reality of me. They preferred the lies I gave them. The fake moans and gasps.

With Grim I was a shadow trying to run from the sun.

And it boiled me alive.

A small, involuntary whimper slid from my lips. Grim responded with a savage smile splitting his lips.

"There it is." One hand knotted painfully—*deliciously*—in my hair as his lips dove to my neck. "Give me more of that."

When I started again, I let myself drown in his hunger and possession. His sweet-painful grip in my hair. His whispers hot against my skin.

Good girl.

Good fucking girl.

His praise slid like heroin into my bloodstream until I was dizzy with it. A moan fell from my lips—

Quicker than a flash, he tugged my head back by the hair, giving me a look both feral and censuring. Using the hand knotted in my hair, he twisted my head to the side to see what he was looking at. My double doors, where Wraith's body made a silhouette.

Oh, right.

After a torturous minute, his grip loosened.

His lips found the crook beneath my ear. "Can you stay quiet?"

I tried to nod, but his grip was too firm in my hair. The up-and-down movements tugged my hair painfully.

"Good girl," he said, and released me.

Grim stood back up between my thighs. The next part played out in slow motion, time passing with the throb of my heartbeat. His hand at his zipper. Metal teeth slowly parting. His thick, tatted cock.

"Don't stop touching yourself." He gripped his cock as he spoke, his command punctuated by the bruising grip.

I obeyed, hand moving back between my legs. I was locked on him, in a trance. I hadn't seen him, *really* seen him, since that night on the beach. Wicked black tattoos slid down the gutters of his Adonis belt, encircling his cock.

It was so painfully difficult to keep quiet.

He tugged his cock with mesmerizing brutality, the flex of his long fingers barely wrapping around his width. I touched myself in rhythm with him.

It grew harder to stay quiet.

I'd never had trouble before; I could always be what anyone wanted. But now? The savage way he gripped his cock, the burn in his eyes, like he was holding himself from plunging into me, had me biting my lip near bloody to keep from crying out.

The muscles in Grim's neck throbbed in stark relief as his head fell back on a silent groan. He coated my lower stomach and inner thighs in hot spurts. The veins in his hand flexed with each final tug. I felt a dizzying mix of emotions.

Marked. Claimed. *Safe.*

Grim's head dropped, chin to collarbone. Black hair fell in a shield. The heavy breaths racking his body, his hand still gripping his semi-hard dick.

He lifted his head, catching my gaze. I nearly buckled under the intensity.

"Did you come, Gemma?" he asked, voice low and strained.

"Ye—" I broke off.

Normally I lied.

Yes. You were amazing. It felt so good. Best I've ever had.

I chewed my bottom lip, then shook my head.

Something clouded his eyes, some kind of emotion, or conflict I couldn't understand, but before I could even try to understand it, he knelt between my knees and grabbed my hand.

He pushed inside me, spreading my pussy with his finger and mine. His come was slippery on my thigh, and Grim pressed it deeper inside me.

I tensed.

"Don't stop," he whispered. "Fuck yourself with my come."

My lips parted. "I'm not on birth control."

He maneuvered my fingers inside me, using his come as lubricant. "I know."

I knew better than to question how he knew the most intimate parts of me. It shouldn't be so hot. I should definitely make him stop, but more than that I didn't want to. I *couldn't*. I was compelled, under an illicit trance spelled by his vicious, ravenous stare.

He crawled back above me, body caging me into the mattress. Grim used me as a doll to fuck myself. Stretching me.

I arched on a cry that Grim smothered before it could leave my lips. On his elbow, he kept one hand pinned against my mouth, the other working inside me with cruel rhythm. I glanced at the shadow darkening my door.

What happens if they catch us?

My eyes found Grim's again, gaze shadowed with inscrutable emotion. My breath was hot and wet against his palm. Pinned beneath his hand, I felt a strange sense of safety. He was watching me so intently, he was focused on me so deeply, I wanted to melt into him. Submit.

My body turned to liquid.

I melted under the pressure of his palm smothering my sighs.

"Yeah, just like that," he whispered against my neck. "So fucking perfect. So beautiful when you surrender. Come on my fucking fingers, Gemma."

I didn't know if it was the command that did it, or the way his irises bruised my fucking soul. Or maybe it was the way his jaw clenched, muscle feathering with restraint as he fucked me with my own hand. Maybe it was just knowing I *could* come, like this, as *me*—and that was how Grim wanted it.

Oh my God.

I can't breathe.

I can't—

Grim inhaled sharply as my teeth enclosed the flesh of his palm. I bit him, *hard*, riding out the orgasm. He didn't flinch or pull away; his eyes encouraged me.

My orgasm stole every part of me, from the tiniest of muscles to the air in my lungs. It shot through me. Rippled down my spine to the tips of my toes, so when I was finished, it was Grim who tethered me to earth.

I was spent. Weak. Strung out.

"*Mi locura,*" he groaned as I came, kissing my cheeks, my neck, my lips. "Good fucking girl."

Grim slid back down my body, between my thighs.

Mi locura.

My cheeks were on fire.

My insides were on fire.

Mi locura.

He hadn't called me that since the beach, and so I hadn't felt this—this *need*—this overwhelming need to do *anything* just so I could hear him say it, in years.

Danger.

My nervous system lit up like a Christmas tree. The last time he called me that, my life changed. Wraith guarded my fucking door; I was a fucking prisoner. Yesterday Grim stole my orgasm only to use it against me.

Not again.

Never again.

I felt a cold certainty envelop my body. This wasn't real. Pretending it was would break me. I *had* to remember that. I *had* to remember why I started the day. If I didn't...

I pushed my feelings aside. Dissociated from his hot opened-mouth kisses cleaning up my come and his.

"Do you like the way I taste?" I asked.

"The fuck do you think," Grim growled.

"It's your Horsemen," I whispered.

It was a second before it registered, but then he froze.

I tilted my head, blinking at him innocently as I slid my pointer finger along my bottom lip. "If you continue to keep me locked up here with them, just know that when you climb through my window, you'll never know if you're sleeping with your Horsemen too."

Grim's lips twitched with a barely perceptible smile, then he tangled his hands in my hair, ripping my eyes to his.

His breath was in my lungs, his chest touching mine with each heavy inhale.

"You think I give a shit whose dick is in your cunt?" he hissed.

Before I could answer, he slammed his lips against mine. A distant thought rode an abandoned carousel in my mind—*this is our second kiss.*

This kiss was different. Rougher. Nothing like the beach. He thrust his tongue deep into my mouth. Obscenely deep. Claiming every corner of my mouth until I couldn't breathe through it, let alone kiss him back. Swallowing. Ravaging. Like he was trying to suck out any taste of another man.

Replace it with him.

I could feel my mind going fuzzy, soft, so I shoved at him. Ripped my lips away. *Fought.*

"Was it worth it, Rich Girl?" He laughed as I continued to struggle in vain. "To try and beat death, you fucked his soldier."

He'd stopped kissing me, but he wouldn't get off me. I elbowed his chest, tried to shove his head away, but nothing stuck. A dangerous glint heated his eyes.

He liked this.

"Or maybe you like swallowing his come. Maybe you like having him in your mouth." His hand slid between my thighs. "Yeah, you have a pretty sloppy cunt right now." His palm was rough and mean and so *right* against my already sensitive nerves. Impossibly, I felt another orgasm rising—

He stood back up, flexing his arms above his head with lethal casualness.

"Invite me next time," he said, stuffing himself back into his jeans. "I'd love to watch them skull-fuck you. Watch your pretty tears fall down your face."

Without another word, he went to the balcony.

"What do I have to do to just make you forget I ever existed!"

He paused but didn't look back. When he spoke, it was with finality reserved for eulogies. "That's a debt you'll never pay off, Rich Girl."

TWENTY-FOUR

GRIM

The club vibrated beneath my feet.

Thump.

He touched her.

Thump.

He touched her.

Thump.

He—

I grabbed Lock by the throat, shoving him against the couch. The girl he was with fell off his lap and scrambled away. A few moments later, the upper deck emptied.

"What the hell is going on?" Raze asked.

"He knows." My grip on his neck tightened. Lock didn't react, bored.

"The fuck did you do this time?" Raze asked Lock.

"You really think I did it?" Lock countered, eyes narrowing on mine.

"I think if it was any other girl you wouldn't think twice," I said.

"Yeah." Lock leaned into my grip. "If it was *any other girl*, I wouldn't."

I stilled.

Fuck.

I yanked my hand back and stepped away, facing the railing. Bodies writhed on the club floor below. I ran my hands through my hair.

Fuck.

Shit.

"Someone better fuckin' talk," Raze said.

"White Privilege Barbie tried to blow me today," he said. "But her mouth was too small. In the interest of full disclosure, I do have a picture of her tits." Lock held up the phone as proof.

I reacted without thought, grabbing it and smashing it against the railing. Raze looked to the shattered phone, then back at me. *What the fuck?* was plastered on his parted lips and twisted brow.

"You're acting like you've fucking marked her." Lock stood off the couch, face-to-face with me.

The muscles between my shoulder blades tightened, about to snap.

It was a dark fantasy that I never let myself indulge. Gemma Crowne marked? She would belong to me. Anyone who touched her would know the consequences. She would be *mine*.

"You can't *mark* Gemma fucking Crowne," Lock said, reading the look on my face.

Of course not.

I rubbed the back of my neck, trying to release some of the tension.

It was never supposed to have gone this far. It was easier when she was betrothed. Not only was that guy like her brother—there was no possible path forward.

"The entire Underworld would want her dead," Lock continued. "It would be really fucking easy to find the Reaper's girl when she's the most famous girl in America."

"You think I don't know that?" I said.

Lock raised his hands, eyes flashing pointedly to his smashed phone, like *Do you?*

Fuck.

He was right.

"Gemma said something interesting to me," Lock said. "Wasn't gonna pay much attention to it, but—"

I arched a brow. "But?"

"But then you tried to take my fucking head off."

Lock stared, cocking his head.

He knew.

He knew I'd lied. He might not know the details, but he'd figured out enough.

Maybe that was why I spoke. Or more likely, it was because possession burned inside me, threatening to turn everything I cared about to ashes. For the first time in my life, I'd lost control.

I exhaled. "She didn't want it."

They stilled, not fully believing what came out of my mouth.

"Gemma didn't ask for a contract," I continued in their silence.

Raze dragged two hands through his hair. "Dude, what the fuck?"

"It wasn't all a lie. I did save her, but she didn't ask to be saved. She didn't want..." I dragged my hand along my jaw. "She didn't want any of it. She wanted to die."

"You've been lying for five years." Raze spoke without emotion, processing. "We're stuck because of you."

I dragged a hand down my face, nodding.

A tense moment passed. I felt Raze's and Lock's eyes on me as the song changed from some up-tempo EDM bullshit to something heavier with a metallic, industrial beat.

Then it shattered.

"We can't shield a weakness until you acknowledge it!" Lock roared, the effort stretching the stenciled hemlock on his neck. In the decades I'd known Lock, he'd yelled a handful of times. Max. Now, he was loud enough that people on the dance floor turned their heads, looking for the source.

"She's not a weakness." I worked my jaw. "I can let her go anytime."

Lock and Raze shared a look, like *sure.*

"Are the rumors true?" Lock asked. "Are you killing people?"

I dragged the hand on my jaw up and down the side of my face. That was all the confirmation Lock and Raze needed.

Raze tangled his hands in his hair, staring down at the floor. "I can't fucking believe this."

"No one from our world is dead—" I started, but was cut off by Wraith coming up the stairs.

"Where the fuck were you?" He spoke to Raze, falling into the couch as he did, kicking his legs up on the iron-and-glass table, pulling out a book. "You were supposed to relieve me of babysitting duty."

"Sorry," Raze said sarcastically. "My mind was busy exploding."

Wraith glanced up from his book, something resembling

curiosity in his emotionless eyes. For the next five minutes, Raze and Lock explained everything.

"That's all?" Wraith made a face like *waste of fucking time* and went back to his book.

"You knew?" we all said in unison. Wraith gave us all a look like, *What?*

"It was obvious." Wraith flipped a page in his book. "You've killed seven people by my estimation. I covered up your tracks when you got sloppy. But...she's made you really sloppy, dude. So the rumors are there."

Lock let out a short, incredulous laugh.

I rubbed my forehead.

"Incredibly obvious if you get off on stalking," Raze said under his breath.

Wraith grinned, feral.

"I feel like I don't know you anymore, man." Raze worked his thumb into the space between his brows. "This thing only works if we're all on the same page. We started this together. We're bound *together*. It's not about you. It's never just been about you."

Before guilt could settle like sludge, Lock continued where Raze left off.

"You kill someone, it's not just you doing it. It's all of us." Lock threw out his arms, gesturing at everyone. "That was the fucking deal."

"So what about the guy whose fingers you broke?" Wraith asked, still busy reading his book. "Was that all of us too?"

Lock looked caught.

"What?" Raze asked.

"When Lock was on babysitting duty," Wraith continued, "he broke one of Gemma's friend's—"

Lock interrupted. "Not a *friend*—"

"*Some guy she kn*ows," Wraith said, irritation battering his normally emotionless words. "Whoever the fuck he was, you broke his fingers."

Silence settled.

Lock exhaled. "He was talking shit."

"So?" I asked.

"So. Shit. I don't know." Lock rubbed the back of his neck.

"She's like a fucking virus." Raze dragged his hands through his black-and-white hair. "Who else is infected? You gonna tell me you bugged her room or something?" Raze directed the last question to Wraith.

"Yes." Wraith flipped a page. "I keep track of liabilities."

I thought back to her room, to the hundreds of times I'd cleaned it for bugs.

Of course I didn't find one. It was fucking Wraith.

So Wraith knew, then.

Beyond the deaths, he realized how fucking far I'd let myself fall—Gemma wasn't the liability he was referring to. I was.

It wasn't that Wraith was being kind in his lack of anger or supportive in his silence. He just didn't care. I wasn't sure if he had any bone in his body capable of feeling.

"Is that all?" Lock asked. "Is there anything else you're not telling us?"

Anything else?

They still didn't know the truth of Gemma's contract, *why* I'd kept us in limbo for five years. Why I couldn't get us out.

I could have let Gemma go that night. Even after I showed up with the tattoo, I didn't have to finalize it. To seal it. But a crazed part of me needed it, needed our lives connected externally to match the visceral, internal connection.

So I made it official.

And I damned the rest of us.

I knew what would happen if I told them the truth, what they would demand of me. So I lied.

"Nothing else," I said.

TWENTY-FIVE

GEMMA

It was the first day of February, the salty Saturday air bitter with cold, and the biggest party of the year for the Horsemen—Heart Eater Day. Every February, two weeks before Valentine's Day, the Horsemen throw a party, some kind of themed, debauched version of the romantic holiday.

The morning after Grim visited me, the Horsemen were gone. Another day passed, and another. They vanished like smoke.

I shouldn't care. I definitely shouldn't be sitting in bed with a bottle of tequila, trying to numb whatever Grim had wakened. I ran my fingers up and down my inner thigh, remembering too easily how he'd touched me.

"Gemma?"

I yanked my hand from my thigh, caught, and turned to the voice.

My sister stood in the doorway. I thought I was seeing things at first. When my sister married her bodyguard, my mother disowned her and banished her from Crowne Hall. Since Grayson, that banishment had been lifted, but still, Abigail rarely came back home.

Couldn't blame her.

I sat up a little in bed. "What are you doing here?" Anxiety twitched my chest—was my mother having another party? Had I forgotten?

Abigail picked at her lip, her slightly crooked front teeth visible. She was nervous.

I held up a bottle of tequila, but she shook her head.

"'Cause you're, like, a mom now?" I fell back to my bed, head at the end. "Never stopped ours."

Seconds dragged, and I could picture Abigail picking her lip in my mind.

"I'm worried about you," she said softly.

I put my lips to the glass rim, muttering, "Gross."

Abigail came to the side of my bed, her face upside down from my view. Brow furrowed.

"So...Grayson filled me in." She picked at her lip. "I knew there was something going on when I found him in your room. That was years ago, though..."

Once upon a time, I pretended to fuck her now husband so I could get his journal and give it to Grim. In that same era, Abby had found me in this room, with Grim.

Still picking her lips, she continued. "I should have been a better sister. I should have dug deeper. Asked questions."

Now *that* I couldn't take. Quiet judgment, taciturn worry, I could take. I could numb that. But her guilt? Like she was to blame for all my fucked-up-ness?

I took a swig of tequila.

Abby grabbed the tequila and put it down behind her, on the nightstand. "Gemma."

"Jesus, what?"

Her brown eyes—so different from any Crowne, except our mother—bore into mine. Staring into her red-brown depths did something to me. Abigail was the only Crowne who didn't inherit our father's eyes. I wondered if he'd be disappointed in me. No less than a second later, something acerbic slid up my throat, like heartburn.

I wasn't even sure my father loved us. He was just lucky enough to die before the question had to be answered.

"What do you want to do, Gemma?"

I rubbed between my brows. "Get coffee. Pop some painkillers."

"No, I mean, I always wanted to open up a jewelry shop. Story wanted to be a poet. For a while, those dreams were impossible. This was...a cage. Do you have something like that?"

I sank deeper into my bed. "It's way too early for this."

We didn't do this, the sister thing. The closest we got to that was one night when we were teenagers and took scandalous photos.

My sister used to hope for our mom to love her, and since dear Mom didn't know how to do that, another vacuum formed. When Mom kept choosing me over Abby, we stopped loving each other.

"It's almost three."

I glanced out my window at what I'd *thought* was hazy morning light but was in fact dusty afternoon. That meant in a few hours I would have to get ready.

My gut tightened.

It was just a party. I went to it every year, and most of the time, I never saw Grim or any Horsemen.

But this time...

I turned back, finding Abigail waiting patiently. What

did I want? My dreams are not normal dreams. I didn't dream of accomplishing something, or being someone. I dreamed of someone who would see inside me and not shrivel in disgust. Who would pick whatever roses bloomed in my shadows, because they loved the pain my thorns brought.

I dreamed of something I knew I'd never feel. As stupid, and cliché, and fucking pathetic as it was, I dreamed of love.

I'd known since birth who I was supposed to be, and so I'd known forever that I was very much not that person. *Gemma Crowne* was loved, but me? I was very much the opposite of her, and very much the antithesis of whatever the fuck was going on with this *new* Crowne image.

Abby stared at me earnestly.

"I don't know," I lied. "A fashion designer, I guess."

Kennedy's dream was to be a fashion designer.

A wrinkle formed between her brows but before she could call me on my shit, my phone rang. A video call from Blaire. Instead of Blaire, Kennedy's face popped up.

"We're on our way," Kennedy said, flipping the camera to show Blaire driving.

"For?" I asked.

"The *Underworld*," Blaire said, leaning closer to the phone. "You said you would handle glam. Don't tell me you forgot?" Her eyes darted from the phone to the road and back.

This holiday was infamous. Anyone who was anyone would be there. What was I going to say? We couldn't go to the hottest party of the year because I was starting to get a little too close to the guy I sold my life to?

"No, of course not."

We hung up after I confirmed I did have glam—I didn't,

but Crowne Hall always had someone on staff—and they promised to see me soon.

Abigail stopped picking her lip and no longer looked nervous, but afraid. "You're going to that?"

"Why wouldn't I?"

A long silence stretched. Waves crashed—or maybe it was the blood rushing in my veins. Abigail worked her mouth into a twist, like she wanted to say something, like it was eating her up not saying it.

Before she could, my two best friends bounded into the room. Their loud laughter crashed into whatever moment had existed. Abigail gave me a lingering look, her brows knit, and then left.

"Was that your sister?" Kennedy asked, flopping on my bed. "Why was she here? Don't you hate each other?"

I never answered. I called hair and makeup, and my friends turned the prep into a party. Kennedy lounged across my bed in a silk robe, sipping champagne straight from the bottle.

There's my girl. My good girl.

I shook my head, trying not to think about what had happened there mere days ago.

Blaire was sprawled on the floor with a pile of jewelry cases, holding each piece against her throat to see what caught the light best.

I sat before my gilded vanity while two stylists tugged and twisted my hair into place, pinning it into something elaborate enough to look effortless. Another smoothed serum across my skin, her hands brisk and practiced.

Just a few short hours later, we were ready.

"The Aston Martin—" Blaire held up her car keys in one hand, as if to offer the choice. "—or a driver?"

The sun had fallen, in its place a clear black winter night. The moon was full, and my skin felt electric.

"Neither," I said. "Let's walk."

After *much* cajoling, we stumbled along the beach, toward the Underworld.

"It's *so* creepy out here—ah!" Kennedy jumped. "What *was* that?"

Blaire started cackling, holding up some kind of long, feathery flower.

"You're such a dick."

Kennedy stumbled in a small dune of sand. "Heels are *so* not meant to be worn in this shit."

"So take them off," Blaire deadpanned. We both held our shoes in our hands.

"But what if someone sees me?" Kennedy whined. "The outfit doesn't work without them."

We walked a little longer in silence, Kennedy tripping every so often. The moon was so full and bright every grain of gray sand was illuminated, shimmering like stardust.

"Are we going to talk about how Gemma brought a Horseman to tea?" Kennedy asked.

"The hot one too," Blaire said.

Their heads turned in unison over their shoulders, back at me. I'd managed to be under the Horsemen's thumb for years without anyone noticing, but now in a matter of days my perfect, pristine reputation had taken hit after hit.

The worst part?

I kind of...well, I kind of enjoyed it. So I knew without a doubt I had to do everything in my power to stay away from that side of me.

"I, um..." I struggled to think of an explanation. "I...I needed a hookup."

"They do delivery now?" Kennedy looked like a kid who'd just learned her favorite toy came in a different color.

"Maybe it's, like, a frequent-flier perk," Blaire said, and they both laughed.

"Someone take a photo of me," Kennedy said. "I look *really* good right now—wait, Gemma?" She paused, staring at her phone, then at me. "Are you sharing our location right now?"

"Maybe..."

"Oh my God! What is wrong with you? You have two hundred million people following you."

"And?"

"And fucking Libby Whitehall was *kidnapped* because that bitch just *had* to let everyone know she got a bigger yacht than Bezos."

Shivers ran up my spine. Libby Whitehall had been returned—barely.

I don't know what's wrong with me.

Why the idea of someone finding me *thrilled* me.

"Um, Libby was kidnapped because she was a ho doing ho things," Blaire corrected.

"Someone's still salty that Sebastian chose Libby..." Kennedy said, underbreath. "But seriously, Gemma, what the fuck?"

"Chill," I said. "I'll turn it off."

I pulled out my phone and went to my page just as we reached the Underworld. Spotlights danced, the lights milky in the sky. The thumping of a bass drifted through the white fog.

We were getting close.

Every sound was magnified. The wire fence creaked in the salty wind. Where the beach met forest, dry blades of grass brushed against one another. Soft sand beneath our feet.

One by one my friends walked up the old boardwalk that led to the club. Behind them, I trailed my fingers on the old iron fence, heart in my throat.

Prick.

I stilled. A small bead of crimson welled on the pad of my pointer finger.

Still open to my page, I clicked to post a story. I painted the blood across my lips like lipstick, then blew a kiss to the camera.

Location, on.

TWENTY-SIX

GEMMA

If the Crownes celebrated every holiday like we were the ones who invented it, the Horsemen celebrated like heathens desecrating the original. The party's theme was "Blood of the Gods." Everyone was to come as some kind of divine tragedy.

It was their version of a toga party.

"I love a theme," Kennedy said. In a lilac dress that barely reached her thighs, her stomach and back entirely exposed, she was supposed to be Persephone.

"You should have gone as Medusa," Blaire said. "It suits you."

Everything was more sinister, sexier. The champagne was dyed deep, blood red. The bottle service girls dressed like a Greek chorus, with short togas and red, glittery blood sparkling their skin.

Kennedy smiled. "And you *still* have time to go as a bitch."

I'd had my dress made months ago, when this was supposed to be just another party. Strings of diamonds and glittery silver draped over sheer fabric. A slit up to my hip gave it a semblance of a toga shape, and more strands of diamonds fell from my hip, down my bare thigh.

Diamond butterfly wings sealed the look.

I was Psyche.

I'd always been fascinated with mythology. My favorite was the story of Psyche and Eros. It wasn't as famous as some, like Hades and Persephone.

But it...stuck with me.

Eros was supposed to kill Psyche, but instead he fell in love with her.

"Do you see that guy dressed as Zeus?" Kennedy asked. "Does he look familiar to anyone else?"

Our eyes wandered to a tall man with blond hair, wearing a toga.

"Oh my *God*, Kennedy," Blaire said. "You dated him for, like, six months."

Kennedy tilted her head. "I don't see it."

The stairs to the balcony were roped off, and tonight the normally unguarded stairs were blocked by two scary-looking men. My eyes traveled up to the second floor. The balcony was empty.

The odds of seeing him, or any of the Horsemen, tonight were low to none. They didn't throw parties so *they* could party.

I stared at the empty balcony, the black railings like a rainbow oil slick under the reflecting neon lights. A sudden, sticky feeling slid inside me, coating my gut and throat like tar.

Was I...disappointed?

No fucking way.

"You called him Trust Fund Freak."

"Oh!" Kennedy's eyes grew. "He cut his hair."

I stood up. "I have to pee."

"I could use a bump," Blaire said, standing as if to go with me.

"I'm actually going to pee."

Her brow wrinkled in suspicion, like I'd just told her chocolate milk came from chocolate cows, but she didn't follow me as I wove through the VIP section. I wore no panties and no bra, so I easily felt the weight of the diamonds and the cool metal against my skin.

Disappointed? I don't get disappointed.

What did I think was going to happen?

That he would be waiting for me? That this time he would explain his absence?

It wasn't like I wanted to see him. Nothing good ever followed—

I stilled. Someone stood in the middle of the general admission floor. Bodies twisted and writhed around him, and he stood still, staring.

At me.

I thought to my shared location, just as someone stepped in front of me, blocking the man.

Wraith.

Goose bumps peppered my flesh. Wraith was my height, maybe a little smaller, but he owned the room. I swallowed, taking a step back. He stepped with me, closing the distance and then some.

"Do you know what it means for a Horseman to leave a contract unfinished?"

"I—" I broke off. "I don't care."

His hollow, tattooed eyes blade-sharp, he barked a bitter laugh. "Of course you don't. Grim knew that when he saved you. He knew that when he tattooed his chest. He knew that when he bound his soul with yours. He knew that when he continued to keep you in debt."

"Why the fuck are you telling me this?"

He stepped even closer, until his subtle, dark scent enveloped me. "If Grim is your reaper, then you're his fucking reckoning. He knows you're going to kill him, and he refuses to let go."

Without another word, Wraith disappeared into the shadows. I stood frozen to the spot, forgetting what I'd been doing.

Oh, right, bathroom.

The bathroom was private and huge, especially for a club. It was all black marble with vines of gold. Velvet oxblood curtains hung on one wall. On the other, a thick-cut sink with gold vining through the black marble.

I pulled my lip gloss out, dabbing my lips.

Grim's reckoning?

Yeah, fucking right.

I shook my head just as the door opened behind me.

"Bruh, occupied—"

I broke off. A person reflected in the mirror. His hair was a mop of messy brown, and he held a knife in his hand.

The guy from the floor.

He took a step closer, and I leaned back.

"I know you make your posts for me," he said, stepping closer. "You've been talking to me. Dressing for me."

His voice disappeared into a sickening groan.

I exhaled. They were all the same. I don't know why that bothered me more than, you know, the threat of imminent death. They were like everyone else, obsessed with the idea of me.

This time I was feeling a little more than the usual numb exhilaration. Feeling...kind of pissed off.

"Is this your big display to show the world Gemma Crowne belongs to you?" I asked, stepping closer. "What a waste of fucking time. *Everyone* owns Gemma Crowne."

Fury flashed in his eyes just as the door opened again, so quiet I wouldn't have noticed had I not had a perfect view of it.

Grim leaned against the doorjamb. None of the Horsemen ever dressed for their theme, so of course he wasn't wearing some kind of toga. He somehow looked more expensive in his simple black pants and black shirt, rolled up to his forearms to show off his tattoos. The buttons of his shirt were slightly undone, messy almost, like he couldn't be bothered to finish it. On that sliver of tan skin I saw the edge of the three scratches that tattooed our destinies together.

I knew who he was really supposed to be. The gold arrow dripping with something that might be blood made it obvious.

Eros.

He rubbed his jaw, a barely there smile tweaking the side of his mouth. Something flickered in his eyes, an emotion like gold glittering at the bottom of a black well.

Humor?

Maybe, but it felt darker.

"I've imagined this so many times," the guy continued, oblivious to the threat at his back. He pressed the knife to my neck and the familiar *rush* overcame me.

I stared at Grim, angling my neck up for the knife.

An offering, but not for this asshole.

Grim's eyes pulsed, locked on my arched neck, and I felt the vibration in my bones. That twisted, dark thing between us shimmered in the air. My teeth tingled like if I'd eaten too much sugar. It landed electric in my gut.

"I bet you're even more beautiful dead—"

Blood splattered my face, neck, and chest. The knife he'd been holding fell from his hands, clanging against the marble. Blood the color of dark wine poured out of the silky straight line from his neck. Behind him, Grim held a knife to his throat, gaze locked with mine.

I barely had a moment to register the promise in Grim's eyes, when the man fell to the floor.

Blood pooled beneath my stilettos, slid like liquid metal down Grim's knife, coating his fingers.

Drip. Drip. Drip.

With each drop of blood, my heart rate slammed against my chest. Grim's eyes were locked on my neck, the vein in his own throbbing.

Something was about to shatter.

TWENTY-SEVEN

GRIM

She'd let me fuck her like this, as a body bled out beneath her stilettos, because Gemma Crowne was not the party girl princess America painted her to be. Gemma Crowne courted death.

Seduced it.

Teased it.

From the very first day our eyes connected in that empty high school room, I knew the truth. She was wrapped in it. I should have seen her for the siren she was then, but I was wrapped in death too.

Maybe that was why I could never let her go.

"Why do you keep saving me?" Her tongue darted out, wetting her bottom lip.

My eyes locked on that, on her pouty pink lips and her wet, red tongue.

When I spoke, my voice was too low. Too dark. Too smoky. "You have a debt."

"That's it? That's the only reason you're keeping me alive?"

"Yeah."

She tilted her head back to hold my stare and hoisted herself onto the black marble sink. Blood fell in drops off her heels as she spread her legs wide for me. Easily. With the movement her dress rose.

No fucking underwear.

I gripped the leather handle of my knife to keep from dropping to my knees and worshipping her cunt, the muscles in my neck spasming.

This fucking killed me. How natural it was for her. The girl with all the walls never had any for me.

I knew she wanted it just as much as I did.

It drove me fucking insane.

That knowledge.

That at any fucking time Gemma would spread her legs for me. The only thing stopping it was me. And, yeah, it wouldn't be healthy or good, but we'd never been those things. We'd never wanted those things.

She scythed her bottom lip, blanching the pink skin.

Fuck.

My muscles already ached with the strain of holding myself back. I would always remember how I felt inside her. How her perfect cunt gripped my cock, like it was made just for me. There wasn't a moment that passed I didn't want to get her back to the point where her nails dug bloody rivers into my back. When she begged, and moaned, and fell to her fucking knees for me.

I could barely see past the need.

There were things Gemma liked—fucked-up things. Shit I probably shouldn't want to do to her, but it was all I could think about as she bit her bottom lip, looking at me the way I'd craved for years.

"You keep scaring away all my monsters," she breathed. Hungry. Heated.

Without thought, only instinct, I stepped between her legs, gripping the back of her neck and angling her so she could feel my words. "I'm your monster. *Me.*"

"Then when are you going to fucking eat me?" It sounded like a beg, a *plea*, ripped from her throat. She wrapped her legs around my waist, baby blue eyes wide.

Her eyes dropped to my hand, widening with realization. She took it in her slender one, lifting it up so she could see my newest tattoo. Fresh. The way she bit me when she came now permanently inked into my flesh.

I couldn't mark her, so I'd cover myself in her. Strung out. Weak? Yeah.

She pressed my tattooed hand between her breasts. "I'll just keep finding someone else to do it," she taunted, voice soft.

I gripped her hips and dragged her flush against me. "You do that, Rich Girl. I need a hobby."

Her bottom lip pushed out in a pout. My spoiled fucking princess.

I wanted her to beg me.

Wanted those spoiled lips pleading me to fuck her.

Her eyes briefly flashed to the body. I gripped her chin, dragging her gaze back to mine. I slid my free hand down her inner thigh, finding her hot and wet.

So fucked up.

So *perfectly* fucked up.

"Did you forget the dead body?" I slid my fingers inside her, my cock bruising against the seam of my jeans as her eyes grew and then drooped. "You want me to fuck you while someone dies at your feet, Gemma?"

She clenched.

"Fuck..." I rolled my neck, bruising my forehead against hers. "I can feel your answer. You're so fucked up."

I sank my fingers deeper, desperate to get inside her. Control wavered. I pressed harder, deeper, faster—addicted to the way she watched me. The dirty, fucked-up thoughts swimming in her hooded eyes, the ones that painted her cheeks red.

"What are you thinking, Rich Girl?"

She opened her mouth, then closed it. I slid my grip to her neck, holding tight as I pushed even deeper inside. Her lips parted on a soft moan that went straight to my cock.

"Say it," I demanded. "Say those thoughts."

"I'm imagining what it feels like to be marked," she breathed. "Tattooed. Claimed."

I stilled.

Her legs spread, eyes wide, entire being vulnerable. Big blue eyes hazy with submission. She'd let me do anything to her. An insane, irrational need blazed through me. I could do more than fuck her like this. I could fucking claim her.

With careful, measured movements, I resumed finger-fucking her.

"And why do you want that?" My throat felt rough, the words sandpaper. "Don't you know that's a bad idea? The princess can't run away with the monster."

"I don't want to run away with the monster." She wrapped her arms around my neck, words a breathless cry that went straight to my cock. "I want the monster to drag me to hell. I dream about how your claw marks feel."

A jagged groan tore through my body.

"You'd wear it here." I ghosted my thumb along the back

of her neck, just beneath her short hair. "So everyone would fucking know."

Her cunt spasmed against my fingers at the image I painted. Her heels dug into my ass, pulling me closer.

Whatever control I had left was being ripped apart, shredded to tiny pieces as I fell into the fantasy.

"Anyone who looks at you will know you're mine," I growled. "Say it."

"Everyone would know I'm yours." She arched into me, voice a husky, breathy promise.

Her body moved against my hand.

Rolling.

Squirming.

She wouldn't just let me fuck her here—she *wanted* to be fucked here. A wild, animalistic urge rippled through my muscles. I could take her here. Take her and never fucking let her go. She would be mine—

Fuck.

The last shred of sanity screamed in my veins. *Stop.* I had to *stop.*

Gemma Crowne *couldn't* be mine. Forget her world and mine were diametrically opposed. Forget that protecting her would be infinitely harder once everyone knew her, that everyone would want her dead, that she would fucking relish it too.

There might come a time when I'd have to choose between her and the Horsemen, between her and my fucking family.

I already knew who I would choose.

And *that* was the problem.

So as Gemma Crowne collapsed around my fingers, nails biting my neck, her moan muffled against my throat in a vibration I would never forget, my words disappeared into a snarl. "You will never be mine."

It felt like ripping a knife from my abdomen as I pulled my fingers out of her. It wasn't right.

I belonged there.

I forced my features into stone, meeting her eyes with a glare. "You'll never wear my mark."

My fingers were fucking drenched with her. My perfect fucking princess and her perfect cunt. I couldn't resist the chance to taste her. Just one last time.

Something like hurt flashed across her face as I slid her taste into my mouth, but it was quickly smothered, replaced by ice.

God, she tasted so *fucking* good.

Too good.

I stepped back, ready to leave and put distance between this destructive need, when cool metal hit my neck.

Gemma had grabbed my discarded knife, now holding it flush against my skin. Her legs tightened around my waist, forcing me closer to the knife. One wrong move and my neck would open.

And fuck if that didn't get me hard.

I covered her hand with mine, gripping the handle, and pressed the knife deeper against my flesh.

"You're in the wrong spot," I said. "You're gonna wanna start here, and drag it here." I dragged her hand slowly across my neck, knife scraping.

She licked her lips.

Pupils dilated, she arched into me. "If I can't wear your mark, then you'll wear *mine*."

Gemma slammed her lips into mine, scoring my bottom lip with her teeth.

TWENTY-EIGHT

GEMMA

Grim pulled back, touching the spot I'd bit him, blood staining the pads of his fingers red. I had half a second to feel the rush of terror, the sane part screaming, *What the fuck did you do?* His gaze darkened into something lethal, and with a deep, guttural noise, his lips crushed mine.

Grim didn't kiss like he fucked.

Grim fucked like he was dying, vicious and violent. Grim kissed like he had already died, and this was heaven. He kissed me like I didn't have a knife biting against his neck. A toe-curling possession oozed from his soft yet demanding lips.

If we were a fairy tale, this kiss would have been under the stars. Not here, while a body bled out at our feet.

But Grim and I weren't a fairy tale.

Grim sucked on my bottom lip, pulling it out with a bite I felt in my toes. I gasped and he pushed his tongue into my open mouth, punishing.

I leaned into it. Addicted to the dichotomy. Somehow both gentle and rough, demanding and imploring.

Possessive.

With each swipe of his tongue, he claimed me. Ruined me for anyone else.

He tasted like some dark, secret liquor. Something spicy but also sweet, heady like good liquor, *illicit* and not meant for human lips.

Ambrosia. The drink of the gods.

I moaned and his mouth slanted to pull me deeper, as if trying to swallow my sounds. One hand slid down my body, around my back, up to my neck, back into my hair—touching all of me like it was the last time.

Grim forced me closer, the knife cutting deeper into his flesh until sprigs of blood dotted his flesh like Christmas holly.

Grim *wanted* this. I couldn't pull back if I tried.

Blood dripped down his neck, and an insane part of me liked it, wanted to mix it with mine so even if he tried to leave me, he never could. I'd be stuck inside him.

Maybe my breathing got too raspy, or my heart beat too loud, because it was like he knew what I was thinking.

His teeth scraped my bottom lip, groaning. "My fucked-up princess."

His kisses grew frenzied and bruising, lips traveling down my neck, mouth a searing-hot brand on my flesh, alternating between tongue, lips, teeth against the muscle.

The butterflies in my belly electrified, shock waves of heat rolling through my body.

Grim spoke a mix of English and Spanish, my skin prickling with each hot whisper against my flesh.

So fucked up.

Jodida princesa.

Te voy a hacer mía.

So perfect.

And when Grim said it, I...I felt perfect.

Our eyes opened at the same time. Lips wet, eyes heavy, the Grim I saw on the beach was back. His mask gone. I wanted to burn the way he looked at me into my brain. My teeth tingled with it. Like he wanted to fuck me. Kill me. Right here.

His Adam's apple bobbed jagged with a swallow.

He was *still* holding back.

"Grim..."

His breath was hot on my lips. "What, *mi locura?*"

I fell apart. Shattered into a tiny, million pieces of pure pleasure as the nickname slid across my skin.

"Please." I scored my nails into his neck. "Please, Grim. *Please.*"

I heard myself as if from underwater. Gemma Crowne didn't beg, but whoever was speaking had no shame. She begged and pleaded with Grim, scythed nails into his neck and repeated it over and over again: *please, please, please.*

Fuck me.

Please.

I need you inside me.

I was scorching. Heated. Twisted.

So maybe that was why I didn't notice the change in Grim until it was too late.

His mask was back. Eyes cold and iron, mouth a solid line. But he gently swiped his thumb down my cheek, almost as if *petting* me.

"Do you think your pussy is so magic I'll forget why I'm here?" His words settled icy on my hot skin. "I've already been inside you, Rich Girl—it's not."

Any lingering warmth vanished.

Whatever spell had been cast shattered like glass at our feet. Grim stepped back, adjusting his cock with a casual indifference that made my throat dry.

As he adjusted, he flashed the fresh tattoo. *My* fucking teeth. My nails were inked into his chest, my mouth on his hand. Why? Why the *fuck* would he do that?

I still gripped the knife, maintaining some facsimile of control. He eyed it and laughed.

I don't understand what changed, why he went from whispering beautiful things against my skin to *this*. At the same time, I knew I shouldn't have been surprised.

Everything was a game to Grim.

So this was worse than anything we'd done over the years, because for a moment I'd let him back inside, into my fucking soul again.

White-hot anger slid inside my veins. I focused on that, on the tightness in my skin and the scream lodged in my throat like a broken tortilla chip, rather than the dull, bruising ache in my heart.

"You ripped me out of the ocean," I said. "Have held me hostage for five fucking years. You can't just—"

He spun, slamming my back against the sink before I could blink, caging me. "What? I can't *what*?"

"I didn't want this contract." With two hands I shoved his chest, but he barely moved. "You put those lines on your chest without my consent."

"What contract was that again?"

My lips parted, but I said nothing—tongue-tied.

"Right..." He dragged the word out, lips twisting up— *fucking cocky*. "Because you can't fucking *say* it. Nah, you'll do what Gemma Crowne does best, pretend you're just like everyone else."

He stepped off like he'd won.

"You promised to kill me, Santos," I said. "You can't put a line on your chest without putting a bullet through my skull."

TWENTY-NINE

GEMMA

Instantly, Grim tensed.

We had a rule—unspoken but clear as day. I had just broken it.

Don't talk about what happens when the contract ends.

Most people who ask something of the Horsemen were looking for revenge, wealth—boring shit like that. So what did I ask for?

Death.

That was why his twisted punishment had been forcing me to live. I turned to face the mirror—and froze. Blood. Everywhere. Smeared on my face, in my hair from the body, on my lips and cheek from him. Just...everywhere...

I turned on the sink.

The silence dragged on as I rinsed the blood out of my hair. I wrung my wet hair until the red water was mostly clear.

Grim slid his hand around my neck, forcing me to stand

straight on my tiptoes. My wet hair dripped to the floor, making pale-pink watercolor streaks in the blood. The heat of Grim burned into my back.

"You really wanna die, *Gemma*?" He said my name with a bite that felt loaded.

I didn't know much about Grim's real name, just that I was never supposed to use it. I'd taken enough Spanish to know it meant saint, which was almost too ironic.

Did I want to die?

"I dunno," I said, his eyes meeting mine in the mirror, grip tightening. "But I'm really looking forward to the day you have to kill me."

I elbowed him off.

"Gonna be pretty hard to marry some rich asshole when you're dead," he said to my back.

That knowing look passed through his eyes, like he was reading parts of my soul I hadn't yet translated.

I hated that look. Especially after he'd just ripped me open like a barely formed chrysalis.

In the mirror, Grim's stare locked on mine, a slight lift to one side of his lips.

"Have you given any thought to how you're going to kill me?" I asked lightly. "Because I have some ideas. You could use a knife..."

I ghosted my touch along his discarded knife.

In one quick movement he shoved the knife away so hard it flew off the counter, smacking into the wall.

"Okay, no knife," I said. "You could use a gun, but, I don't know, it's so impersonal. I want to feel the life leave my body."

He eyed me in a bored, disaffected way. The only indication what I was saying might be affecting him was the muscles beneath his shirt flexing with my words.

"Know it's you doing it." I licked my lips. "So...so, I thought you could choke me—"

He was on top of me before I could finish.

A grin slid across my lips. "Was it something I said?"

His thumbs slid slowly into place on either side of my neck. The air was soft and heavy with our breaths.

He pressed his thumbs into my jugular. "Is this what you want?"

Grim wasn't a reckless person. He wasn't like me, emotional and impulsive. He was almost infuriatingly calm. But things happened when he got that rasp in his voice, when sandpaper scratched the back of his throat.

It was like he was feeding off me.

The air around us drunk.

"This what you want?" He pressed his thumbs into my neck.

Yes.

Fuck.

I opened my mouth on a silent, choking gasp, arching into him.

"You want to die?" His voice shredded with smoke as he kneed my legs apart. "Should I fuck you until you die? Feel your cunt squeeze me until your life drains around my cock?"

Oh, *fuck.* My thighs ached with need, with the fucked-up fantasy only Grim gave me. His teeth scraped down my shoulder, and my breath turned ragged.

"Promises," I gasped.

He lifted his head, and he was like an old Hollywood star, eyes shadowed under silky, wavy black hair.

There was something in the dark irises, something I couldn't name, only *feel.* Feel the too gentle way his thumbs stroked my neck, how his jaw clenched and nostrils flared.

Then all at once he dropped me. My heart raced, my vision blurred. Lightheaded. Dizzy.

"You're not in control here, Gemma." Grim pressed me deeper against the sink, my lower back cutting into the marble vanity edge. "You never were. You never will be."

His eyes softened with *pity*. I once again got that feeling that I'd started to associate only with the Underworld.

It didn't matter that I'd been in this world for five years. I still felt like a little kid thrown in the deep end for the first time.

I angled my chin higher. "Then kill me, Grim."

"Nah, baby, you crave that too much." He placed his finger under my chin, tilting my head to find his eyes. "When you cease being useful, I'll give you what you want."

Words whispered seductively, but they settled like jagged shards of glass in my gut.

His grip on my chin was tight. Unable to turn my head, I stared at his chest, refusing eye contact. Three jagged scratch marks were visible through his unbuttoned shirt, glowing on his olive skin.

The tattoo Grim had used to steal everything.

It felt like it was mocking me.

He released my chin but didn't step away. There was something in his eyes. That throbbing, aching something that had me hooked like a fish that kept swimming back to the same barb, begging to be hooked again and again.

He looked like he was about to say something.

I leaned for it. *Ached* for it.

Stupidly.

"Stay away. Don't leave your world. Don't come near me. If we need you, we'll find you."

I worked my jaw, staring at the jagged red lines on his chest. "But the contract—"

"That's an order, Gemma," he growled. "From now on whatever bullshit we had is over. I don't wanna fucking hear you, see you, know you."

Anger, indignation, fucking *rage* made my teeth hurt, my jaw ache.

Fuck you for making me feel this.

Fuck you for taking it away.

Fuck you.

"You made me a promise," I gritted.

He pushed the hair out of my face. "Don't go looking for monsters anymore." His palm lingered on the side of my face. "Where were you, Gemma?"

"With a boy," I spat. "Some asshole, whose name I'd like to fucking forget."

THIRTY

GRIM

The hurt in Gemma's eyes lingered like stale cigarette smoke in my lungs.

From now on whatever bullshit we had is over.

It wasn't over. It would never be over, so long as the ink still stained my chest. Killing Gemma has become our fucked-up fantasy. Not the actual death—she could have killed herself in the past five years, she could have found a way, I knew that.

It was refusing to take her life in her own hands, instead trusting me with it, obeying whatever I said.

And that drove me nuts. Her soul-deep submission.

"We had a fucking plan." Lock's voice dragged me back to the present.

We'd waited until the club closed before starting cleanup. Bleaching the bathroom, moving the body. Now Lock leaned against my bathroom wall, arms folded, eyes on me. Raze watched me with a similar expression, and Wraith sat on the toilet, reading a book. Behind them, a body dissolved in acid.

"We had a plan," Lock continued.

With my thumb and forefinger, I massaged the arch of my jaw. "I'm aware."

"Are you? You were supposed to distance yourself from Gemma—*there! There it fucking is.*" He pointed at me like he'd just discovered something.

"What? There is *what?*"

"I thought I was seeing things at first, but every time we talk about letting Gemma go, you tense the fuck up, like you're getting ready to fight."

I relaxed my shoulders. He was right. *Fuck.* I didn't know how I'd get myself out of this, but I did know it wouldn't happen if I kept seeing Gemma. She had ensnared me and whenever I was with her, I didn't want to leave the web.

I rubbed the back of my neck. "Are you saying I did this on purpose?"

"I dunno," Raze said, stepping forward. "But, somehow, anytime she's with you, shit goes sideways."

I rubbed the groove between my brows, looking at the barrel holding a rapidly decomposing body.

"Let her fucking die," Raze continued. "Let someone take her. Stop fucking saving her. Her contract is void. There's no real tie to us. So we let America's fucking Princess leave our lives."

Another wave of involuntary tension corded my muscles. I breathed through my nostrils, focusing on the moment.

"It's not that simple," I said, voice strained with tension.

"Why the fuck not?" Lock demanded.

You promised to kill me, Santos.

I'd opened my mouth to tell them the truth, the *entire* truth, of that night, when the reason waltzed in.

Vander Archeron.

The man above us. The reason the police or FBI never came sniffing around. The reason for the ink on our backs. The Horsemen stilled as he walked in, sitting on the edge of the tub like he had every right to be there.

"What the fuck do you want?" I said.

He folded his arms, a lazy smile on his lips. "Is that any way for a son to talk to his father?"

A different, spiky tension wrapped barbed wire around my fascia.

Vander eyed the black barrel, sniffing at the now familiar smell of acrid, soapy rot. "You boys have learned a lot since the first time we met."

I shifted, rebalancing on my feet. "What. Do. You. Want?"

"What I've always wanted," he said. "You."

I worked my jaw. "I'm paying your tithe. I'm doing your contracts. What the fuck else do you want?"

"I have you the way someone has a dog. Throw meat and it snaps at the right thing." I ignored the obvious bait at calling me a dog, as he continued, "I don't want a dog. I don't *need* a dog. I need a successor."

"Tough shit."

He laughed, bitter and humorless. "You've had five years to kill the Crowne girl. I'm starting to think you want this life. Secretly."

A nearly imperceptible shift happened in the room. I could feel the question, the burning glares, as Vander revealed the truth.

"Either finish your contract and kill Gemma, or join me. Permanently." He stood up, brushing at nonexistent dirt on his thighs. "You have until the fifteenth of this month. If she's alive, I'll assume I have my answer." He walked to the door, pausing, his fingers curled around the frame. "You can't have both, Santos. You don't get Gemma and your little family."

Then he left.

Silence followed, the creaking of the Ferris wheel in the wind loud.

"You're gonna explain what is happening," Raze said. "Right fucking now."

"What did he mean you have to kill Gemma?" Lock added.

I exhaled.

"That's the contract," I said. "That's what she demanded for the ink."

I tell the story, the entire story. Me stalking Gemma, finding her as she tried to kill herself. The look in her eyes after I saved her. Knowing the minute I left her alone, she would find a way. Tattooing myself. Showing up, showing her her life was forfeit, her only agreeing if once our contract ended, I ended her.

"I knew," Lock said. "I fucking *knew* something was up. Five years ago you told us she tricked you into this contract. You said you would figure a way out of it. That we would be free. You—" He broke off in disbelief and indignation.

"Not only did you drag us into this," Raze continued for him. "You knew there would be no way out."

"There is a way—"

"You will never fucking kill her!" Lock raged, his voice hoarse.

A moment later, the anger drained out of him. He slid down the wall, to the marbled tile floor, arms over knees.

Resigned.

Fuck.

Fuck, fuck, fuck.

"And he knows?" Raze said, drawing my attention back. "Vander knows?"

I rubbed my jaw. "He figured it out. I don't know how. Probably the same way he found us that day."

"And you didn't try correcting him?" Raze asked. "Lying?"

I could have.

I *should* have.

I might even have convinced him long enough to get myself out of it. But that was the problem, the dirty, fucked-up truth. I didn't *want* out, not if I had to give up my only tether to Gemma.

"So what now?" Lock asked. "You gonna go be your dad's pet?"

"He's not my fucking dad," I growled.

"Maybe you could mark her." Wraith spoke for the first time, flipping a page in his book.

Raze looked at Wraith like he was sprouting heads. "*How* are you so cool about this?"

"Because I've known for years. At least it's out in the open. We can deal with it. The whole 'let's pretend nothing is happening' thing clearly isn't working." He eyed the barrel in the center of the room.

"So what do you suggest?" Raze threw a bloody towel—used to clean up the bathroom floor—at Wraith. "He actually mark her?"

Wraith caught the towel with ease and shrugged. "Maybe it will cancel out the contract. You know, a double-negative thing."

"Or," Raze stressed, "maybe it will make everything

worse. Maybe nothing changes, and now we have a spoiled, suicidal brat on our hands."

"That's also a possibility," Wraith conceded.

I'd been holding, white-knuckled, to my last shred of control. Today, with her taste still on my lips, I could feel that grip slipping.

Mark Gemma Crowne?

Lock laughed. "You only think this is a good plan because the idea of bloodshed gets you hard. And that plan has a *lot* of bloodshed."

"Look, I don't care what we do," Wraith said. "Mark her, don't mark her, kill her, ship her off to the Galápagos. But—" He turned his attention to me. "—whatever happens, don't put your life on the line for a girl willing to die."

THIRTY-ONE

GEMMA

I had that feeling again. That hurricane feeling. That twisted one that my mother called attention seeking, but to me felt like a sandstorm in my chest. It carried me through the cold winter night, past Main Street, to a small tattoo parlor.

My entrance was announced with a dainty-sounding bell at odds with the rough interior.

"We're closed," the tattooist said without looking up.

He was like something out of *Sons of Anarchy*. With blond hair in a low ponytail, big and burly, even hunched over, I could tell he surpassed six feet.

"I've got five thousand that says you're not."

He glanced up, an interested arch in his brow. It didn't take him more than a second to recognize me. He exhaled, stretching big arms over his head.

"You looking for a flower or some arrow?"

I pulled out my phone, showing him exactly what I wanted.

His eyeballs popped. "Yeah, fucking right. Good luck finding someone to ink that."

"Ten thousand," I upped.

He swallowed. "You have any idea whose mark that is?"

I had a really good idea. I guess you could say it was *inked* in my brain. The horse, skull, and scythe shining with briny ocean water, rippling across his shoulder blades and dripping down his muscles.

"Twenty—and I won't say shit about where I got it done."

Grim Reyes doesn't love me. He never did. He saved me because he saw an opportunity to keep the perfect Crowne princess hostage forever like a broken doll to play with.

Every word, every action, was calculated.

But he didn't get to end it this way. He didn't get to end it, period. He didn't get to turn my world upside down over and over, and then call it quits. Leave me in the dust.

Again...

I swallowed, realizing I'd been quiet for too long, the tattooist eyeing me uncertainly.

"Thirty, fuck."

He looked away, but said, "Where you want it? Lower back?"

"No." I pointed at the nape of my neck, where my hair was just short enough for it to be seen always. "I want it visible."

He sucked in a breath. "You got a death wish or somethin', girl?"

"Or something," I muttered, sliding face-first into the leather chair, legs spread on either side.

The needle hit my skin, and I swallowed a gasp as I

permanently inked Grim into me. I played with the cracks in the leather chair, the night with Grim replaying over and over again. A numb sort of calm spreading through my veins.

You will never be mine. You'll never wear my mark.

With each prick of the needle, I felt that already blurry line between my world and his dissolve.

I couldn't stop thinking back to the day I first met Grim —not the day our fates collided, but the day we first spoke— and wondered what would have happened had he not seen me, and I not talked to him. If we hadn't tumbled into our fate, and our lives stayed separate.

I'd been too complacent. Too foolishly hopeful. I'd lived five years on the crumbs that Grim gave me. Not anymore.

It didn't take long for the tattoo to finish, or maybe I was just so in my thoughts that I didn't notice time pass.

He handed me a mirror that reflected against the one he held to see the fresh ink on my neck.

"They'll know," he said. "Doesn't matter if you try and hide it. They always find out."

"I'm counting on it."

My mother always said happily ever afters didn't exist, and I should look for opportunity.

THIRTY-TWO

GEMMA

The door slammed open, my head pounding with it.

I rolled over, pressing my forehead into my pillow and groaning into the satin fabric. "Fuck you too."

Without a second to breathe someone grabbed my bicep, yanking me out of my warm, soft bed and into the cold morning. I blinked blearily into earnest blue eyes, so similar in color to mine, if not icier.

Grayson, my brother.

I shoved his hand off me. "Excuse you."

"What does he have on you?"

I rubbed my eyes with the heel of my palm, trying to clear out the harsh morning light.

"Who?" I asked through a scratchy throat.

He shoved a phone in my face, and I squinted at the blaring blue light. It was a news article—multiple articles, actually, all sharing similar headlines.

Gemma Crowne Hard Launches New Boyfriend: Who is the Mysterious New Beau?

Beneath the blocky black print was a blown-up Instagram post—*mine.* My chin rested on my bare shoulder, eyes at the camera, and you could clearly see my new tattoo. The caption read:

For my new boyfriend...

Oh.

So that actually happened? It wasn't a dream? For the first time in five years I felt something other than nothing.

Dread.

Guilt.

Excitement.

I shoved Grayson away, swinging my legs off the bed. "You're the one who said I could date whoever I wanted."

"That's..." My brother broke off, looking like one of those cartoon heads about to explode.

"He saved you," I said—*why was I defending this clearly drunk and insane decision? Defending* Grim? Without reason, the words kept coming. "He saved your wife and child. Is the man who saved your daughter not good enough?"

Behind my brother, his wife stood, an inscrutable look in her stony green eyes. It wasn't judgment, it was more... curious. Story was someone who took in the scene before reacting.

"Whatever he has on you, we can fix it," Grayson said. "You're not alone in this."

"I'm not some endangered woman. I did this. I got the tattoo. I posted knowing what the media would do with it."

He stepped back, looking left and right, and dragged his finger along his bottom lip for an uncomfortably long time.

Finally he managed, "Why?"

I paused, tripping over my tongue. Why? Because I wanted to have control for once. Because I wanted to make *him* squirm. Because—

Anyone who looks at you will know you're mine.

This was all happening too early, without caffeine, and much too hungover.

"Bored. Crazy. Pick one, combine them—I don't care."

My brother inhaled audibly. "You know Mom is going to have a fucking heart attack."

That made me stop.

Her perfect daughter, her last fucking hope, had tied herself to a criminal.

I knew what would happen when she found out, and it wasn't a heart attack.

I pushed those thoughts away. "Huh, didn't peg you as giving a shit about what *Mother* thinks of my or anyone's love interests. Guess I forgot how fond she was of Story."

He worked his jaw. "That's different."

I laughed. "Oh, okay. So I get to marry whoever I want, *unless* you don't approve—"

"Fucking *marriage?*" That finger on his bottom lip worked overtime, eyes about to pop out of his head.

"At least Mom and Grandpa never pretended to be—" I gestured at him. "—I don't know, Gray, what were you trying to be? Different? They were always crystal clear about the rules and what would happen if I broke them. She was kind enough to give me my first tampon when she sold me to Horace, so do you have a present prepared for when you put me back in my cage?"

Grayson's fingers curled hard into his palm, blanching the knuckles. He took deep, uneven breaths through flared nostrils, jaw clenched. Story placed her hand on his shoulder. His entire body tensed, then relaxed. He turned to face her, the muscles in his back rolling with the movement.

They spoke low, too low to really hear anything. I did catch *I will fucking end him before...*

Then Story handed their child, Sonnet, to him. "It's a nice day out."

"I know what you're doing," he growled.

She smiled. "Is it working?"

He didn't answer, but kissed her on her forehead. I rolled my eyes.

He glared at me, Sonnet in his arms. "If you think he's living in our house, you've really lost your fucking mind."

I shot him a smile. "That's cool, I can go live with him."

His jaw clenched so tight the muscle in his cheek popped.

"Grayson," Story murmured, and Grayson left.

Then it was only Story and me.

She tilted her head.

"I can't even begin to imagine what lecture the maid who ruined my brother's marriage is going to give me."

"No lecture." She leaned against the wall, ignoring my obvious attempt to rile her up, stony eyes seeing too much. "You once told me he was both your villain and your hero."

I reached for the cigarettes inside my nightstand, then stopped.

Don't smoke, Rich Girl, you taste better.

The moment she spoke of came rushing back. It was right after our grandfather went to jail, when Grim had saved us and taken my brother's contract. Story saw me talking to Grim. Story saw *everything* when we were trapped at the compound. The memory fluttered like autumn leaves in my mind. Colorful. Fragile.

Someone once told me the villain and the princess have a

relationship too, even if it's unwanted. Is he your villain? Or your hero?

I rubbed my eye, head throbbing. "I don't remember that."

"I've also been talking to Abigail and apparently this has been going on since before she left here."

"Cool, sounds like you know everything, so I don't know why you're even here, babe."

It was a minute before Story spoke again. "I never thought your brother and I would end up together. He was *engaged*. We were from two totally different worlds. Everything we wanted hurt others."

I looked up, meeting her gaze.

"Grayson thinks Grim has something on you, that he's forcing you into this," she continued.

"You don't?" I asked.

"I think I know what it's like to want someone, even though it could ruin everything. I think maybe there's a world you want to be in, but feel stuck in another. When you're ready to talk about it, I'll be here."

Honestly, if any other person tried to have this conversation with me, I'd call bullshit. Story wasn't like any other person in my world. She was, like...the kind of person you could tell a secret to and not have to wonder who was going to hear it next.

I stayed in my bed after she left.

It wasn't until the sun fell again that I got out, took a shower, and threw on a different pair of clothes. My mother never came by, and I wasn't sure if I should be happy about that, or worried.

I resisted the urge to rub my aching neck.

Because of the fucking tattoo.

A twisted kind of tingle spread in my gut. The kind I

used to get when I shoplifted. I'd done something wrong. I knew I was going to be punished for it. For some messed-up reason, I felt alive because of it.

The icy, brackish winter air drifted into my room, my curtains fluttering.

He'd come.

I picked up a matchbook, toying with the fragile wood.

Snick. The flame lit.

I stared at Grim through the small, passionate flame. "The Reaper comes to visit, but I don't have any more souls to give him."

"You really fucked me, Rich Girl."

THIRTY-THREE

GEMMA

"Does making the king of the Underworld an overnight celebrity cause...issues?" I licked my bottom lip.

"You think you're cute, huh?" Grim stepped closer.

A new moon darkened the sky to something black and wicked. Grim was a chiaroscuro of emotion. Shadows sharpened his jaw while the little light from the moon set the hunger in his eyes ablaze.

"Mmm...I'm sorry." I batted my lashes. "You wanna take it out on me?"

"You'd like that too much," he said.

He traced a line down the nape of my neck, and I gasped at the raw sensation. His gaze shadowed, the word in them practically setting the air on fire.

Mine.

The thing between us—the irrational, reckless, *hungry* thing—ignited.

I wanted more.

I was so tired of fighting it.

He thrust me against the wall, and the painting beside me quivered. Then he dragged my hands above my head, clasped in one of his.

I let him.

His eyes flared at the easy way I surrendered.

"I've been holding back." His grip on my wrist flexed, as if he was still holding back, and he parted my thighs with one of his. "You should have taken the fucking out, Rich Girl. You brought the Reaper into your pretty little world, and I'm gonna tear it the fuck apart."

"Not if I set yours on fire first." I smiled.

I could feel him. Even through his jeans, he was like a lead weight on my thigh.

Hard.

I was talking about ruining him and he was fucking *hard* for it.

His lips steamed my ear. "You think I can't play with you while the world watches?"

He bit the lobe, barely, just enough to ignite goose bumps along my spine that I could feel in my teeth.

His hand slid around my back, pulling me closer, his breath a hot, seductive promise against my flesh. "I can be your boyfriend, and I can be your worst nightmare, Gemma Crowne."

I gasped. "Promise?"

Boyfriend.

I had a split second to feel that deep in my marrow, Grim *finally* staking some kind of claim, when he spun me around, pressed me flat against the wall, his chest on my back.

He kept my arms pinned above my head.

Then he slid his tongue up across the fresh tattoo on my neck, starting at the top notch of my spine, ending at the base of my skull. Goose bumps peppered my flesh. Even his gentle lips felt like a scrape. The act was primal, raw.

His soft kiss transformed to teeth scraping along my neck.

A *bite*.

It was so fucking painful against my freshly wounded skin—and so fucking addicting. I saw stars. The world blurred, and I became a puddle of hot liquid. A mindless, drugged pleasure that felt like stardust in my veins. I gasped, or maybe moaned. I squirmed against him, and his free hand slid to my abdomen, pressing me against his cock, holding me in place.

"Please," I gasped, not totally sure what I was asking for.

The hand at my stomach slid lower, between my thighs, where the skin was bare from my shorts. He pinned me like that, the heat of his hand searing my flesh.

He alternated between biting and licking and kissing, teeth and tongue and just *too much*. He whispered Spanish against my neck. Words that I think meant *perfect* and *beautiful*, words that I *felt* more than heard.

I couldn't think through it. Through the mix of pain and pleasure. I was all sensation. I squirmed into his hand. He was going to do it. He was going to finally fuck me—

He froze, groaning against my neck, the vibration sending illicit shivers up and down my spine. It sounded rough and ragged, ripped from him.

"Not yet, *mi locura*." The grip between my thighs tightened, his lips hot and wet on my neck. "Did you realize by making me go into your world, you'd have to come into mine?"

If I wasn't so strung out on him, I would have laughed.

Instead, my voice came out breathy, low. "I've *been* in your world."

With his hand still between my thighs, he released my wrists and knotted his fist in my hair, stretching my neck backward until our eyes met. The sinewy muscles in his jaw twitched, flexing with an inscrutable emotion.

"You've never known what it means to be the Reaper's girl."

Then he kissed me. Still pinned against him, arching in a way that would have been uncomfortable if my body wasn't already on fire.

His lips were demanding, cruel, *intoxicating.*

I gasped and his tongue slid into my mouth. I gripped his wrists, nails digging into the flesh, needing something to keep me steady. He dragged my bottom lip out with a bite.

The kiss was a claim.

A promise.

He didn't stop until I was squirming on his hand, until I was certain he could feel me dripping down my thigh.

Then he released his grip in my hair. My head fell forward to the wall, heavy. I took in deep, ragged breaths. Everything was blurry. My heart slammed against my chest.

He spun me around so we were face-to-face.

My breath disappeared down my throat. Grim was always a bit too much like some fallen angel, some god hell-bent on revenge. But now there was a reverence in his eyes that made my throat thick.

Like the angel had fallen *because* of me.

He was unashamedly hard. His eyes on fire. His hair wavy and messy like a villainous movie star. His nostrils sharpened. The shadows made him grow larger and untamed.

"Enjoy your last night of freedom, Rich Girl. Tomorrow..." His eyes traveled down my face, settling on my lips. "You're the Reaper's girl."

THIRTY-FOUR

GRIM

Five Years Ago

Gemma Crowne was acting strange. Her family's famous Fourth of July party was happening at Crowne Hall. But instead of joining kings and actors and whoever the fuck else, she was at *my* beach, staring off into the black ocean, her silky white dress swirling in the wind.

This bad habit of mine started years ago.

Gemma has been a secret obsession since the day I found her crying in that empty high school room. It started slow, watching her in class, figuring out what she liked and what she *pretended* to like. Making sure her favorite cheat snack appeared in her locker (Cheetos with ranch, fucking weird).

When some jock asshole tried to grab her and force her

into his lap, it escalated into breaking his good throwing arm the day before a college scout was supposed to see him.

I would have done so much worse, and had.

After we graduated, and I no longer had her in my sights, it escalated further. From following her on every social media she had, to spying through her window, watching her cry when no one thought she was looking.

Finding out who made her cry, and making them pay.

It was hacking her computer, finding the porn she watched, and jerking off to the same video that made her come. It was studying the erotica she read. It was memorizing her secret fantasies.

It was definitely fucked up. Amoral. I should have left it—*us*—in that empty classroom. But my world had always been like an old movie, seen in black and white, where some parts had faded into time and lost sound completely.

But Gemma?

She was Technicolor.

And when I was with her, the world was Technicolor too.

Gemma took a step toward the ocean. I was ripped out of the past, locked on her movement. She walked until the waves hit her thighs, dress sticking to her skin. She stayed like that for a moment. The moon rippled on the black ocean waves.

Then she dove, head disappearing under the black.

One wave crashed.

I knew I should leave it alone. Let it be. We'd had one interaction almost three years ago and had never spoken since.

Another wave crashed, still no Gemma.

She didn't know who I was beyond the rumors. Our

worlds were so far apart they may as well have existed in different timelines.

Except that one moment three years ago was enough to tattoo her inside me indelibly.

A third wave crashed. Before I could think, I was in the water. My jeans sticking to my legs and weighing me down. I waded quickly to where she'd been, then dove.

Gemma floated above the ocean's sandy floor. Moonlight illumined her in the black ocean water, pale and ghostly. Eyes closed, she almost looked...peaceful.

I ripped her out, throwing her to the sand.

She was still.

"Fuck."

I bent over her, pressing my hands into her chest. What was the song you were supposed to sing? "Stayin' Alive"?

Ironic.

I pushed and pushed against her chest. She didn't move, her face frozen in uncanny peace. *Shit.* I tilted her head back, placing my mouth against hers, and breathed.

It took three breaths and two more rounds of pumping, but then Gemma convulsed, coughing up brackish water. She turned to her side, purging the Atlantic from her lungs. After three rounds, she fell to her back on the sand.

For a moment she stared up at me without walls. Eyes wide and teary, glossed in wonder. Something passed on her face then, a look that would haunt me forever. Like she knew this would happen. Like she was waiting for me.

Then she blinked, and it shattered.

She shoved at my chest. "What the fuck are you doing?" I stood and she scrambled to lift herself up to her elbows, gaze burning with anger.

I turned from her, facing the ocean, and reached for the collar at the back of my neck. I pulled the wet shirt over my head, dropping it to the sand. She could see the tattoo I was never supposed to show.

Twistedly, I *wanted* that.

The waves crashed in a cathartic, preordained order. Their bruised blue color was too similar to the dark rings circling Gemma's baby blue irises. I was content to have watching her from afar be my life. Knowing her without ever revealing myself. Content with the small windows I'd carved for myself into her soul. But then she tried to end it.

And I felt something inside me snap.

I spun around. Gemma hadn't moved. Her white dress stuck to all the illicit, mouthwatering parts of her, nipples pink beneath the fabric, a small triangle of hair visible between her thighs. I wanted to bury my face in it.

I'd imagined this for a while. I'd seen glimpses of Gemma when she changed—the blade of a tanned collarbone, the side of her naked thigh. Like the fucked-up pervert I was, that was what I get off to. I jerked it to glimpses of Gemma Crowne.

"Fuck you," she bit out. "You had no right." Her eyes dropped to my cock, where the bastard was hard.

The venom she spat didn't match her fiery, hazy gaze, like morning sun caught in fog.

Hungry.

A better guy wouldn't even consider taking her after she nearly died.

Over my jeans, I rubbed the hard outline of my cock. "Run, Rich Girl."

"No," she said. "This was none of your fucking business. *You* leave."

She hadn't lifted her eyes from my cock, mouth parting, as I continued to stroke myself.

"You sure about that?" I gripped the metal zipper. "Sure you want me to leave?"

I tugged the zipper down a few inches.

"You're a fucking pervert," she said, but her voice was husky with desire. A fucking supermodel voice. A voice that could sink ships.

I dragged the zipper down the rest of the way, pulling myself out. She dragged her bottom lip between her teeth, biting so the soft flesh turned white. I took a step forward, legs on either side of her hips. I palmed my cock, getting off at the look in her eyes, like she was in a trance.

Gemma slid to her knees, my cock eye level with her.

So close.

So fucking close she just had to move an inch. The same thought rippled across her eyes.

"Is this how you get off?" Her tongue darted out to lick me. So slight, just enough to tell me I wasn't in control of this. "Finding fragile women to take advantage of?"

I knotted her hair in my hand, pulling her head back from my cock, using every last shred of control I had not to take her. The submissive haze in her defiant eyes almost tipped me over.

"Gemma Crowne is a lot of things." I laughed. "She's not fucking fragile."

I released her hair, pushing her flat against the sand.

I wanted her beyond sex. I wanted to fuck her until she gave me her life so I could protect it and care for it in ways she couldn't. Fuck her into submission so she wouldn't even think about killing herself without my permission.

I pinned her beneath me. That soft, pliable haze glazing her eyes once more as I pulled her wrists above her head. Her eyes dropped, her lips parted.

Then she blinked, features sliding back to anger.

"Get the fuck off me, psycho." I dodged a knee headed straight for my cock. Her dress rose with the effort, up past her thighs, too fucking close to my cock.

I pinned her legs between my thighs, immobile.

"Stop," I gritted.

She did, for a moment, that act of obedience going straight to my cock.

Like I said, I'd studied Gemma Crowne. She didn't get off to something usual. She wanted to be taken, to be forced, to be bent into submission. She didn't want violence. She wanted a desire so consuming she couldn't listen to the voice in her head.

Gemma redoubled her fighting. Keeping my grip on her wrists, I slid my hand down to the crease of her thighs. So tantalizingly close to where I wanted to go.

"What will I find when I spread your cunt?" I played in the crease between her thigh and pussy, smoothing goose bumps under my thumb.

"You're disgusting—"

She broke off, breath catching, as I slid my hand across her bare pussy. The moment felt illicit. Beyond her status and mine, beyond the fucked-up reason we were in the sand. Secret desires, desires she pretended didn't exist, reflected in her heavy-lidded gaze. Desires that I wanted to fucking unleash.

So I teased it, teased her.

"You're trapped, Rich Girl." Her body melted at the threat. I squeezed her wrists, emphasizing my hold on her. "I can do whatever the fuck I want with you. You can't stop me." I slipped a finger inside the seam of her cunt. "But you don't want me to stop, do you?"

A million feelings ripped through me when I touched her.

This wasn't getting off to the same porn she watched, this wasn't watching her through a window. I was *finally* touching Gemma Crowne.

I lost composure, forgetting the game we were playing, head falling on a groan. "You're already so fucking wet."

"It's not for you," she said, but her thighs pressed against mine, trying to spread against my hold. I shifted my legs, giving her more space.

Her thighs fell open instantly.

"Really?" I slid a finger inside her. I thrust in and out in a slow, controlled rhythm. Getting off on her, on the way she battled her submission. "This isn't for me?" I asked, punctuating with a thrust, and the slick of her made an audible sound. "Feels like it is. Feels like you're being a really good girl and getting fucking soaked for me."

Her lips parted like she wanted to contradict me, then melted into a hazy sigh. Still, she shook her head wordlessly, battling the feeling. I could feel a smile on my lips as her pussy clenched around my finger. She was so fucking perfect. I could have gotten off to just this. I could have come on her thigh like a kid with the way her pussy gripped my finger and her eyes grew heavy with submission.

She arched, trying to get my hand deeper. I paused, finger still inside her.

"Tell me what you want, Gemma. Say it clearly." She hesitated. I slid my finger out of her, ignoring the way her whimper went straight into my bloodstream.

"Say you want this." I fisted my cock and pressed the head to her lips, spearing her with just the tip. Her spine bowed again, trying to push me inside her.

I pulled back.

"Say it," I gritted. "Fucking beg me." My neck ached with the strain of holding back. She was on the verge; she wanted to give in and submit. I saw a glimpse of her need in that empty room, and I'd been hooked ever since.

The way Gemma submitted to me went beyond logic. It was instinctual.

But she just rolled her lips between her teeth, silent. I wasn't going to go further until she gave in and asked. So I released her, starting to stand up—

She gripped me by the shoulders, forcing me to stay. Her icy-blue eyes stared into mine, wide with a plea she wouldn't speak.

"Say it," I said.

She spat in my face.

I wiped the spit, a savage, unhinged need electrifying my veins. It must be evident on my face, because Gemma blinked rapidly, swallowed audibly.

Well, fuck. Best-laid plans and all that.

I slammed inside her. She arched up on a cry, nails digging into my shoulders.

"*Fuck.*" The curse slipped out of me on a hiss.

Her pussy was perfect.

Magic.

Fuck.

"Oh yeah," I groaned. "This is definitely for me." I pulled my cock out, and back in, over and over, the slick sound of her louder than the waves at our back.

Her rose gold hair fanned around her head. Her mouth parted, soft whimpers escaping on each thrust. I pressed my face against her neck. Until I could smell her skin, the real her, not the expensive candy flower shit she tried to hide behind.

Fuck.

She was headier than any drug I sold.

Shit went straight to my head.

"What a good fucking girl," I groaned.

Her cunt gripped my cock like it was made for me, which was maddening.

Because it wasn't.

No matter how fucking right, how fucking cosmic she felt, we only had this night. I wrapped my hand lightly around her neck. Gemma didn't like choking. She didn't actually want violence. She wanted to feel the threat, the power, and give in to it.

Her eyes rolled back in full submission, body accepting me. The walls in her mind, fucking gone. Obliterated.

"I'm going to ruin you," I said, pressing my thumb deeper into her jugular, thrusting harder inside her. "Fucking ruin you for anyone else."

I lifted her leg up to my hip, getting deeper inside her cunt. She let me without hesitation, body soft and pliable, spreading easily for me. Her eyes hazy and starry, like the ocean right at sunset. The one I thought I imagined—no, the one I *recognized* and have been trying to forget for years.

"So fucking perfect." The words scraped my throat, rough and breathless. "So fucking good opening up for me like this."

A strangled moan that sounded suspiciously like my name slipped from her lips.

"Santos," I corrected.

She stilled beneath me, confusion arching her brows.

"Call me Santos," I explained. "That's my name."

"Santos," she repeated, like she was licking the flavor off my name, and it made me feral. I thrust harder and deeper, wanting to mark her forever with me. So even when I'm gone, anytime she comes she remembers my fucking name.

"Say it again," I said, and thrust harder.

"Sa-antos!" she cried out, my name breaking into a cry

that slid under my skin, rippled and vibrated through my blood. I didn't care if it was fucked up and selfish and wrong. If I had to be strung out, so did she.

She scraped my back, nails digging blood. She arched up, meeting each thrust. She bit her lip, trying to keep from crying out again.

I knew Gemma's favorite foods, her favorite books. I knew that she secretly loved spiders and she hated cute things. But I never thought I'd have the privilege to memorize how Gemma looked as she was about to come. The way her baby blue eyes widened and drooped when I tested the grip on her neck. The way she groaned when I thrust inside her just right. The flush on her cheeks. The haze in her eyes. The pain of her nails in my flesh as she reached for something, anything, to ground her.

I stopped.

"If you want me to let you come," I said, "fucking beg me."

I wanted her fucked up on me, her soul tainted with mine.

It was selfish. Fucked up. All kinds of twisted.

I thrust in a deliberate movement until her pussy clenched with anticipation.

I paused. "Fucking beg, Gemma."

Her eyes found mine. I waited for her to spit at me, tell me to fuck off.

"Please," she whined. "Please. Please. *Please.*" I nearly came at that. She broke off into a reckless whine. Thrashing her head back and forth.

Was there any sound better than Gemma Crowne begging me?

"Please let me come. Fuck me, Santos. Punish me with your cock. Make me cry. *Please.*"

Yes. There was. And it was Gemma Crowne begging me to do filthy things with her.

My grip tightened on her neck—still not choking—and I resumed thrusting.

"You want this?" *Slam.* "You want me to force it out of you like the little slut you are?" *Slam.*

"Yes," she choked out, tears forming in the corners of her eyes. "*Please.*" A sweet agony twisted her words.

But she still wouldn't come until I let her. A realization settled heavy in my blood at her complete and total submission. Gemma Crowne couldn't belong to me, but I would belong to her. Forever. I would protect her until the day I died. If by some unlucky break I died before her, I would make another deal with the devil to stay around long enough to torment anyone who dared look at her.

"Your pussy is mine," I said. "Your sighs? Mine. This is all fucking mine." I worked the grip against her throat. "Say it."

"Yours," she cried. "Your slut. Just for you. Only for you. I'll never come again if it's not your cock."

I didn't ask her to say *that*.

Fuck.

Gemma Crowne was going to kill me.

"Good girl," I groaned, and she clenched at the praise. "You're such a good fucking girl. Now be a good girl and come on my cock."

That was all it took. A cry ripped from her throat, her nails scythed bloody rivers into my pectoral, and she came apart on my cock. My balls tightened with my own release, but I held it long enough to memorize the flush on her skin, the way her eyes rolled back, her mindless, breathless whispers.

Thank you.

Oh, please.
Do anything to me.
Oh fuck, I'll do anything.
Thank you.
Thank you.

Then I came violently. Brutally. The thing that existed taboo and stolen between Gemma and me ripped out of my soul to find hers.

"I'll kill anyone who touches you and fuck you on their dead bodies," I said, my thrusts wild and uneven as I came. "Everyone will know what happens when they touch you." Unhinged. Animalistic. Saying shit I had no right to.

With one final thrust, I finished inside her.

And *this*—this was the image I would take home with me. Gemma's wide blue eyes, lips parted. Her features soft and open. Vulnerable.

This was what Gemma Crowne's trust looked like.

And she was giving it to me.

I captured her mouth in mine. Kissing her brutally, bruising her, memorizing her with my tongue, marking her with my bite. Her mouth, her cheeks, her jaw, her neck, over and over again, trying to steal a lifetime's worth of kisses in one night. Her sighs fogged my flesh, her lips searched for mine.

"*Mi locura,*" I breathed against her lips.

My madness.

Because that was what she was.

I was mad with her.

Mad with want.

Mad with need.

Fucking *insane.*

I licked the side of her neck, up to her ear, then back to

her lips. She clenched, and shit, I was ready to go again. Her nails dug deeper into my chest.

"Santos—"

Fireworks blasted off in the distance—the Crowne family Fourth of July party. It was booming, thunderous popcorn in the sky. And it shattered the moment.

I could feel the change.

Feel her walls build back, brick by brick.

Feel our stolen moment leave and disappear into history.

I slid out of her, ignoring the way her eyes widened at the reminder of me. I slid back into my wet jeans, zipping them up as I stared down at her in the sand. Her dress was tangled around her hips. Naked. My come leaked milky onto her thighs and into the sand.

In a final, reckless moment, I knelt down, shoving my finger inside her, pushing the come back inside. I knew everything about Gemma, like I knew she was on birth control. She got the injection every few months.

Her mouth dropped.

"Don't do this shit again," I said, pumping my come deep inside her.

"You don't fucking own me," she hissed.

"That's not what you said a few minutes ago." I smeared my come across her clit, causing her to arch and shiver.

Then I stood back up.

She got to her elbows, still open for me. I stared down at Gemma, legs spread—waiting for me. She'd let me take her again. She wanted it.

Her rose gold hair was wild and knotted, mascara smeared black beneath her blue eyes. Her freckles faintly visible beneath all the crap she piled on. And fuck if that didn't get me hard, again.

God damn.

My fucked-up princess.

With a clenched jaw, I left. Left before I did something neither of us could come back from.

I left the beach in a daze, still mindless as I walked into the house and up the stairs. The rest of the Horsemen were out—out where I was *supposed* to be—prepping for the Underworld Fourth of July party.

I walked past my room, into Wraith's. He was the Horsemen's tattoo man, and kept a tattoo gun in his closet. I took the gun back to my room and propped it up on my bathroom sink.

In the mirror, Gemma's scratch marks reflected bloody on my chest.

I dug the needle into them.

She would do it again, she would try to kill herself again. I saw it in her defiance.

That sealed it for me. Gemma Crowne was always going to be with someone else. She was fucking engaged tonight.

So I would be her reaper. I would keep her life safe. She would live in my soul. Entwined.

THIRTY-FIVE

GEMMA
Present

They say never take a contract with a Horseman. They didn't take your money, they took your soul. So what did it mean when you belonged to one?

Tomorrow, you're the Reaper's girl.

The morning came and went. Afternoon disappeared into red sunset. And then I was supposed to get ready for a party.

Like nothing happened.

Like I hadn't inked the Reaper on my neck.

My image reflected back at me from my floor-length mirror. The girl in the mirror looked exactly the same. Same rose gold bob, perfectly applied makeup, and couture dress.

Maybe nothing had changed.

"You look nice."

I froze at my mom's voice. Swiveling my head, I found

my mother in the doorway. A sense of relief washed over me. Like me, she was the same.

Same icy countenance and effortless, regal air.

"Um..." I tugged at the silk of my dress. My mother and I always threw up mirrors and smoke to avoid anything real. Grim's brand was still raw on my flesh, impossible to hide or ignore.

This was uncharted territory.

She took a seat on my chaise. "Did I ever tell you the story of my first love?"

I nearly choked on my own spit. First love? Since when did Tansy Crowne *love*?

"Years ago, when your sister fell for...that boy, I told her the story. I tried to warn her. Get her to see reason."

"Abigail is happy now," I whispered.

"Maybe," she said, though her nostrils flared, almost imperceptibly. "There was a time not too long ago where I would have warned you that you don't get both," she continued. "You don't get to live this life and love whoever you want. But after giving the same speech to both your brother and sister..."

She trailed off into silence, the only sounds the beach below, a soft hum of the heater.

It was a moment before she spoke again. "My first love worked for my father. I never thought we would be together, but I didn't dissuade the fantasy. He died shortly after I married."

Another silence. I stared at her. She stared into the distance, into some memory. In the low light, my mom seemed younger. Naive.

"Maybe your siblings did get a happily ever after." She stood up, like that was where she was going to end it.

No threat.

No guilt.

It settled sticky in my gut. Tansy Crowne didn't give up. She didn't concede.

"Mom," I said as she started to leave.

She stopped for a moment, then continued without looking back.

Downstairs in the ballroom, I stared at the wedding portrait of my mother and father, lined up with a series of similar Crowne wedding portraits.

Today's anniversary party was to celebrate the long lineage of Crowne marriages.

I couldn't find it in me to laugh at the irony as I studied the line of portraits dating back to before the Romanovs fell. All had the same cold melancholy painted into the oil.

My mother's first love died. Then my father.

My father never loved her, and she was never able to love the one who did.

Maybe in her own twisted way, these rules were meant to protect us.

"I thought you were taken now." The guy I was supposed to be paying attention to took a sip of his whiskey.

I turned away from the portraits and affected my *Gemma Crowne* smile. "Oh, you know the tabloids. They'll say anything."

I lightly touched his shoulder, laughing.

Flirt, laugh. Flirt, laugh. Nothing had changed.

I was still in a too tight, too expensive dress designed not for my comfort, but strangers' opinions. I was still in my house, still smiling demurely at men whose names I couldn't remember.

"If I was taken, could I do this?" I ran a hand up and down his arm.

It was supposed to be different. I was supposed to have

broken the five-year loop. I let anger burn my throat, rather than taste bitter disappointment.

At least this I could control.

The way his eyes grew at my suggestion, the way he practically panted. Yeah, I could control that.

My insides felt like they were locked inside a sound-proof box.

He looked around the ballroom. "Do you want to get out of here?"

I didn't know anything about him, didn't even know his name. Did it matter? I was no more real to him.

"Maybe—"

Over the guy's shoulder, I saw him. His body was shadowed in the dark of the hallway, but still unmistakably *him*.

My heart throbbed in my throat. He wouldn't be here, not during a party. He only came with shadows and secrets.

You brought the Reaper into your pretty little world, and I'm gonna tear it the fuck apart.

I plastered a smile, focusing on the man in front of me. "Upstairs. After the party."

Grim walked into the room. His black jeans and hoodie at odds with the glittery dresses and pressed suits. Despite that, he walked with a swagger that only came from owning everything and everyone in the room.

The conversation changed to hushed whispers as heads turned to watch Grim. All except my mom, who stared at me.

I did what I usually do—I dissembled. I smiled. I held my pink martini up to my lips, ignoring Grim getting closer and closer, instead focusing on the man in front of me.

Whispers turned to roars. Grim stopped just behind the man I was talking to, tall enough to stare over his head and straight into my eyes.

Grim crooked his finger.

A heady mix of adrenaline and fear buzzed in my body.

If I didn't acknowledge him, he'd go away.

But if I did…

I focused all my attention on the guy in front of me, oblivious to death at his back. I think he said something flirty, because he reached out to touch my cheek.

It happened so fast. One minute he was touching me, the next blood splattered my haute couture dress. I blinked through the spray. The guy fell in a heap.

On the ground.

Blood jeweled the handle of Grim's gun where he'd smashed it on the guy's head. Before I could react, Grim grabbed my bicep, dragging me across the body. Screams sounded, and my world went up in flames.

"Is he dead?" I asked.

The blood was slippery at my feet, and I nearly fell. Grim yanked me upright, and my shoe came off, stuck in the red puddle.

"Did he die?" I repeated.

Grim pulled us out of the ballroom at such a speed I had to either run to keep up or lose an arm. I looked over my shoulder, at people bending down to the body, at my disappearing world, at my lonesome shoe lost in the blood.

It was almost like the end of a fairy tale, when the prince rescued the princess. Except… I stared forward, at Grim. In this world, the princess ran away with the monster.

Grim stopped only when we were outside. A black car was waiting, Crowne security mysteriously absent.

I ripped my arm out of his hold. "What did you do?"

Grim grabbed my chin, tilting my neck so I had to meet his black gaze.

"What did *I* do? Nah, baby, what did *you* do?" His touch was gentle, too gentle for the edge in his voice. Smoky, sliding inside me, until I couldn't see or think.

I nearly choked on it.

"This is on you." Still with one hand free, he pointed his gun toward the house at my back. "You're the Reaper's girl. Does that guy look like the fucking Reaper?"

The Reaper's girl. His.

Grim let me go and yanked open the back car door. Wraith and Raze sat on black leather seats, staring at me. I stepped back.

"I thought the whole point of being, you know, *you* was staying low-key. There's no going back from this!" The car rumbled, filling my nostrils with the sharp smell of gasoline.

Grim snaked his hand around the back of my neck, and I swallowed at the sensation of him against my tattoo.

His jaw clenched, eyes lethal—he was *pissed*.

And it filled me with excitement.

"You thought this was another one of your Rich Girl games." Grim pressed his fingers into my still sore tattoo until I gasped. "You have no idea what you've done."

Still holding me by the neck, he shoved me into the car. He placed his other hand above my head, protecting me from the top. I had a half second for my gut to squirm at that, when I was in the car, in the clutches of two other Horsemen.

"But you will," Grim said.

With one last searing look, he slammed the door, shutting me into darkness.

THIRTY-SIX

GEMMA

Sandwiched between Wraith and Raze, I replayed the events as the car rumbled farther away from my home. Blood. Screaming.

I felt another panic attack coming.

My mom.

My brother.

My sister.

My world—

"People will talk," I said. "The police will come. You can't just...just hurt someone because he *talked* to me." And what was wrong with me that I liked it? That I had goose bumps?

At my side, Raze laughed, like what I'd said was ridiculous.

I always knew they were powerful. They were the darkness in Crowne Point. Seen but unseen. Felt. But there was no way they could have so much power that they could beat a man in broad daylight and get away with it. Right?

Lock's blue eyes fastened on me in the rearview. "Afraid yet, princess?"

A few moments later we pulled up to the Wharf. Raze tugged me out of the car, shoving me toward the Underworld.

The Wharf was divided into parts. The famous Underworld, the club, was originally an old lighthouse. Sometime in the nineteen hundreds, a hurricane hit and the lighthouse was destroyed. After that, the Wharf ended serious functionality, and the lighthouse was reconstituted into a church. The result was a Frankenstein of architecture, an uncanny mix of stained glass shoved into concrete and industrial purpose.

A few yards behind the club sat the only other functional building: the Horsemen's home. Like the club, it dated back almost as far as Crowne Hall. When the Ferris wheel was operational, it was a haunted house. Before that, it was the preacher's residence. Before that, the lighthouse keeper's home.

They pushed me through a door of black wood and jewel-stained glass.

I'd been to this part of the Wharf once before, when I needed Grim's help and he kept me as collateral. But even then, I'd been blindfolded, shoved into a dark room.

Opulent wasn't the right word for their house. *Rich*, maybe, like a good wine or expensive steak. I expected the inside to be as cold as the people who lived here, but it was filled with a delicious warmth that came from fireplaces and wrapped like a blanket.

It was well kept. Black, exposed brick lined the hallway. Great windows overlooked the Wharf and beach where the ocean was an inky-black void, and a reckless wind blew, loud and rushing. It was impossible to tell if the roaring came from the trees bending to the wind, or waves crashing on the sand.

I caught a glimpse of the kitchen and living room as they shoved me down a short hallway, up black wooden stairs, and into a room on the second floor.

Floor-to-ceiling mullioned windows overlooked the old pier and the rusted Ferris wheel, while a vaulted ceiling with exposed ribs of black wood gave the room a feeling of ghostly sanctuary.

There was a bed, not neat, not messy—silky black sheets, heavy blankets, metal frame.

Scattered remnants of normalcy lingered. A chipped mug, a lighter, a gun on the nightstand.

Someone *lived* here.

"Time you learned the rules, princess," Lock said.

I blinked out of my thoughts, into Lock's cold blue eyes. Lock and Raze faced me, blocking the exit. Wraith leaned against the doorframe, partially obscured by their bodies. To the left, Grim leaned against the wall, one foot up behind him, hands in his pocket.

They looked...relaxed.

"Rules?" I asked.

"Pretty sure you've figured out the first one," Raze said. "Don't fuck other people."

"I wasn't *fucking* him—I was talking to him."

"Don't talk, don't look, don't think about people who aren't the Reaper."

I put a freshly manicured finger to my temple and stared directly at Lock, licking my bottom lip, before sliding my gaze back to Grim.

"What happens if I break them? Gonna kill someone else? Me?"

"Yes," Wraith growled from behind Raze and Lock, his tattooed face obscured half in shadows. "We know all about your games. The monsters you court for attention. The death you put on Grim's hand."

As Wraith continued, I glanced at Grim, uncertainty wrinkling my brow.

They knew?

"Any man who touches you," Wraith said, stepping between Lock and Raze into the room, "monster or not, we will kill. We will all kill for you."

Wraith had the same tone in his voice as Grim held in his eyes. Not bitter or angry, but resolved. A man at the gallows.

It made my chest tighten.

It felt different, like it wasn't a game anymore.

"Well." I shrugged. "You're going to be killing a lot of people."

"Maybe," Raze said.

"Definitely," Lock added.

They laughed like this was just a regular day. As if they hadn't kidnapped the most famous girl in America, as if it was normal for that girl to lure monsters to their death.

The game had ended. That nice buffer between us and reality crumbled.

So I searched for something, anything, to build that defense back up.

"Five years ago you stole my life and promised to kill me," I said, attention on Grim. "If you won't do it willingly, I'll *make* you."

Grim laughed. "Good luck with that."

"You don't believe me?"

He arched a brow. "I believe you'll try."

"We won't let you die, princess," Lock said.

Wraith stared. "We're your monsters now."

Oh, wow, there it was. Fear. In the five years I'd been under Grim's thumb, I'd never felt it. I was starting to think I was immune. But you could always count on fear. It was your emotional period, coming at the worst possible time, in the worst possible place, and likely involved a boy. Or in this case, four.

The Horsemen shared a knowing look with Grim, and then they left, shutting the door as they did. The room transformed. The air heady and thick. Grim leaned against the opposite wall, one leg propped up. His pose gave an illusion of calm, easily shattered by the tension threading his neck, the ravenous glare in his eyes.

Everything I'd done landed on me at once. It was always a game between Grim and me. We pushed to see who would crack first.

There was no game in his eyes.

"Say something," I demanded.

"You have that look in your eyes," he said, dragging a hand over his mouth.

"What look?"

"The one you had with a knife to your neck. Like you're daring me to do something." He stood off the wall. "It's fucking hot."

I swallowed. "I'm not—"

"I've thought about this moment a lot, Gemma." In three quick strides, Grim closed the distance.

"The moment when you kidnap me?" I joked.

"What I would do when I had you again." He thumbed the blood on my collarbone, smearing it. "It wasn't supposed to be like this. I was going to be sweeter."

The idea that Grim had been fantasizing about me as much as I had him—that he wanted it...*sweet?*—made me hot. I couldn't breathe. I shouldn't want this, but then that was Grim and me, a sky of starry shouldn'ts that somehow made a constellation.

He gripped the back of my neck, forcing me to look at him as he did so. I hissed at the pressure on my tattoo, and his eyes grew heavy lidded. He dragged my lips down with his free hand, and forced his thumb into my mouth, tasting lingering blood, sharp and coppery.

"You deserve sweet." He pressed against my neck, soft yet hard, and the pain transformed into hot, twisting pleasure. A small sound fell from my lips without my consent.

This was the moment I should turn back. Where I fought, where I said I'd made a mistake.

Back at my house, blood spilled garnet on the marble.

The foundation beneath my feet was crumbling.

Maybe Grim felt it too.

He dragged me to him by his grip on my neck, forcing me to arch into him.

"Last chance to get out, Rich Girl." He dragged a bloody hand down my face, waiting.

"I don't want sweet," I said. "I want you."

His eyes went dark. Black.

Everything changed in an instant. He reached behind his back, gripping the collar of his shirt and pulling it over his head.

Ripped.

Each muscle brutally cut.

That tattoo I hadn't seen since the night that bound us, vivid. Three blood-red lines, shadowed in black. Scratch marks—*mine*.

Then his lips were on mine.

THIRTY-SEVEN

GEMMA

Grim's kiss was a heady mix of rough and gentle. The scrape of stubble against my cheek. Gentle, worshipping lips. Dragging out my bottom lip with his teeth only to capture my sighs with his mouth. His tongue slid across my lips, and I opened for him, slanting my face so he could get deeper access. He took it greedily, pressing me deep into the bed, mattress dipping.

Like he wanted to devour me.

Consume me.

His kiss moved to my neck, to the area beneath my lobe, biting at the soft flesh, before soothing it with his tongue. He trailed kisses down my neck, to the hollow of my throat, and then between my breasts. He paused, my dress preventing him from going further.

With two hands he ripped, butterflying the fabric. He stilled, eyes darkening at my bare chest—the dress had a built-in corset. Then he shoved me to the bed and ripped the rest of the fabric down past my belly button, to the hem. I lay naked and exposed, dress ripped to my sides.

I had a half second to register the way my heart skipped at the ravenous gleam in his eyes, when his lips landed on my flesh.

He kissed down the now exposed skin. My collarbone. The wing of my ribs. Above my belly button. My hip bone.

Anywhere but where I needed.

He drew a line down the middle of me with his tongue, from chest to my lower abdomen, then back.

I grabbed his hair, forcing him to look at me. "Grim."

He quirked a brow, licking a hot line underneath the curve of my breast, from rib to sternum. "Yeah, baby?"

"I—" I broke off as his kiss turned into a bite, tugging at the thin skin above my ribs.

"Please."

"So polite." He groaned. "You sound so good when you beg." *Finally* his mouth found my breast. I arched up into him, and his hand slid to my lower back, holding me in the arch against him.

"You're not afraid of me, Rich Girl?" His gaze caught mine, taking a nipple into his mouth, rolling it around, biting it. "Even after today?"

He slid a hand up my body, smearing the blood from the man he'd assaulted across my skin—as if to punctuate his words, like he was marking me again.

"I knew who you were before you were king of the damned," I said. It was meant to be a joke, but I was too breathless. As he bit and teased my nipple, my thoughts scattered into fireworks, bursting in a thousand different sparkly directions.

I couldn't think past the heat in his eyes. The way his hand lingered on my stomach, possessively.

A smirk quirked his lips, his eyes flashing back to mine. "Then you must be fucking terrified, Gemma." He bit my hip, sliding kisses down my body. The dip between my stomach and pussy, the top of my thigh and inside. He slid his tongue along the crease of my inner thigh.

"I'm not—" I broke off as he planted a hot, open-mouthed kiss on the center of me. His stare found mine, locked.

I couldn't breathe.

The room melted away. Past, present, and future dissolved. All that existed was Grim on his knees, a look in his eyes that went beyond hunger and desire—vulnerable and open. I saw him—*Santos*—and I felt the depth of him, reaching inside and tugging at the bond we had.

He broke the stare, sliding his tongue between my pussy lips.

"So fucking good," he groaned, the sound vibrating against my flesh in a delirious way. "I've wondered how you'd taste." He punctuated each sentence with a deep thrust of his tongue, as if trying to consume the very soul of me. "I've only ever got a taste. It wasn't enough."

His voice was shredded and raw, angry even, like I'd kept this from him. He dragged one lip between his teeth, sucking and pulling until I saw stars. It felt like a reminder, like whatever he gave me was for *him*.

He gripped my ass, pulling me deeper into his hungry mouth. "You are perfection. So fucking good."

He plunged a finger inside me as he licked and sucked my throbbing clit. My spine bowed on a gasp. The room went blurry. I heard things distantly.

So fucking wet.

Such a good girl getting so fucking wet for me.

But the words were like trying to pinpoint rain in a rainstorm. I could only feel how he kissed and licked and bit me while his fingers worked inside. I melted into the feeling, into him.

"You're too tight," he gritted.

I lifted my head, delirious, finding his eyes. "For?"

"Me."

The thought, as much as the low snarl with which he'd said it, made me clench. He was going to be inside me. After years of nothing, I would have him again.

"I told you—" My words disappeared into a gasp as Grim dove his head back between my thighs. "There hasn't been anyone since you."

He froze, slowly lifting his head up. The room vibrated and pulsed between us. His lips wet with me. Then he climbed on top of me and grabbed my hand, pressing it against his pec, against the three scratch marks that started everything.

"Why?" he repeated the question he'd asked days ago when I'd first confessed. I couldn't give him the truth then. But now? I hesitated, the words on my lips.

He let go of my hand and slid his back down. Out of sight. The moment hung on the shared breath between us. Then I felt him, his cock at my entrance, spreading me slightly.

My spine bowed.

"Why, Gemma?" He pushed a little bit more inside. I closed my eyes, body melting into a hot pile of need.

Oh, God, finally—

Grim grabbed my chin and my eyes shot open. The muscle of his jaw twitched, control about to snap.

"Why haven't you fucked anyone else?" The grit in his voice, the power in his gaze, burned the answer out of me.

"You know why," I breathed, arching, trying to get him

inside me. "I wasn't lying when I said I'd never come again without your cock. You fucking *ruined* me."

His eyes flashed, searching mine, looking for the truth.

He cursed under his breath.

"I'd planned to get you off first," he said. I had a half second to process the regret in his voice, before he was inside me.

Oh, *wow*.

"But then you go and say that." His voice was strained, the rough edge sliding into my veins, making my blood fizzle and pop.

What happened next was a blur. It was Grim inside me, it was his lips against my neck. It was that delicious, delirious fullness. It was my body singing for him. It was rough and hard and perfect.

"Your sheets will be destroyed," I gasped at another thrust, realizing we were still covered in blood.

"Good. Fuck up my sheets," he growled. "So when you come to your senses, I'll still smell you."

I disappeared into Grim. Into the smell of him, masculine and strong, earthy and dark. Into the feel of him, like the ocean at night: all-consuming, powerful, a depth that can never be seen, only felt.

His thrusts were ruthless and calculated.

He lifted up my leg, pushing my knee to my chest, driving deeper.

His hand encircled my throat with that always perfect amount of tension. Never violent. Never too soft. Just enough to remind me *he's* in control.

He whispered things I couldn't quite hear, but felt nonetheless.

I didn't know how to describe the thing between Grim and me. Grim stole my life. Grim held me hostage. I barely knew him when we first had sex. But what we had defied logic. Before Grim, I could lie to myself. Say this was just how sex was supposed to be.

But after...

Grim had shown me what it was like to feel safe. I felt comfortable giving him my submission because I knew he wouldn't weaponize it. I felt safe with his hand around my neck. I knew he would listen if I said no, but the beautiful thing was I didn't need to. He sensed my hesitation before I did, and he switched it up.

Like now.

I didn't need to tell him the position was starting to get uncomfortable. He was already sliding out of me, shifting us to the side, him at my back.

"This better?" he asked, sliding back inside me.

Oh...fuck.

I went cross-eyed at the sensation. Better? It was amazing. I melted into him on a sigh.

"Yeah." He laughed. "That's better."

His hand slid back around my neck, pinning me tight against him as he continued driving into me with a slow, torturous rhythm.

"Arch for me," he commanded. I did and he groaned, felt him twitch inside me. When he spoke, his voice was hoarse. "Yeah, just like that. Good girl." He licked at the tender flesh of my tattoo—his mark—groaning against my neck. "So perfect."

I felt my orgasm build with each deliberate thrust.

I was so close. My body tightened. But I needed something. I didn't know what. I just—I needed—

His grip tightened on my neck. "Come."

That's it. With his permission, I came apart. I disappeared into hot Spanish words against my flesh. I became nothing save shivers and sensation and rippling, electric currents.

When it was over, when I was nothing but raw sensation, Grim didn't stop.

I grew hazy. I became a doll. Grim flipped me onto my stomach, pushed into me from behind. He flipped me back to my side, positioning me how he wanted. He grabbed my thigh, pulling and bending my leg at an impossible angle, so I could feel his cock deeper.

I was weightless. A pile of needy goo. I could only moan and come again.

And again.

Until the world was a delirious blur of Grim's soft, coaxing whispers. Until I was sweat and need. Until I couldn't take it anymore.

"I can't," I said. "I can't come again."

I tried to squirm away from him. He stilled, stopped moving inside me, but he didn't let me go. His hand pressed into my stomach, keeping me in place.

"Yeah, you can. Breathe." He thumbed circles above my belly button, waiting. I took a deep breath and he rumbled his satisfaction against my neck. "Good girl. Just like that. Take another."

So I did.

And on the third deep breath Grim started moving inside me. The dichotomy of his gentle words and hard thrusts. How safe I felt in his arms. It spun me out.

"My slut," he praised. "My good little slut. So obedient. Still so open for me."

I've had guys try to call me a slut in bed before, but it never did anything for me. I didn't get off on degradation. The guys in the past would say it with venom, like a punishment. Grim said it like it made me the most precious thing in the world. I got off on *that*. On being *his* slut. I would do anything if it made him purr that I was a good girl.

I felt it building again.

Could feel the tightening of my thighs, the clenching of my abdomen. On a cliff's edge, about to dive into the water.

"Don't stop breathing, Rich Girl."

Not realizing I'd stopped, I sucked in a deep breath and fell off the cliff. The orgasm tore through my body. Grim pumped harder and harder and I cried out, trying to bury my face in the sheets, but he tangled his hand into my hair and pulled my head back against his chest. He swallowed my screams with mouth, his tongue diving deep into mine. I scratched at anything. His hand in my hair. The bed, pulling the sheets into a knot in my fist. The world went black, and I disappeared into sensation.

When I came to, I was no longer on my side. I was on my back, and Grim was on top of me. He stroked his fingers through my hair.

"Welcome back." He smiled—a real fucking smile. My stomach did a somersault at the way it stretched his cheeks. It was like the sun breaking through, shining on a bloody battlefield. The light inside the darkness so clearly visible.

So perfect.

Without thought, I lifted my fingers to his smiling lips. He pressed his head into my palm, still smiling.

"Did you come?" I asked, his still hard cock like hot lead on my thigh.

In response, he lowered his head and planted a soft kiss on my shoulder, on the cluster of freckles. "These freckles? Mine." He moved lower, kissing above my stomach. "This mole? Mine." He dove lower, to my hip. "This dimple in your hip? Mine." He kissed my hip, then bit it, teeth clamping softly over the bone.

"Yours," I breathed.

Grim kept moving lower, planting kisses all along my flesh. Into the soft thatch of hair on my pussy. Lower still—

I sat up, grabbing his hair.

The look he shot me was fearsome, like I'd just ripped away water from a dehydrated man.

"You need to come." I released my grip, attempting to bargain with the look in his eyes.

His eyes softened. "I *need* to taste your cunt." He bent down, kissing the seam of my pussy. "I *need* to make you come again."

"But—"

"Let me be selfish," he growled. I opened my mouth to protest when he took one pussy lip between his teeth, dragging it out. It wasn't painful, it was *electric*. It made me want to give in.

So I did.

I sank back into the mattress and let Grim be selfish.

THIRTY-EIGHT

GEMMA

The sun had long since set, the pier moonlit. Grim held me tight to his chest, like I would disappear. I traced his tattoos with my finger, distantly wondering what was happening in my world. Blood still caked my fingernails, splattering across my soft manicure.

I was giddy, excited. Finally the outside matched the chaos inside me.

I traced the outline of a tattoo just below his collarbone —an upside-down cross. It stood out, a slightly different style than his other tattoos, but like all the others, there was a line drawn across it.

"Why is this one different?"

He didn't have to look to know what I was talking about.

"That was my first." His hand covered mine. "Before I took my ink. When I was still Santos."

I looked up the meaning of his name after the night on the beach, the first time Grim asked me to call him by it. On its surface, it meant *saint*—irony of all ironies—but the name itself was rich with meaning and history.

Some tales spoke of a cursed "Santos" bloodline, descendants of a saint's betrayer, doomed to bear the name in irony.

In old Spanish superstition, invoking "los santos" could ward off curses or bad luck, but using it carelessly or mockingly could invite divine retribution.

Holy name, unholy fate.

"What happened?" I asked. He tensed a little, and I quickly added, "You don't have to tell me."

"I killed someone," he said.

There was a hollow ache in his voice that I didn't understand. Grim was no stranger to murder, after all.

It was more vulnerability than I'd *ever* seen from Grim. I wanted to press. I wanted to dig into him.

But I kept quiet, wanting to keep this moment even more.

He dragged a hand lazily down my arm to the elbow, then back to the shoulder. For what must have been the hundredth time since last night, I couldn't believe I was here. I couldn't believe I was with Grim, in his bed, and his touch was so *gentle*.

Knowing how violent those hands could be, that hands that murdered were caressing me gently, made my stomach do flips.

"Do you ever think about it?" I asked. "That...that night." His jaw was sharp from my angle, eyes staring ahead.

I waited for it. For him to lie or tell me no, that I was the delusional one.

"Every day," he said.

I shivered.

"I knew you would always be with someone else," he continued. "You were fucking engaged that night. At the same time, that night sealed something I already knew. It was always you. Would always be you."

He flipped me to my side, his body cradling and imprisoning mine. He slid his hand between my thighs, and something between a groan and growl slipped out of him as he found me wet. His cock branded my ass, and I reached for it, sliding him back inside me.

Our groans harmonized.

"You feel so fucking good."

His hand slid around my neck in a gentle, possessive hold that had me seeing stars. I arched against him. His rhythm was nothing like the savage energy of earlier. It was slow, deliberate. I felt every inch of him inside me.

He tilted my head and crushed his lips against mine. My sharp gasp heated his mouth.

He kissed me as he rode into me.

Thrust his tongue into my mouth in a slow, brutal rhythm that matched his cock.

He licked the side of my neck, up to my ear, then back to my lips. I was twisting, coming undone, breaking under the need. My nails dug into his arm.

"Please," I begged.

"*Please* what, Rich Girl?" His words were a vicious heat on my ear.

"Please, let me come. *Please.*"

A rumble of approval shook his chest, and his pace picked up into something violent. He slammed into me, harder, demanding.

My abdomen tightened. Small, helpless whimpers fell from my mouth. Undignified. Very much not becoming a Crowne. But I was so close. I couldn't see past this need.

"That's it," he rasped. "That's a good girl. Come on my cock."

His praise, coupled with the way his cock swelled and throbbed inside me, pushed me over the edge. We came together, in a mix of groans.

"You're mine, Gemma Crowne," he said. "I'm never letting you go. *Ever.*" The last word disappeared into a low growl.

He held me tight to his chest as he finished, one arm wrapped around my chest, the other still on my neck. Still inside me, his come dripped along my inner thighs.

Slowly, the hazy afterglow of my orgasm faded.

I'm never letting you go.

My gut twisted at the possession in his voice. I *wanted* that, I wanted it too badly. But he'd have to let me go, eventually. The nightmare still waited outside this dream.

"I should probably get going," I whispered.

I tried to pull away and his grip on my neck tightened. "Why?"

"It's been hours," I added. "People are probably freaking out. Maybe I can clear things up."

"And what are you going to do about it, Gemma? What's your solution? How do you rewind and go back to before?"

I opened my mouth but said nothing.

I don't know.

He slid out of me and I felt empty. Hollow.

I sat on the edge of the bed, my back to him. I felt the mattress dip with his weight as he got out of bed.

That familiar coldness crept in, the one that always followed any type of intimacy with us.

He came to stand in front of me, and my throat went dry. His abs slick with sweat, outlining every cruel, rigid detail. His inked cock meeting my eyes. Dirty, reckless thoughts swept my mind.

It would be so easy to put him in my mouth. So easy and so *right*.

I shook my head.

"I'm the Reaper. I live in hell." He bent down and thumbed my chin. "You don't get to leave hell."

My lips parted at the intensity in his eyes. At the soft way he spoke.

Just as quickly as it came, it vanished.

"You chose this." He stood back up, folding his arms. "Don't start acting like a damsel now."

"But..." *How will this work? What about my family? What about his very real job as the king of the Underworld?* I didn't ask any of this, my tongue tied. Instead I asked, "But how?"

He shrugged. "People will die."

"I can't...I can't stay here. People will wonder."

"It's been one day. Pretty sure your family will think you're off getting drunk somewhere."

That hurt, so I laughed. "Fuck my family. They wouldn't notice if I were gone for months. I have more followers than the president, than Ariana Grande, than fucking Beyoncé. *They'll* notice."

One time I went twenty-four hours without posting and people thought I'd died.

By my count...we were about twelve hours away from that.

"Tell them the truth."

I blinked.

"You traded in your pretty crown to fuck the worst man in town."

His voice was hard. The gentle rasp I'd felt against my skin now replaced by cold iron.

The anniversary party was coming up. My mom—

Oh God, my *mom*.

Was she okay?

Grim grabbed his pants, sliding into them. Then he turned, like he was just going to leave.

"Wait—I can't stay here. I have a life! I'm the most famous girl in America. People will notice if I'm gone."

"You shoulda thought about that before you tattooed death on your neck," Grim spoke, his voice rough.

Goose bumps went up my spine. He'd said it like my life was ending.

I stared at where blood still caked and splattered on my body. "Our two worlds will never work together. You said it yourself."

"You're right." A soft grin quirked his lips to the side. "Welcome home."

He slammed the door shut.

THIRTY-NINE

GEMMA

"Are you planning on keeping me locked up here forever?" I yelled through the door. "I have certain responsibilities."

I sighed and slid down the door. I'd been yelling on and off for hours to complete silence. Grim had locked the door when he left. The sun was rising now. A sliver of orange above the icy-blue ocean that lit the black sky iron blue.

I will memorize every part of you. Map your uncharted territory. Make it mine.

Last night Grim had been so different. So gentle. So... *not us.* My skin was still ablaze thinking about it.

But nothing ever changed between Grim and me, not *really.*

I watched the sun rise and light the rusted Ferris wheel a blinding, blazing copper.

The problem with our love story was there were no monsters, no villains and evildoers. There was no fate to fight or dragon to slay.

Because the problem with our story was *us*.

It had always been *us*.

We were the monsters, we were the villains, we were wrong for each other.

Poison.

The real reason Grim Reyes and I never got together? It had nothing to do with which side of town we lived on. Deep down, we knew the truth. Our lips were coated in the same venom.

We're your monsters now.

I banged the back of my head against the door, Wraith's words spinning around and around.

Back.

I'm not letting you go. Ever.

Forth.

It's a game. It has to be a game.

Back.

Grim was only a dark fantasy that throbbed between my legs. A nightmare I fell asleep to. There was never a time I really thought we could end up together.

Forth.

I'm not sure what game they're playing, but I know the minute I stop playing, I'll lose.

Back—

I fell onto my back as the door swung open. Raze towered over me, shirtless, his black tattoos upside down from my view.

"Do you have a death wish?" he asked.

I sat up, rubbing the back of my skull. "Yes."

He blinked, then frowned, suspicious. "Time to eat, Barbie."

I followed him through the hallway and down the stairs. With his back to me, his tattoo was fully visible. It was a black horse just like Grim's, but instead of a skull and scythe, the horse was surrounded by fire. The line work was amazing—but I wasn't supposed to see this.

No one saw a Horseman's tattoo and lived.

Downstairs, Raze led me back to the kitchen I'd caught a glimpse of the night before. With marbled checkerboard black-and-white flooring, a circular wood table, and appliances built into antique-looking wood counters and cabinets, it was both luxurious and oddly cozy.

Lock got something out of the antique black fridge, and Grim sat at the table across from Wraith, talking about something I couldn't discern. I felt like a teenager again, back at boarding school and sneaking into the boys' dormitory.

Upon my entrance, the conversation died, and all three turned to me. Grim's eyes met mine, blazing. Raze pulled out a chair and gestured for me to sit. I looked at it, nonplussed. Since when did the Horsemen act like gentlemen?

"Sit," Raze barked.

That was more like it.

I sat, more and more uncertain about the game they were playing. Grim hadn't spoken to me, but neither had he stopped staring.

A quiet, discomforting possession radiated from him.

"If I'm going to be your prisoner," I said, "I'm going to need access to certain things. I'm accustomed to a certain lifestyle. Like what is the thread count in those sheets? Negative five?"

He tilted his head. "You don't like my sheets?"

"I..."

His sheets?

That was his room?

But...of course it was. Somehow this felt more intimate than anything we'd done before. This was him without any pretense. The bed had been made by him. The book open on the nightstand—he was reading it.

"Is there a breakfast menu?" I asked, changing the subject.

"Here's your menu." Lock slammed down a box of off-brand cereal. I looked between all of them.

"Do you have any almond milk?"

"That shit's terrible for the environment," Lock said.

Lock turned away and I saw his tattoo. His Horseman had crystal blue eyes to match the owner, and instead of a scythe, Lock had a sword and crown. *I shouldn't see this,* some distant self-preservation whispered. I shouldn't have seen Grim's, let alone all of theirs.

But I couldn't stop staring.

Grim gripped my jaw, dragging my gaze from the tattoo and into his eyes.

"Eat." He shoved his bowl of cereal in front of me.

"Not hungry," I said. He said nothing, his eyes punishing. "I don't eat breakfast," I continued. "Let alone sugary treats disguised as breakfast—"

He shoved his thumb between my lips, forcing my mouth open, a hot weight on my tongue. A moment later he shoved a spoon in my mouth. A slow smile split his lips when I swallowed.

Grim pushed another spoonful into my mouth while the conversation continued around us. This shouldn't be lighting me up. Want shouldn't curl in my gut and drip down to my thighs. He pushed another spoon into my mouth, and I fought the urge to squirm.

His nostrils flared, like he knew.

"Someone forgot to replace the vegan butter." Lock shut

the fridge door. "Wasn't me, Wraith. So kill one of these two."

I blinked, nearly choking on my cereal. *Wraith was a* vegan?

"Not me." Raze laughed. "Like I'm going to fuck with a guy who'd gut a man but won't eat a steak."

They started talking about all kinds of sundry things, like who used what video game and didn't return it, if anyone noticed the shower was making a weird noise.

It was all so...normal.

Grim dragged my attention back to him with another bite of cereal. You could never say Grim was a *tender* person, but a softness smudged the feral possession in his eyes.

I get hot and twisty from it.

Grim set the metal spoon against the bowl with a clank, and horror spread through my limbs.

I'd eaten an *entire* bowl of cereal.

Before I could dwell on it, Grim stood up, holding out his hand for me to take. I took it. Without words, Grim pulled me up the stairs and back into the room—*his* room. Blood roared like the ocean in my ears.

The look he was giving was too intense. Too not what we are. By now he should pull away, do something to get control. Instead he just stared, sending shivers down my spine.

So I tried to break it.

"So what am I?" I asked. "Your fucking captive now?"

"No," he said simply. "You're mine."

Another excruciatingly long minute of eye contact, and then he turned as if to leave.

"Where are you going?" I asked.

"Business," he said without turning around, nearly at the door.

"Are you going to lock me in here again?"

He turned around, arms folded. "Depends, you gonna leave?"

No.

Yes.

I have to go, I can't stay here.

A vicious smile split his lips, as if he could see the words in my hand. "You know what? Go ahead, leave, Rich Girl. Wherever you go, I'll find you and drag you back."

My lips parted, mouth suddenly dry. His eyes dropped to that, hunger darkening the irises, but he only turned back around. He paused in the doorway. "Good girls who stay get rewarded, though." He tapped the doorframe, and without another word, left.

I could leave.

I could walk right out.

Good girls who stay get rewarded.

I shook my head. I was alone, in *Grim's* room...and I wasn't above snooping. That was the only reason I was staying.

His room was meticulous. I had cleaners morning and night, and even mine wasn't this clean. The only thing messy was the bed. Shivers ran up my spine.

Fuck up my sheets.

I pulled out a dresser drawer and found clothes perfectly folded. Beyond me there was an open doorway that led to a walk-in. I headed over, then paused, a book on the nightstand catching my eyes.

What kind of reading was the Grim Reaper into?

Frankenstein?

The book was old and beat up. The insides had words

scribbled in the margins. I was having a hard time picturing *Grim* annotating *Frankenstein*—

Wait.

I looked closer at the annotations, at a little purple heart drawn in the margin.

No way.

This was my fucking book. I lost it in high school.

No fucking way.

I noticed it was missing the day after...

The realization landed like rocks in my gut. I'd lost it the day I met Grim.

No way he'd kept it.

Why did he keep this?

Fuck.

Fuck, fuck, fuck.

"Big Brother Grim," a soft voice called out. "Have you seen the—"

I turned to find a young girl frozen in the doorway. She stared at me like a deer caught in headlights. She was petite, with straight black hair. About sixteen or seventeen, she looked a little like Grim.

"Who are you?" she asked. "How did you get in here?"

"Who are *you*?" I countered.

"I'm *Zabby*." She said it like I was supposed to know what that meant.

"Am I supposed to know what that means?"

"I'm Grim's sister."

I paused. I knew Grim had a sister, but the idea of the Horsemen with families still felt wrong, like the sun out at midnight.

She stepped closer, peering at me. "You don't look like a murderer. But...that would make you a good murderer."

"I'm not a murderer. It's not my fault they didn't tell you I'd be here."

She huffed an exhale. "They don't tell me *anything*. I'm not a little girl anymore, but they all still treat me that way." She tilted her head, taking me and the room in, then a second later her face split in joy. "Oh, *oh*, you're *her*! You're the one he claimed."

I rubbed the back of my neck, unsure what to say.

"I didn't think they would do it," she said. "Not after Vander."

"Who is Vander—" I started to ask, but was cut off by a voice rough as nails.

"Sabrina," Lock said. "Go."

Lock stood behind Zabby—*Sabrina*—in the doorway.

Zabby spun. "You—"

"Go," Lock repeated.

She clenched her jaw. "You guys don't tell me anything." With one last look at me, she turned and left. Lock watched her go down the hallway, only turning back when the footfalls faded down the stairs.

"So..." I said. "Who's Vander?"

Lock visibly tensed, but only said, "Go change."

"Change? For what? *Into* what?"

He nodded to the left, where an open archway led to a walk-in closet. Eyes narrowed, I walked toward it.

Rows and rows of pink met me, except for a small corner of black. Pink dresses, soft cashmere loungewear, and a small section of Gothic and lacy black dresses. All in my size. All brands I would wear. I knew these brands. This would have cost hundreds of thousands.

Was this entire closet for me?

Shivers peppered my skin. It was like Grim had been preparing for this.

"Hurry up, princess," Lock called.

I grabbed a relatively simple pink A-line minidress. It had a corset with a semi-sheer lace bodice scalloping my breasts.

When I came out, Raze had joined Lock. They shared a look.

"We should make her change," Raze said.

Lock shook his head. "We're already late."

"What's wrong with what I'm wearing? This is couture."

Lock's blue eyes locked on me. "You look like bait, princess."

Bait?

They stepped aside, making a clear path for me.

"Where are we going?" I asked.

To my surprise, they answered. "The Underworld."

It was barely ten in the morning. The Underworld didn't open until eleven at *night*. With Raze at my back, I followed Lock down the stairs, and then down another set of stairs into a basement I didn't know existed.

It was rare for a basement to exist so close to the beach, but this one appeared carved into stone. Inside was a plethora of cars. Expensive sports cars. Bikes. But the antique black one Grim used sat revving, metallic gas filling the air.

Lock opened the back door for me and I slid inside, sandwiched between him and Wraith, just like yesterday.

"We're driving the two feet it takes to get to the club?"

They said nothing, pulling out of the garage and up into the bright, wintry day. I craned my neck, following the foggy pier until it disappeared in the rearview, stomach sinking.

Swallowing, I stared forward. "I thought you said we were going to the Underworld?"

Grim eyed me in the rearview but said nothing.

Minutes passed in silence. We drove past a blue-and-white painted wooden sign: *Now Leaving Crowne Point.* My throat tightened. We entered a forest, and trees whisked by. Soon an hour had passed, then another.

I must have fallen asleep. Suddenly the car jolted, and I woke up in the middle of trees—somewhere I didn't recognize at all. The car was running, rumbling beneath me, gas filling the vehicle and burning my nostrils.

Maybe they're going to kill me here.

Two flat knocks sounded on the window, and I nearly jumped.

Raze lowered the glass, and someone shone a light inside. It was so bright I felt it in the back of my skull.

I had a second to get a glimpse before Wraith gripped the back of my skull, pushing me forward so harshly the muscles in my upper back screamed. He'd been covered in tattoos—as in face, eyelids, lips. The color was different, maybe it was the night, but they glimmered—

I stilled as I felt someone, probably Lock, brush the hair at my nape aside.

They're showing my tattoo—

The car jolted forward, and Wraith released me. I sat up with a jerk, hand flying to the back of my neck as if that would protect me. Wraith and Lock stared forward, as if nothing had happened, as if this was all fucking normal.

I crossed my arms. I'd act as if this were normal too.

We drove through inky black. I could barely see the shadows of the trees against the sky. How did the light from the city not reach here? It reached even Crowne Point.

I heard a creak—heavy wrought iron gates were opening. Then...it appeared.

I nearly gasped.

Crowne Hall had been called palatial, but this was like the castles our ancestors *hoped* to emulate. Grand obsidian towers and spires swept up into the shadowy sky. Stone gargoyles perched on ledges, the onyx in their eyes glittering.

Invitees streamed through pointed arches, their dresses better than any bespoke item I'd ever worn. Black diamonds glimmered on necks and wrists.

There was something off about everything. The shadows were velvet and every person was tattooed.

Even still, I knew this dance, even if it was more ominous. I'd been raised for this dance. Beauty is armor, that was a lesson my mother taught me early.

"Don't look at anyone," Raze growled. "Don't speak, even if someone talks to you."

"Where are we?"

"We already told you, princess," Lock said. "The Underworld."

FORTY

GEMMA

So this was the Underworld—not the glamour they sold to my friends for a thousand dollars a bottle or the illusion that had girls and boys lining up at the bottom of the stairs—the *real* Underworld.

Everyone was in black tie, wearing inky, muted colors like scales.

I glanced down at my pink dress.

You look like bait.

I followed Grim with Lock and Raze at my back. I didn't know where Wraith had gone—this place was almost entirely shadows—he could've been anywhere.

The Underworld—the *real* Underworld, apparently—was a wicked Greek bacchanal, complete with dancing on pedestals next to ancient columns sweeping up to the skeleton vault ceilings. It was shirtless men adorned with golden black horns, and girls with only diamonds covering their breasts, rubbing against each other as they danced.

Every movement was sensual, leaden, like a silk scarf caught on a breeze.

Grim wound through bodies, and something overcame me. I began to feel leaden as well. I blinked, trying to steady myself. The flames blurred and slowed, and in front of me, Lock seemed to grow taller, more shadowy.

You okay, princess?

"Did you say something?" My voice sounded underwater.

Lock didn't turn around.

Dancing stilled, heads turning to watch us as we walked by. In the shadows, thick-lashed cat eyes stared, illuminated by the burn of a cigarette.

At first I thought they were watching the Horsemen, but no, they were looking at *me*. Hair pricked the back of my neck. I was used to being watched—I was a Crowne, after all—but this was something else. There was a glimmering in their eyes I couldn't decipher.

But the feeling, yeah, I caught that. I was a cow walking into a slaughterhouse.

We turned left—right into a naked woman arching on a black chaise. Over her curved belly, the tips of golden black horns were visible. As we continued to pass, I saw why. A demon had buried his face between her thighs. She gripped his horns, pressing him deeper into her.

But right before he was to obey and bury himself into her, he jerked his head to the side and locked eyes with me. His eyes were white—no black at all.

Lock yanked me forward into his blue glare. "What did we say about looking?"

He didn't let me answer.

Every society has a hierarchy—a caste. It wasn't hard to

see where people fell if you took a moment to look. Even in the Underworld, people betrayed themselves.

The important people, whoever they were, stuck to the balconies, veiled and much less crowded.

And then there were doors, stuck behind massive Grecian pillars. Those were guarded. The very important people must be behind those.

The Horsemen walked through the doors, and we entered a circular room featuring a raised floor with an ornate, black wingback.

"Stay here and don't move." Before I could say anything to that, Grim gripped my neck, forcing my eyes to his. "If you don't act like you're mine, I'll have to *show* that you're mine. Got it?"

"Am I?" It slipped out before I could stop it. "Yours, that is."

He thumbed my tattoo, his brush sending a shiver of sweet pain. His eyes softened slightly, and I saw something in his eyes, a glimpse of the boy behind Grim. As quickly as the softness came, it vanished back into iron.

They left, disappearing back into the party.

Not after Vander?

As I sat against the wall with nothing to do, Zabby's words came front and center.

And *why* did Grim still have my book?

The room was packed, but no one was mingling. In fact, it was eerily silent. The sensual music from outside muffled. I heard something, though—*moans*. They seemed to seep from the walls.

In the center of the room was an empty chair. That wasn't quite right—a *throne*. It was breathtaking, ghostly, and ornate. It was made of black scales. Onyx snakes wound up the arms, arching over the cresting back, their eyes a bril-

252 MARY CATHERINE GEBHARD

liant white. There was also something written along the back crest in gold, but I couldn't read it from so far away.

"How's that tattoo treating you?"

I turned at the familiar voice.

Prince HSOG—who, I realized, I still didn't know his actual name—leaned casually on his arm against the wall, like this was normal.

"Isn't it obvious?" I tilted my head. "It's great. I'm getting out, meeting new people."

He smiled. But it was like he knew something I didn't. I wanted to ask him so badly what he knew, but I worried that if I did, I would give up all my cards.

So I kept playing pretend.

"Are you going to tell me how someone like you keeps showing up in a world like this?"

"How do you know it's not the other way around? Maybe someone like me keeps showing up in your world." He stepped closer, my back against the wall. Over his shoulder I saw heads had turned, watching us.

"I don't think you're allowed to touch me," I said.

He put his hand beside my head. "That so—"

"This looks cozy."

From behind the prince Grim's smoky voice edged. The prince stared at me a long time, *too* long for when someone like Grim is at your back. He gave me a wolfish smile, then stood up.

"Grim." The prince turned to face him, all playful humor gone.

I slid along the side of the wall, trying to put distance between me and HSOG. I braced for whatever Grim was going to do. He'd nearly killed someone for just speaking to me.

Instead, Grim just smiled, a deeply vicious and terrifying smile. "I'm trying to figure out what part of *off fucking limits* wasn't clear."

"Funny thing about prey, Grim," Prince HSOG said, taking a step to Grim. "Leave it alone too long and someone else takes the first bite."

"*Someone* will crack their teeth on that bite."

A weird tension threaded between them. I wasn't an idiot. I knew *I* was the prey in this metaphor.

The prince threw a look over his shoulder, giving me a smile. "See you next time, Gemma."

I watched him walk into the crowd, and then it was just me and Grim...well, me, Grim, and a mansion full of people. Though they were just feet away from us, they didn't look in our direction.

Grim stepped to me, caging me against the wall.

"I warned you, Gemma." He slid down my body, eyes locked on mine. Hungry.

I barely had a second to register Grim on his *knees* before the meaning of what he said hit me.

I'll have to prove you're mine.

He was going to eat me out, here, in public. I put my hands on his shoulders, trying to move him.

"I didn't do anything," I said. "He talked to me."

I fisted his hair, pulling him off me, and a vicious, inhuman sound escaped him. His eyes flashed to mine, determined. In this moment, it wasn't about proving something, he just *wanted* this.

Hands slid around the backs of my thighs, up to my ass. Grim fisted and kneaded the flesh, pressing a hot kiss to the inside of my thigh.

"People will see," I whispered, fight draining from my body.

"No one will dare look at you," he said against my flesh.

I looked back out to the sea of people. They still weren't watching, but it felt like they were fully paying attention, even as they spoke to their neighbor.

Grim slowly peeled off my panties. All care in the world. As if it were just the two of us and not whatever the fuck this place was.

A different kind of panic hit me. The kind reserved for being a perfect, beautiful doll.

I gripped his shoulder. "I haven't showered yet."

"Good," he growled, and then his lips were on my flesh.

I almost buckled at the sensation. As if sensing that, his hands tightened on my ass.

"You taste so fucking good," he groaned against me.

He grazed his teeth along my lips and lightly tugged. This time I did buckle, but his tight grip held me up. I looked over his head, to the crowd. In the middle of hundreds of heads studiously avoiding us, the prince stood.

"He's looking," I gasped.

For a brief second, Grim tensed. Then his fingers flexed on my ass, pulling me closer to his mouth. I gasped, completely enveloped by him. Sliding one hand down my ass, to my pussy, Grim fingered me as he sucked.

I *shouldn't* like this. But my body disagreed. I was so wet. So achy. Grim's tongue disappeared briefly from my cunt to lick up the evidence on my inner thighs.

I was boneless. Jelly. Grim's grip the only thing keeping me from sliding to the floor.

"I want you to come, Rich Girl." His words vibrated deep in my pussy. "Show people who you belong to."

I *wanted* to. I was so fucking close. But that little, annoying voice was still in my head. Pointing out the people. Pointing out that *America's Princess* didn't do this—

Grim's teeth enclosed the tender flesh of my inner thigh.

For a moment the world was bright and blinding, my heart slamming against my chest.

Then it all melted away into something soft and hazy. I disappeared into his mouth. Licking and sucking. Biting and thrusting. Devouring me, marking me internally.

Anyone could have been staring at me and I wouldn't know or care. All I knew was Grim.

I fell apart to him speaking worshipping words against my pussy.

FORTY-ONE

GEMMA

No one spoke on the way home—no, not *home*, I quickly corrected myself. This was not home. The drive lasted most of the night, and by the time we got back to Crowne Point, it was morning. I wasn't sure where we'd gone, probably somewhere out of state.

Lock got out and held the door for me. That would never not be weird—the Horsemen being gentlemen.

The Horsemen started talking as they got to the foyer, about mundane and sundry things like whose turn it was to do the laundry.

Where was I? What was that place? Why was the fucking prince there again?

I followed Grim up the stairs, to his room, mind spinning, tongue tied.

"Tell me what that was," I said before the door had even shut.

He paused, the muscles in his back twitching beneath

his black shirt. He shut the door with a soft click, then turned around, face a mask.

"The Underworld."

I took a breath, trying to calm the tiny, scratching fingernails clawing at my chest—

Anger.

Oh, I'm angry. Again.

Hmm. I'd spent the majority of my life numbing my overactive emotions, but with Grim, they bubbled up and over.

Because how dare he?

How dare he upend my life? How dare he whisper sweet promises to me while he was inside me and *keep fucking lying.*

He glanced at my clenched fists, like he could see the thoughts in my head, and smiled.

"You keep saying that," I said. "But you know I know of the Underworld as that fucking club."

He dragged a hand across his jaw. "You got a lotta questions today, Rich Girl."

"And, like always, you have zero fucking answers."

Cool.

Fucking *great.*

Of course nothing was changing. I went to move past him and open the door, needing space, needing a quiet place to question my life and my choices. Because, like, what the fuck was wrong with me that I *knew* this was our reality and I kept hoping for something different?

He grabbed my arm. "Wait."

I stared at the inked fingers curled above my elbow, traveling up to meet his gaze. Some kind of foreign emotion clouded his eyes. Fear?

No, that couldn't be right.

"There are things I can't tell you, Gemma."

"Can't or won't?"

His jaw clenched. "Won't."

A moment passed, marked by the shattering crash of the waves on the beach and the cawing of a lone seagull who didn't get the winter memo.

Anger dissolved into heavy, thick disappointment. In him. In myself. In the fact that I accepted this. I had his mark on my neck, he'd been inside me, and I still didn't get to be in his world.

"I have to go," Grim said, but he didn't let go of me. His grip tightened.

"Business?" I cocked my head, knowing full well he wouldn't tell me where he was going.

He didn't respond.

He didn't have to.

A moment later he left. I stared at the empty doorway.

One heartbeat.

Two.

Fuck this.

I stomped downstairs—yes, stomped. I wasn't above being petty. But downstairs was empty, so wherever Grim had gone involved the Horsemen. I walked into the kitchen, bare feet cold on the checkered marble. They had to have alcohol somewhere.

My eyes scanned the antique, hand-painted cabinets. A crystal bottle glinted at me from behind the cabinet's glass pane.

Bingo.

I grabbed the bottle. Patrón Lalique series. Expensive. I popped off the crystal top, taking a drink as I left the kitchen.

There was a heaviness in my heart that reached my limbs.

It choked me.

Sniff.

I paused at the sound, following it to the living room. Zabby sat next to a black metal fireplace, on a deep burgundy Persian rug with intricate floral and geometric motifs.

"You okay?"

She startled, turning to find me, eyes wide. "I'm fine."

Her eyes were shiny, nose red.

I held up the tequila. "Wanna get drunk?"

We got through half the bottle before either of us said anything. Zabby turned on the fireplace, the heat and crackle warming a deep ache in my bones that had nothing to do with the cold. Out the floor-to-ceiling mullioned windows, the rusted Ferris wheel sat beneath a wintery gray sky.

"Wanna tell me why you were crying?" I asked.

She quirked a brow. "Wanna tell me why you stole the tequila?"

We stared at one another, neither blinking.

"Fine," I said, taking another drink. "Grim is lying to me. Or...keeping things from me."

Zabby exhaled. "He does that."

Curiosity replaced the heaviness in my limbs. This was Grim's sister. She grew up with him. She *knew* him.

"What was he like?" I asked. "Growing up?"

She stood up on her knees, suddenly animated. "Well, one time when I was in grade school, I asked a boy to be my Valentine. He said yes, but the day came and he completely forgot about me. Laughed at the present I got. I came home crying. Weirdly," she continued, "later that night, the boy showed up with a dozen roses and two boxes of expensive chocolate."

I bit my cheek to stop my smile. Grim was always protective, even then. For the next hour Zabby told me all kinds of stories about Grim.

How he used to let her fall asleep on his shoulder during cartoons. How he was never mean like her other friends' brothers. How he would read to her, doing all the voices. How he slept with a light until he was twelve—

"No!" I interrupted. "No way. *Grim* was afraid of the dark?"

She nodded excitedly. "Our life was totally different before Vander."

There it was again, that name.

"Who is Vander?"

A look clouded her features, like she'd said too much, and she quickly changed the subject. "Aren't you afraid?" she asked. "Being, you know, claimed. People will want to hurt you. To kill you. Just to make a point."

Was I afraid? Maybe. Deep down I knew Grim would never let anything happen to me.

But also, deeper down, a part of me didn't care if something did.

"Kind of," I lied, and took another swig from the bottle. "But I don't know if it matters. I don't know how it's going to work. This thing. Obviously I can't stay here. I don't know why they're keeping me here."

"It's not up to them, you know. They have to report to someone."

"Wait, wait, wait—they report to someone?"

"It's more than that…they're captive."

I choked on my liquor. After a good minute of Zabby

drunkenly slapping my back, I sputtered, "The fuck did you just say?"

She looked startled, like she'd let something slip she shouldn't have. "I thought you knew! It's because of you."

"Me?"

Because of me? How could it be because of me? I barely knew them. I said as much to her, confusion making my throat hot. She stayed quiet, that look still on her face, like she'd just revealed my aunt was my mother.

"Look," she said. "I don't know much. I just know they were almost free of their debt, then Grim took yours. I think it's even more complicated now that he claimed you. You're not...really supposed to do that with someone in your debt."

That was *five* years ago. He was almost free?

I took another drink, willing the room to dissolve.

After a few more, it did.

Somewhere in our drunk logic, our clothes came off. Zabby said something about her being a witch, and that if we wanted to get rid of the negative energy of the day, we needed to burn it. So we tossed them into the fire.

It *did* feel good.

Now we lay naked on the soft rug, staring at the swirls of the ceiling's intricate crown molding. Only in America were people weirdly prudish. No one batted an eye in a Japanese onsen.

There was something...grounding about it. Like beneath the clothes, inside the flesh, we were the same fucked-up pieces of stardust.

Zabby swished the bottle around. "Aw, empty—"

"Where the fuck are your clothes?"

We turned to find Lock standing in the doorway.

Zabby sat up, swaying. "Hi, Big Brother Lock."

"Where are the other members of the boy band?" I asked.

Lock's eyes were trained on Zabby, jaw clenched. I swore I saw something in his eyes.

Something *way* beyond brotherly.

It was as if he'd been hit by a bus, and was also trying to lift the fucking bus.

"Where. Are. Your. Fucking. Clothes."

We both shared a look, laughing.

"It's a secret," I whispered.

And we laughed harder.

"Are you drunk?" Lock demanded. If steam could come out of his ears, it would have.

We both laughed. "Maybe."

"You let her drink?" He shot me daggers. "It's a fucking school night and she's seventeen."

I looked around. *The fuck?* Was this the Underworld or a goddamn church?

Zabby shot up, fists clenched, before I could respond. "I'm not seventeen anymore! I haven't been seventeen for *months*. Stop treating me like a fucking child!"

Lock's eyes flashed.

Whoa. Am I really drunk or did something just *pop*?

Lock reached over his head, pulling his shirt off by the back of his collar. "Put this on."

Zabby stuck out her lower lip. "No."

The muscle in his jaw twitched. He took a step toward her, and she took a step back. Lock's stare sharpened, and then he was after her. She sidestepped him, running around the couch.

The chase was short-lived. He reached across the couch and threw her over his shoulder.

She waved at me as he carried her up the stairs.

Right as Lock left, Grim came into the room.

"You're ruining the game." Zabby's slurring words disappeared up the stairs.

Damn. There goes my drinking buddy.

Grim leaned on the doorjamb a moment, watching me, a softness in his eyes that was still too much even with my drunken haze.

He came over.

Wordlessly, he bent down and lifted me into his arms, carrying me out of the room and up the stairs.

"Is it true?" I asked. "Am I the reason you're condemned?"

His eyes flashed down to mine. Blazing. But he said nothing. When we got into the room, he placed me in his bed. Pulling the covers up.

"Since when does the monster tuck the princess in?" I asked.

He came down, lips a breath from mine, so I felt the heat of his words on my flesh. "Since the princess started flirting with them."

"You wanna know a secret, Grim?" I asked. He stilled, waiting. "You're the one who flirted with a monster."

Some emotion flickered through his eyes, but whatever it was, I wouldn't get access to it.

He pulled the blankets up to my chin. "Go to sleep, Rich Girl."

FORTY-TWO

GEMMA

I woke up, head pounding. It was dark outside, and shadows danced on the ceiling. I turned my head to the right, where outside spotlights made luminous circles in the clouds.

I sat up, and another round of throbbing slammed into my skull. My hand flew to my forehead, trying to ease it with pressure.

Jesus Christ.

I hadn't been this hungover in...years. Zabby must be wrecked—*Zabby.* Our conversation slammed into me.

Who is powerful enough to keep the Horsemen captive?

I slowly stood out of bed, bare feet hitting the hardwood. Looking down, I saw I was wearing an oversize black shirt—Grim's. I knotted the fabric in my fist, feeling oddly... warm.

The house was just as dark as Grim's room. There was only small, soft light from a wall lamp. It made the shadows fuzzy, the furniture warped.

Am I still drunk?

"Hello?" I called out, coming down the stairs.

Silence answered.

"Zabby?" I tried.

Still nothing. I walked into the living room where Zabby and I had drunk. Through the window, the club lit up the room in neon. A dull vibrating thrummed beneath my feet from the music.

I walked out of the living room and back upstairs, to Grim's bedroom.

Go to sleep, Rich Girl.

The memories felt fuzzy in my mind, but I remembered the feeling. Safe. Cared for.

I took a quick shower, not bothering to blow-dry my hair. A foreign sense of freedom overcame me. I *always* had a blowout. Now my hair started to dry in natural half curls and waves.

My feet padded along the cold floor, to the walk-in closet. Scratchy glitter and soft silk danced along my fingertips as I searched for a dress. I picked out a pale-pink mini.

It was a short walk to the club, what with the house being behind it. I entered through the back doors, weaving through the floor like I'd done hundreds of times before with my friends. Distantly, I wondered what the fuck they must be thinking.

Were they rejoicing?

Finally Gemma Crowne has fallen.

I wove my way through bodies until I reached the stairs. Oddly, there was no line tonight. The upstairs was empty.

No Horsemen. No Grim.

I went to the railing, leaning over and looking down at the club floor. I felt like I'd been split in two. Like, down there, in some other timeline, Gemma Crowne was still dancing to the beat.

I wasn't sure how long I stayed up there, but it was longer than a few song changes. I headed toward the exit just as the DJs were switching out.

"Gemma?"

Downstairs, I paused at my name, turning to find my friends. In sparkly pastel minis and strappy metallic pumps, Blaire and Kennedy were dressed for a night out.

"Uh, hey," I said.

"Hey," they said in unison.

"You missed the party," Blaire said.

I used to have a constant mental loop of which party to go to, what my goal was there, what the headline should be when I left.

Now?

I wasn't even sure what party she was talking about.

"Yeah," I said. "I was busy."

"Oh, right," Kennedy said, bright. "The Crowne anniversary party is coming up."

"Right," Blaire added, elongating the word to *righhhht*.

We had perfected the art of ignoring the elephant in the room.

When Blaire came back from holiday with a new nose? We asked her if she met anyone cute skiing. When Kennedy's parents' divorce was tabloid fodder, our conversations never strayed far from high school gossip.

I was so sick of it.

"No, actually," I said. "I've been fucking the head of the Horsemen."

Their eyes grew, sharing a look.

"Oh, um, congrats?" Kennedy said.

"Yeah, slay, girl..." Blaire trailed off. "So when are you coming back?"

Back?

Of course. They probably thought I was just getting it out of my system. Like when Kennedy fucked a guy who had just gotten out of jail.

"We have that interview next week," Blaire continued.

"And we're behind in content," Kennedy said. "Because your family didn't do their vacation, we don't have any PJ photos—"

"God, who the fuck cares?" I couldn't do it anymore. Couldn't talk about private jets and who fucked who and which designer was loaning which person what dress.

I was getting too comfortable like this, starting to like being indebted to Grim more than I liked being free. That was a problem, because we had an expiration date.

I would have to go back.

Back to my world. Back to endless, plastic parties. To never saying the real thing out loud.

"Would you have ever been friends with me if I wasn't Gemma Crowne?" I asked.

"Um..." Kennedy worked her mouth to the side. "What?"

If I had to go back, I couldn't go back to *before*. I couldn't say my best friends were people who thought my favorite food was caviar. Who didn't know my favorite book was *Frankenstein*.

"I'm so fucking sick of pretending," I said. "Tell me the fucking truth for once in our friendship."

Blaire laughed. "Okay, like you? Dude, we're all just following your lead."

"I *know* you're only friends with me because I'm Puerto Rican," Kennedy said. "You know how I know? Because every Cinco de Mayo we always have to do a special picture together. That's fucking Mexico, bitch."

We stared at one another.

She was right.

This was all so...fucked.

"This is who we are," Blaire said. "This is what *you* created. Why are you being so fucking weird?"

"Did the Horseman dickmatize you or something?" Kennedy asked.

Or something.

"I don't think friends should sell secrets to tabloids," I said. "I don't think friends should be held hostage by follower count. I don't think we're friends."

Kennedy blinked, but it was Blaire who spoke. "I have no idea who the hell you are anymore, Gemma."

I nodded, because, *yeah.* I wasn't sure who I was anymore, either.

I left without another word, pushing open the heavy metal door into a cold winter night.

I'd never ended a friendship before. Even when I hated someone's guts, I still smiled and acted friendly. Trinity started a rumor that my father wasn't my real dad, and I still hugged her at every party.

It didn't matter if my friends didn't know me. They were like everything else, a commodity. The more you had, the richer you were.

But something had changed. I didn't want that anymore. I wanted *real*.

Halfway between the club and the house, I paused. Five men came from the beach, now blocking my way. They didn't look like my usual crazed stalkers. They were meaner. Covered in tattoos. The middle one's tattoo covered half of his face and snaked down to his neck.

Our eyes locked.

People will want to hurt you. To kill you. Just to make a point.

I took a step back as they walked toward me. The club was too far away to get to before they reached me, and they blocked the house.

Fuck.

Two came to my back, another two at my side, and the one with the face tattoo stood front and center. I was surrounded.

I smiled, affecting my light, breezy Gemma Crowne voice. "Usually people form a line for autographs."

Humor died in my throat as I felt one of them step to my back. I'd called many monsters before, but this was different. I didn't *want* to die.

"Nothing personal," the tattooed guy growled, pulling out a knife. "This is a message for your man."

"Hey, pretty boy!" At Lock's voice a visceral part of me sagged. "Don't you know it's rude to play with someone else's toys?"

Tattoo Face turned to his left, where Lock stood. Next to him, Raze and Wraith. Before he could respond, Wraith threw a knife, hitting him square in the chest.

He fell to the ground.

And it wasn't about me anymore. All four of them rushed the Horsemen. Two went to Wraith, the other two split between Raze and Lock.

It was four on three, but the Horsemen weren't bothered. Wraith took on the two easily, a right hook slamming into one jaw, while he ducked from the second guy's punch. Raze took the guy with him to the ground, smashing his head into the asphalt. Lock played with the other guy. Dodging. Dancing.

I started to relax. They had this—

Suddenly Lock was on the ground, a knife to his neck. I spun around—was someone going to help him? Raze had someone pinned to the ground. Wraith was still fighting two people.

So I did the only thing I could think of. I ran to Lock, taking off my shoe as I did, and slammed it over the guy's head. It didn't take him down, but it was enough to startle him. Lock reversed the pin, the guy getting a slice at his shoulder first.

"Thanks, princess." Lock shot me a smile, then sliced the guy's throat.

Wraith finished playing with his prey. Then it was over. Five bodies lay on the ground. Lock's arm bled red rivers down the muscles in his biceps, across his ink, but he laughed. They all laughed. Like this was nothing.

A moment later, the rumble of a car engine sounded.

"Shit," Raze cursed. Our eyes followed his, to the source of the sound—a car driving away.

"Whoever it was will take back the message," Lock said.

While Lock and Raze joked about something I couldn't hear, Wraith walked up to me. I braced myself for anger. He thumbed my cheek, swiping blood I hadn't realized was there. It was...*sweet*. That terrified me more than anything. The Horsemen weren't *sweet*.

"I told you," he said. "You don't get to die."

FORTY-THREE

GEMMA

I dabbed antiseptic onto Lock's shoulder. Grim had arrived ten minutes after everything went down, helping to clean up. Now they all joked as bodies dissolved in acid. There was a tension in Grim even as he laughed with them. He'd dragged a chair next to me, one hand wrapped around my upper thigh, as if making sure I was still here.

I looked through the kitchen door, brow furrowing at the gallon-size drums in the hallway.

Like five men didn't just try to kill them.

Like they weren't covered in blood.

I pressed more of the cotton into Lock's gash. I felt a strange combination of numb and wired, like an electric wire shoved into cotton.

"Where did Gemma Crowne learn how to clean a wound?" Raze asked.

Raze had a cut under his eye that I'd managed to clean.

His knuckles were bloody, and I'd had to take out the individual pieces of gravel. I looked at the abrasion on his knuckles, remembering him shove a guy to the asphalt. The head breaking open on the gravel. His grip white-knuckled.

"Yeah, I'm curious about that." Lock tilted his head to find my face.

I remembered my mother on the bathroom floor, shattered glass surrounding her. It was hard to tell if she'd dropped the vase because she was high, or if getting hurt was the point.

"Camp," I lied.

"Camp?" They laughed, like that was the most insane thing in the world.

While they laughed, Grim stared at me. His head slightly tilted, a softness in his eyes.

Like he could somehow see my mother bleeding.

"Sabrina is on her way," Wraith said, coming back into the kitchen. "Should get there in three hours."

Wraith was the least injured, but his lip was still bleeding, and he'd probably have a black eye, even if the ink hid it.

"She must be stoked," Lock said. "She hates winter."

"Zabby is leaving?" I asked.

Maybe I didn't speak out loud, or maybe I was too quiet, because they continued as if I hadn't. They were sending Zabby away, to some friend of Lock's in the South. A place that was safer.

Because of what was happening.

Because of *me*.

It was all because of me. The chaos was because of me. And if Zabby wasn't lying, then their debt was because of me too.

"I can leave," I said.

The laughter stopped abruptly. Grim's grip turned hard, bruising. The other three shared a look.

"This is too much, this is too dangerous," I said. "You got hurt."

Lock laughed. "Princess, this is not hurt."

"You might need stitches."

Another laugh.

I felt something shift. It wasn't like a few weeks ago when they held me captive in my room. There wasn't anger or resentment in their eyes. This was something different entirely.

It was too close to affection.

Which made it so much harder. Anger made sense. This? I didn't deserve it. Any of it.

"Everything is falling apart—"

"Let it," Wraith said. "You're ours, Gemma. The time for second-guessing passed a long time ago."

My throat felt thick. Wraith didn't say it with sweetness, just matter-of-fact, but still. A declaration like that coming from *Wraith*?

"I am curious. You got some kind of fetish for making bad guys angry?" Lock asked, turning to me. "What number is this now? Eleven? Twelve?"

"Thirteen," Wraith answered.

"Like I said, fetish."

I dropped the bottle. Burnt-orange liquid poured onto the marble. They were joking. I know they were joking.

I watched as the sticky liquid seeped from white tile, to black.

In my out-of-control life, monsters were the one thing I could control. I made them come when I wanted, where I wanted.

And I knew Grim would handle it.

It was all in my control.

I once read control was an illusion. I never really got it. Until now. It wasn't...fun anymore.

"S-sorry," I said, bending down. Absently, I noticed my hands were shaking. I *saw* the tremors but didn't feel them.

The room went quiet. Gemma didn't shake. She didn't *apologize*.

"Gemma," Grim said. I kept trying to get the bottle. "Gemma, look at me."

It was the authority in his voice that had me lifting my eyes. Some deep, primeval part of me wired to obey him. I didn't hear them go, but the rest of the Horsemen had left. Grim leaned forward on his chair, knees on his elbows.

That *Grim* thing happened. Where I couldn't breathe. Where all I saw and felt was the lethal fire in his eyes. Gleaming. Intense.

His lips tilted.

"Come, Rich Girl."

No.

Don't do it.

But I stood up, my legs moving involuntarily, until I was between his legs. His gaze never strayed from mine. I was too open right now. Too vulnerable.

But I couldn't look away.

Our breaths were one.

He tilted his head, peering into me. Goose bumps shivered along my arms and legs and spine.

"I should go," I said. "I need to leave. If I leave things will get better."

"You don't want to belong to me, *mi locura?*"

I do. I *so* do.

"No."

One side of his lips tilted up, like he'd read my lie. But he said nothing, running his open palm up the back of my thigh, curving over my ass to the small of my back.

Again I felt like a thing. A very precious thing. That belonged to Grim. And I was weak with it.

I can't be the reason your life falls apart.

"You were never supposed to kill them." I shoved him, and he gripped my wrists with both hands, keeping me close.

"So I should have let you die?" he growled.

"Yes!" I struggled in his grip, but it was iron. "Let me go. I'm not good for you. I'll ruin you. I'll ruin your life. I'll destroy everything."

"And?" he demanded. "Since when do you care about that, Rich Girl? Why do you care what happens to me?"

I tried to turn away, but he gripped my chin, dragging me back.

"Do you love me or something?" His eyes searched mine.

Love?

Love was too shallow a word for what I felt. Grim consumed me. My blood. My marrow. He was rooted so deep inside my soul I could feel the tangled roots.

His palms slid into place on either side of my face, caging me. His eyes sharpened, like he was reading my mind.

Then he crushed his mouth against mine. His thumbs dug into my cheekbones, pulling me closer to him. The kiss was rough and commanding—I couldn't move under his grip—and over too soon.

"I will never let you go," he said, pulling back to snarl against my lips. "Never."

He didn't let me go, grip still bruising my face. Under a lock of black hair, his eyes were black, fathomless pools. The words Wraith had said to me weeks ago reflected back in the hungry, visceral emotions shimmering in their depths.

If Grim is your reaper, then you're his fucking reckoning. He knows you're going to kill him, and he refuses to let go.

FORTY-FOUR

GEMMA

The first time I met Grim was the one time I didn't feel alone. I couldn't remember exactly what had instigated the crying, but I had a few guesses. It was my first year at Crowne Point High, but my grandfather ripping me out of boarding school and shoving me into public school wasn't the cause, just a symptom. That suffocating buzzing I used to smother at boarding school with pills and sex had nowhere to go. It clawed out of my chest daily, screaming.

That day, I couldn't control it.

Tears fell in a deluge, so I skipped class and ran to an empty room. I swiped furiously at my eyes and dug my nails into my palm. Nothing worked. I couldn't stop them. On the floor, I dug my head into my knees, hating myself. Hating that I was like this. Hating that I had nowhere to hide.

Then I heard a book fall.

I moved to get off the floor when Grim came out from behind a shelf. Still on my knees, I froze.

"You can't tell anyone about this," I said.

His hands came to my face. Silent. Smearing the tears beneath my eyes. His palms were big, encapsulating the entire span of my face. I felt...safe.

Maybe it was how his body eclipsed everything and became the only thing I knew. Or maybe it was how he held my face with a kind of knowing possession that should be reserved to past-life lovers, not two kids who just met. Like even back then he knew I belonged to him.

So when I should have been standing, shoving him off, and running, instead I leaned into it.

He didn't ask if I was okay or if I needed help. Just stared at me with a knowing look that excavated parts of my soul.

Then he dropped to his knees too.

I still had to tilt my head to find his eyes. I remember my brain screaming at me to leave. That this was *not* what I should be doing. But then he took my hand in his and pressed my nails into his neck.

The same way his dark stare told me he knew what I needed, I knew what he wanted. I scythed my nails against his flesh.

"Who made you cry?" A threat lingered in the rough, rocky tone of his voice.

"No one. I'm..." *I'm fucked up.*

I expected him to press me, or say he felt sorry. Instead he pushed my hand deeper into his neck. His eyes grew, then drooped into something heavy with promise. I felt something more than sizzle between us; a part of me broke off and latched on to him.

Then the bell rang.

Grim stood off his knees, but I stayed frozen.

"*Frankenstein*, huh?" He nodded to the book that had fallen out of my bag.

"It's my favorite," I said.

Why am I telling him this? No one knew about my secret love of *Frankenstein*, and I definitely hadn't told them. Gemma Crowne was supposed to be untouchable—not aloof, but so very above everyone else. As if possessed by someone who had never met Tansy Crowne, I kept talking. "The author wore her husband's petrified heart as a necklace. I don't think there's anything more romantic."

His eyes sharpened, like he was homing in on some great treasure.

Then he turned to leave.

"Wait, will you—What just—" I broke off. What the *fuck* was I doing? Despite my brain screaming at me not to be such a fool, I asked, "Will I see you again?"

Pathetic.

Grim placed a knuckle beneath my chin, lifting my blurry gaze to his.

"My insides are radioactive. I corrode whatever and whoever I touch." He stroked the side of my jaw with his thumb. "I'm poison, Gemma. Stay away."

We never spoke of what happened in that room, but my starving soul feasted on the memory for years.

I will never let you go. Never.

I was that teenage girl again, frozen and on her knees, knowing she should run, but leaning into it anyway.

The only time I saw the Horsemen today, including Grim, was for breakfast. Zabby was gone, like they said. I spent the day alone. I read, I took a bath in Grim's massive black marble tub, then hours later came to the club. It was weirdly touching to be left alone. Like this was my home, and they expected me here.

It was just a few days until Valentine's Day. As wrong as it was, it was nice being away from my mom, from Crowne Hall—

Someone was behind me.

Terror slid icy into my stomach as the mystery person bunched my dress up to my hips, fingers sliding between my thighs to where I was bare.

People will want to hurt you. To kill you. Just to make a point.

I swung my elbow into the mystery man's stomach. A startled, slightly amused grunt shivered on my ears. My terror transmogrified into heat.

I knew that voice.

"Your cunt is sloppy for some man," Grim growled, sliding his fingers inside me.

I gripped the railing as he slid one, two more inside me. The club below blurred into a bokeh of sparkly dresses and neon lights.

"Not some man," I gasped. "The Reaper. If he finds out you touched me, he'll kill you."

"Oh, yeah?" he rasped. "Does he own you or something?"

His fingers curled up inside me, hitting that perfect spot as we played out a dark, twisted fantasy.

"*Yes*," I groaned, arching into his touch. "He'll kill you just for looking at me—"

I broke off. Down on the main floor, nearly obscured by shadows, was Kennedy. Kennedy with *Wraith*. Wraith pressed her against the wall, touching her cheek—

Grim slammed inside me and the room blurred. All I knew was that perfect, delicious fullness. Grim stretching me, taking me, owning me. The pounding of the beat, the energy of hundreds of bodies below, thrummed inside me.

When I managed to blink open, Kennedy and Wraith were gone.

"If someone sees you come, I'll have to kill them. So be good. Be quiet."

I clenched at that image, and Grim's answering groan on my flesh let me know he felt it. He wrapped his arm around my waist and hauled me backward, down to the couch.

"You're mine now, Rich Girl. I can touch you whenever." Grim gripped my inner thigh, spreading me wider. "Wherever."

I couldn't think. Soft, helpless sounds slipped from my lips.

As Grim spread me wider, it was like fireworks went off in my body. His cock hit the perfect, aching part of me and I'd never felt so full.

I glanced at the stairs. My silky pink dress slid over my thighs, shielding what was happening. But anyone could walk up the stairs. They would know. They'd have to know.

The thought sent wicked shivers down my spine.

I could feel release building, mounting with each slow, torturous thrust.

"You took that choice away the day you took my ink." He licked the back of my neck—the tattoo. "So be a good girl and come when I say."

His teeth closed around the skin of my tattoo, and that sharp pain, mixed with the delicious ache of him inside me, pushed me over the edge. I fell. Shattered. Came apart. I groaned, moaned—nearly screamed. At least, I must have, because his hand covered my mouth.

I fell apart on his cock and Grim came with me, his

jagged groan seeping into the skin of my neck. Then I felt him, hot and wet, dripping out of me onto my thighs.

"There's my good girl," he said, hand sliding between my thighs to my pussy, massaging his come against me. I jolted at the sensation, still throbbing, too overstimulated.

He bit the lobe of my ear, whispering sweet words as I came down.

His words slid like wine into my blood. He pressed soft kisses up and down my neck, teeth and tongue and lips creating a delirious potion, and I couldn't help but feel... home.

Right.

I stared out at the empty balcony. I'd been here so many times before, but never like this. Never with a sense of belonging.

The truth was, it felt like an oasis. No phone. No contact with the outside world. Not wondering how many followers I lost, what the tabloids were saying. Here, I could just...be.

I'd gone on many vacations, to private islands, exclusive resorts, palaces in Switzerland—but I was always *on*, always *Gemma*. When I was on the beach, I was thinking about the best photo to take. When I was at a club, it was, *who is watching?* Who was going to send some stupid blind about how Gemma was drunk with so-and-so?

So of course it had to end.

"*Gemma?*"

I froze at the disbelieving voice, willing reality to change. Grim's lips didn't leave my neck, but he tightened his grip on my stomach, and with that I felt it—felt the violent, possessive glare he shot my brother.

"Grayson?" I squeaked. "What are you doing here?"

I tried to get up, but Grim pinned me. Even if my dress

draped and hid the most illicit parts, he was *still* inside me. His come leaked rivers between my thighs.

Grayson's attention shifted over my shoulder, to Grim. "Let her go."

Grim bit my neck. "Gemma can't go anywhere right now. She's too busy taking my cock."

I'd seen my brother this angry only once—the night his wife nearly died. A calm, detached cool slid across his body that didn't at all match the fury in his eyes.

Grim kissed my neck in that same slow, lazy way he had been. As if my brother wasn't right there. As if it didn't fucking matter, because this was his *right*.

Grayson clenched and unclenched his fists. "I will use the full force of Crowne power to destroy you."

"Gemma Crowne belongs to me now," Grim said. "She's never going back. Accept it."

Grayson took a step toward us, his glare reckless. Violent. This wouldn't end well. Grayson didn't know when to tap out.

I didn't know if Grim *could* tap out.

"Grayson," I said. "Please. I'm fine."

Grayson's glare ripped away from Grim, softening on me. "It's been two days, Gemma."

"I'll be home soon," I said, not sure if it was a lie. Grim tensed at my back, his grip on my stomach even harder.

Grayson's jaw clenched. His eyes slid back to Grim. "This is not over."

Then he left.

FORTY-FIVE

GEMMA

The sun was streaming when I woke, a high afternoon light and—oh God, what *was* that? I squirmed at something delicious between my thighs.

A moan slipped from my lips.

"Good fucking girl," Grim growled.

I startled at the voice vibrating against my thighs. Grim was there, shoulders pushing my thighs apart, muscles coiled with the effort. I tried to sit up and he gripped my hips, keeping me pinned against his mouth.

His tongue slid inside me and *oh fuck*.

I melted into the mattress, letting it happen. He ate me slow, building it up until I couldn't take it anymore. Until my hands found his hair and I pressed myself against him, forcing him to go faster and harder.

He rumbled in approval.

Seconds later I fell apart.

I was still panting, still seeing stars in the ceiling, when Grim crawled above me.

He smiled, lips glistening. "Good morning."

Then he kissed me, thrusting his tongue in my mouth so I tasted myself. He knotted his hands in my hair, yanking my neck into an arch to get deeper.

This isn't over.

They're captive.

It's because of you.

All the unanswered questions shot through me like lightning. Grayson, Zabby—everything.

"Wait—" Grim found my neck. Kissing and sucking the hollow beneath my ear in a deliriously distracting way. His cock pressed against me, and I spread my thighs on a groan—

No, fuck.

I pushed him off me and he pulled away—on his elbows, leaning over me in the most distracting way.

Hair messed. Lips glistening.

"We need to talk," I said, words too breathy, chest rising and falling.

We didn't do any talking last night. I couldn't live in this pattern anymore. Where the things unsaid between us piled like shipwreck debris, cutting and heavy and blocking. Where we ignored it until we no longer saw each other.

"Someone told me you're captive."

Grim's stare narrowed. "Who are you talkin' to, Rich Girl?"

I went silent. I might have been a lot of things, but I was no snitch.

Grim was too smart—he figured it out in seconds. "Sabrina."

He rolled to the edge of the bed, ink stark in the morning light. It slid like silk over his corded back muscles.

His debt.

"Is it true?" I asked. "Are you indebted? Were you close to getting out of debt?" *Before me*, left unsaid in the lingering air between us.

Grim gripped the mattress, knuckles white. "You don't need to worry about that."

"Who is it? Who owns your debt?"

Before I knew what I was doing, I reached out and feathered my touch along the ink. He tensed, before sinking into it.

Still, silence followed.

I pulled my hand back.

"Fine." I stood up, walked over to where I'd found my book. I held up the weathered and beaten thing. "Will you tell me what this is, then?"

He stared at the book, jaw clenched with some inscrutable emotion. After what felt like an eternity, he spoke. "What does it look like?"

It *looked* like Grim had been pining. But that couldn't be right.

He was *Grim*.

I set it down. "Is it true I'm the reason? That you were almost free, until me?"

He stood up, and for a moment I thought he would come to me, tell me everything, put a hatchet to the distance between us.

Instead he reached for his pants, sliding them over his hips.

"If you'd let me die, everything would be fine. Why?" I went to him, grabbing his arm. "Why did you—"

In a flash, Grim pinned me against the wall. "You really

still asking that?" The little flecks of amber in his fathomless black-brown eyes flamed. He leaned close, close enough I could taste the words from his lips. "You know why."

Before my heart had a chance to slam into my ribs, he stepped back.

"You need to change," he said.

"What? No. What I *need* are answers."

"You want to see your family, right?" he asked.

I jerked in surprise. "I didn't— I never said—"

He cut me off with a too gentle touch to my cheek. "Go get dressed."

A quick change, a trip downstairs, and a short car ride later, we sat outside Crowne Hall, the car idling on the cobblestone driveway.

I picked at the fabric of my skirt.

I *did* want to see them. I *was* worried. I didn't know how Grim picked up on that. But...I didn't want to go back.

Pick.

I don't want this to be the end.

Pick.

Grim grabbed my jaw, pulling my gaze to his. "I'll be back. Don't make me drag you out."

My heart skipped.

His thumbs dug gently into my flesh. My lips parted at the heat in his stare, at the soft way he spoke.

"You're mine, Gemma," he said. "I just bought you time."

"You gave me a few pomegranate seeds," I whispered.

A slight smile speared his lips. "Something like that."

Grim didn't leave until I was in the house. Even then, I saw him through the windows, lingering.

I turned and faced Crowne Hall. It was a few days before the anniversary party, so vendors were setting up. I walked past them. In their starchy, white uniforms I felt like I was walking through ghosts.

That was sort of what it felt like now, like going back in time, to a different world. I remember the parties, remember how just a month ago it all revolved around this.

Now?

It was like when I'd seen my mirage on the club floor. This was my life, but it felt like it belonged to someone else.

Every Crowne had their own wing of the house, and once upon a time, we stayed there. We didn't visit.

I walked toward my brother's wing, but paused at the sound of voices coming from my mother's. The voices got clearer the closer I got.

"Mom," Grayson pleaded. "Get out of the closet."

"I don't think I will," she called back, or...slurred. "I rather like it in here. My dresses are the only members of this family that haven't betrayed me."

I entered my mother's ivory-and-gold wing. Grayson held a finger to his forehead, standing outside the frosted doors of my mother's closet. To his left, Story rubbed his back.

"Mom?" I called out.

"Gemma?" Grayson spun, features twisted in shock and...no, that couldn't be right—relief? "Are you back?"

Tansy flung open the door, and all three of us stumbled away so we weren't hit in the face. Her dress room illumined her in pale-white gold. She wore a *wedding dress*, a plush fur coat, and a furry ushanka on her head.

My mother was drunk.

Story and Gray looked stunned. For them, it was probably like seeing Bigfoot. You'd heard about it, but you dismissed it as myth.

"I seem to have run out of champagne," Mom said. "And wine. And cognac. And wine."

She glared at us like we were the problem. She walked toward the other side of the room, toward the wet bar, her foot-long ivory train trailing after her.

"Mom—" Grayson reached for the champagne in her hand, and she smacked him.

I stepped between them. "*Mom*."

"*You*." Tansy looked up at me reproachfully from beneath her lashes. "I don't need help from *you*." Gone was the stoic, regal woman of all the servants' nightmares. In her place was someone I thought belonged only to midnight.

Broken.

Human.

"If someone tries to take my champagne again, you will see why everyone calls me *Führer Tansy*—you think I don't know they call me that. I know you call me that." She spun around the room, raising the bottle high. "I didn't used to be this way." Her eyes watered and she took a huge gulp.

From the bottle.

Then she looked at it, brow furrowing, realizing once again it was empty. Something on her dress caught her attention. She poked a small red stain on her white dress. Wine, most likely. "My dresses have betrayed me."

"Mom, come on." I pulled her to the bed and she fought me off. I shot Grayson a pleading look. A moment later he was behind her, gripping her elbow and pushing her toward the bed.

"Oh, how lovely, just like my wedding." She threw her arms in the air. "Are you going to force me up the aisle like Daddy too?"

But my mom stopped fighting and climbed into bed.

"Thanks," I said. "You can go now."

Grayson blinked, bewildered. "Go?"

I crawled into bed, lying sideways to see her like always. Her cheek pushed into the satin.

"You left me," my mom whispered.

I rubbed her arm, up and down, until her eyes closed. I wasn't sure how long I stayed like that, but the light in the room changed, the shadows grew. Eventually my mother snored, and I sat up.

Grayson and Story were still there, and they stared.

I ignored the questions in their eyes and went to the bathroom. I yanked open drawers, emptied the wicker baskets that held towels.

"What are you doing?" Grayson asked. "What was that?"

I looked at the mess. No pills. *Nothing*.

But they had to be around here somewhere.

I dragged a hand through my hair, looking around the room. The mirror, the now empty drawers, the toilet, the ottoman—I paused, zeroing in on the soft white fabric.

"Seriously, Gemma—" My brother grabbed my arm, and I shoved him away.

I pulled the top off the ottoman and sighed.

Orange bottles littered the inside, piling one on top of another. I fisted as many as I could in my hands, and headed to the toilet.

"How did you know about these pills?" my brother continued. "Are you back? What's going on?"

As the pills dissolve in the toilet water, a realization struck me. I was doing the same thing my mother had done to me. I was holding Grim hostage with the threat of death.

Fuck.

I flushed the toilet.

"Gemma, answer me."

"What the fuck do you think that was, Grayson?" I screamed.

A moment later, a vicious, sticky sob clawed its way out of my throat. I fell to the ground, hands splayed on the marble.

Orange bottles littered the floor.

There were still bottles to empty. There would *always* be bottles to empty.

Another sob.

What the fuck is wrong with me?

STOP FUCKING CRYING.

I couldn't stop. I couldn't fucking stop. This was coming from somewhere too deep to see.

I was sick of being perfect so she'd be happy.

I was sick of it never being enough.

I was so fucking sick of it. Sick of hiding who I was so someone would love me.

My mother's feet were visible on her bed through the bathroom door. Nothing I did would ever make this stop. Just like nothing Grim did could ever help me.

My sobs grew sharp. My breathing too fast. I clawed at the marble, trying to ground myself.

The room was blurring.

"We can help you," Story said. "Whatever he has on you, we can help. You don't have to stay there."

I laughed through my sobbing. An insane, hiccuping sound.

Of course they thought this was about Grim.

A moment later, Grayson snapped. "What are you doing here?"

Black boots obscured my vision. A moment later, Grim bent down. With his knuckle he lifted my chin, eyes to his.

"Ready to go home, Rich Girl?" He smeared the tears away from my cheek.

I nodded.

Grim lifted me into his arms, and I melted into the warm heat of him. His chest sturdy against my cheek. His arms tight on my body.

Grayson stepped in front of him.

This time, when Grim spoke it wasn't threatening or taunting. There was a sober, dark edge to his words. "You don't know what this is," he said. "You never did. You never paid attention to her. So step aside, Grayson."

A moment later, Grim carried me out of Crowne Hall.

FORTY-SIX

GEMMA

Violent sobs had left me, but tears still poured. I couldn't stop them. It was like something had burst in my soul, leaking out of my eyes. Grim carried me back to his room. The Horsemen froze when they saw me, an audible silence corrupting their previous conversation.

The tears wouldn't stop coming. Hot on my cheeks. My chest clawing with something I couldn't describe. Inside the room, Grim set me on the bed. I thought he'd leave, shut the door, and probably question his life choices.

Instead, he sat down next to me, pulling me into his lap.

He wrapped his arms around me, pressing my head to his chest. I don't know how long he sat with me like that, silent, letting me soak his soft shirt with my tears. He dragged his knuckles along my neck, perfectly content.

"I don't know what's wrong with me," I whispered, voice muffled by the soft fabric of his shirt.

"There's nothing wrong with you," he said simply. "You feel."

I lifted my head, skin between my brows tugging as I processed what he said.

He lifted up my chin, swiping away my tears, then bringing the taste of them to his lips. "You see what no one else does. You *feel* what no one else does. The world wants to erase that. Your world, especially."

My shoulders sagged.

Yeah. That's it.

Emotions were always a shameful thing in my home. Having zero control of them? Unthinkable. As a little girl I was called too sensitive, too *much*. I don't remember the exact moment I started hiding.

I peered at Grim.

I didn't understand him. How he could keep secrets from me. How he could lie and rearrange my life, while also being everything I needed.

"Don't you want someone, you know, not broken?" I asked.

Softness creased the corners of his eyes, but not with pity. He stared at me a long time—too long, so I felt like squirming. Then he laughed. *Laughing?* I pushed at his chest to get away, but he gripped my hands.

"You think I'm doing you a favor? I'm not. I'm selfish." I stopped struggling, settling back into him. There was that word again. *Selfish.* Grim's selfish wasn't like my selfish. "I'm so fucking selfish I had a thousand opportunities to let you go, and I didn't. I won't." With both hands he gripped my face, possessive and bruising, eyes searing. "I don't feel. Or, I didn't...until you."

I turned away, unable to compute the sincerity in his eyes. "What if I'm always like this?"

"Good." He dragged my gaze back to his. "When it gets too much, don't hide. Let me help you forget. If I can't, you hurt me."

Hurt me.

The first time we met flashed into me. The strange, aloof boy who'd taken my nails against his neck. Who'd given me a brief taste of peace.

As if remembering the same thing, he placed my hand to his neck. "You hurt me as much as you need."

"I can't—"

"You'd be doing me a favor," he said with a growl that slid into my bones.

"Despite what our history may suggest," I said, "I don't actually want to hurt you."

"Don't be greedy, Gemma." He pressed my nails into his skin. "What are you feeling? I want to feel it too. Put it inside me."

Muscles coiled in his neck, his jaw working with restraint. His eyes throbbed, savage and ravenous.

And because of that I scythed.

He let out a jagged groan as the skin broke. After a tantalizingly long minute, he inhaled, rough and broken, lids hooded, jaw clenched. "*Good* girl."

Good disappeared into something rocky, and I felt the praise abrade my blood.

He pulled me tighter onto his lap and I felt him, hard iron between my thighs. Like everything else about us, I know this is fucked. I *know*. I should probably be in therapy. But the thing was, I'd done that. All it ever did was make me feel even more broken.

"Tell me what you're feeling." It wasn't a request, but a demand.

"I'm...I'm mad."

"More," he demanded instantly.

"I hate how I have to do mental contortions, rip apart pieces of me to be accepted. I want to scream at the world, strangle it until they understand the problem isn't me, it's them."

I dug into his neck, bright pebbles of blood sprouting beneath my nails. At the increased pressure, his cock jolted against mine.

His jaw was taut, eyes rapt.

Hungry.

Doing this, wanting him while pain still scratched my insides, was doing something to me. His cock on my ass, his words on my lips, were a whip on my soul, grazing teeth along the flesh of my heart.

It was like...emotional BDSM.

"You would be distressed, too, bitch," I yelled.

I didn't know who I was talking to.

I didn't know where this anger came from.

It was definitely not for Grim, but his eyes gleamed, urging me on.

"You would be so fucking distressed." I dragged my nails down his neck, four jagged red lines following. "If everyone wanted to pollute the very essence of you just so you would smell like them."

One arm slid around my waist, pulling me tight against him.

"But instead I have to learn how to live with you."

"No, you don't." With his free hand, he lifted my chin. "You're a queen, Gemma."

The earnestness in the black depths of his eyes was disarming. *Queen.* I'd heard some version of that my entire life. But it was never like this. A power behind it, a reverence.

When Grim said it, I felt it.

More than that, I felt like it belonged to me.

He pressed a deep, hungry kiss to my lips. "The world bends to you."

Grim lifted me off him, onto the bed. He got to his knees, fingers coming to the hem of my skirt. There was hunger in his eyes, but his touch was gentle and unpressured. He dragged the skirt off my body, then gently lifted my shirt over my head.

He pushed me back into bed, pulling the blankets up.

It twisted me up. This brutal criminal was treating me like I was made of glass. He sat next to me, back against the headboard, and pulled me to his side.

"Go to sleep, Rich Girl," he said, tracing his fingertips through my hair.

I must have fallen asleep. When I woke, the sky twinkled early-morning iron. I felt leaden, limbs heavy, eyes swollen. The kind of heaviness that came with too much emotion and too little sleep.

Grim was no longer in bed. I sat against the headboard, pulling the silky black sheets with me.

Ready to go home, Rich Girl?

I thought back to Grim's words. *Home.* In a perfect world I would stay here. This *would* be my home.

But everything was so messy.

As long as I was a Crowne, I couldn't just disappear.

Antsy, I hopped out of bed, throwing on one of Grim's black shirts. It came just to my thighs. The house was quiet in the morning, the creak of floorboards beneath my soles the only sound.

"Cutting it real close to the deadline."

I paused at the top of the stairs. That voice sounded familiar. I peeked around the corner and froze.

It was Prince HSOG.

I quickly darted back before anyone saw me.

"I already told you no. I showed up at the Underworld. I gave you what you wanted."

The prince laughed. "As long as you have that tattoo, you jump when I say jump. Unless you want something to happen to her—"

A large thud sounded, like a body had been slammed against the wall.

Prince HSOG laughed. "Is that any way to treat your father?"

Father?

The prince was Grim's *father?*

"If anything happens to her, I'll end you."

"You can end this anytime, Santos. Finish her, or keep your pet and come join me, finally." The sound of shuffling followed, like bodies moving and clothes being straightened. "You have until the fifteenth."

The door opened with a creak, then slammed shut.

Finish her or keep your pet.

I couldn't move. My heart hammered, frozen in place. Even when footfalls sounded on the stairs, I was stuck. The floor had become tar, and I was sinking into it.

Grim stopped short on the top step, looking like a deer in headlights.

"Father?" I said. "He's your *father?*"

FORTY-SEVEN

GRIM

Shit.

Gemma wore one of my black tees, the shirt barely reaching the tops of her thighs, and it was fucking distracting. I liked her in my things. Liked her in my house.

But she'd definitely heard what I said.

Hopefully we could shove it down like all the other shit we buried.

"My shirt looks good on you." I tugged at the fabric, pulling her closer.

She blinked rapidly, mouth open, and swatted my hand away.

"Your shirt looks good?" she repeated. "Are you kidding?" She shook her head, taking a deep breath through her nose. "I don't know why I thought things would be different. Why you would ever tell me the truth."

Her brow caved over blue eyes. She turned to leave.

"Wait." I grabbed her arm. Her eyes bounced from my

hand encircling her bicep, to me, and back. "Fuck." I dropped her, raking the same hand through my hair.

She folded her arms, waiting.

Okay. Guess I'm telling this story.

The hallway was empty. It was quiet in the early morning, the pulsing beat of the club fading into the ever-present hum of the ocean. The guys were out, either at the club, doing business, or doing someone.

"I'm not doing this here." I grabbed her hand, dragging her back to the bedroom.

Right as she came into the room, I turned and shut the door at her back, my hand above her head. I didn't immediately step away, keeping her pinned.

She leaned against the door, neck tilted to see my eyes.

Gemma Crowne was more than beautiful, she was ethereal. Like some lost fairy, but the old-school kind, not Disney shit. The fairies whose beauty made you follow them into another world, trapped forever.

Her lips were a pouty, dusty pink. Her eyes a deep, devouring blue. Whenever she felt, emotion glimmered in them like sunlight dying on the waves. Right now, irritation shimmered in the blue depths, but there was something else there, too, something betrayed by the way she parted her lips, the soft inhale she made.

Fuck.

Even now, her body still gravitated toward mine.

I bent my elbow, arching my head lower, snuffing out the little light between us.

She arched toward me, her hips meeting mine—

I pushed off the door, walking to the other side of the room, putting distance between us. Gemma Crowne was fucking distracting, and I couldn't be distracted for this conversation. I fell into my black velvet wingback.

Gemma stayed where she was, leaning against the door, one leg crossed over the other. She had the longest fucking legs. The way she was angled made my shirt ride up on one side, past her thigh, so I could see her delicate hip bone.

My bite had since faded.

She needs another one.

"Well?" Gemma asked.

"What do you want to know?" I asked, tearing my gaze from her legs.

"Everything?" she said. "Are you in debt? Is it my fault? He's your *father*? What the fuck?"

Questions tripped out of her rapid-fire. I leaned forward, elbows on my knees, and studied the knots in the hardwood.

I thought I could protect her from this.

My need to protect Gemma went beyond saving her from random assholes. I didn't just want to guard her from the world, I wanted to save her from the stained, ugly part of myself.

"I didn't know my father growing up," I said. "I assumed he was one of the many drug addicts or dealers my mother went through. A deadbeat. Then, around sixteen, he showed up. Wanted me in the family business. Wanted someone in the bloodline to inherit."

A bitter-tasting laugh left my lips at the memory. My biological father, standing in the rotted wood doorframe of my childhood home, an ice-white sky behind him. His clothes nicer than anything I'd ever seen, the trailer park at his back.

Like the devil himself.

"Your dad," she repeated, processing. "He's your dad. So you're royalty. A prince."

My face twisted at that. "That's Vander Archeron's world, not mine."

"Vander," she repeated. "I've been calling him HSOG." At my face, she clarified, "Hot and Scary Older Guy..." A sheepish look in her eyes subdued any jealousy about to flare. "But you said he wanted you to inherit—"

"Not whatever fucked European province he came from. His *real* kingdom, the Underworld."

It was a moment before Gemma spoke again. I heard her shifting, pictured her folding and unfolding her arms, one long leg unwrapping and then wrapping over the other.

"That place you took me to?" she finally asked.

The Underworld, the real Underworld, was a hub for society's worst. A place to do deals without scrutiny. Where truces were made and broken. Drugs and money laundering were child's play. There, they got into organ and sex trafficking. Slavery. At the center of it, my father, raking in power and wealth.

I nodded.

Her brow furrowed. "Wouldn't you want that? You already kind of do it."

We used our power to play "Robin Hood," as my father had put it. Though he'd tried, we never set foot into any kind of trafficking. We existed as the boogeymen in bad men's eyes, so everyone in our community could be safe.

My father?

It was only ever about one thing: power. At any cost.

"I told him to fuck off, and he did—for a while. A year passed without seeing him, and I thought he'd fucked off back home."

"But?" she asked.

I dragged a hand down the side of my face. "I told you I killed someone."

The creak of the floorboards. Soft, bare feet padding across the hardwood. Then Gemma took a seat opposite me, on the bed. Eyes wide, waiting, without judgment.

"Sabrina's father was abusive." I stared into her deep blue eyes, focusing on the way they softened, and not the memory I was unearthing. "I took as many hits as I could..."

I touched the half-moon scar on my lip, a memento from the time my stepdad slammed a belt buckle into my face.

Her fingers came to my lip a moment later, feathering the edge of the scar. "That's how you got this?"

I nodded. "It didn't matter, he fucking *wanted* her to bleed. If I left for more than a few hours, I'd come back to blood and bruises." At the horror in her eyes, I quickly added, "Lock offered to take shifts to be in the house when I couldn't, and Raze and Wraith eventually joined in as well..."

Memories of that day came back.

Wraith, Raze, and I had left to pick up dinner. We'd been gone less than an hour. When we got back...

He touched her.

My stepdad was beneath Lock as he hammered into him, punching an already-passed-out body. Lock's entire body was clenched, knuckles white, eyes on fire. As if he wished he could bring him back to life, just to beat him again.

Behind them was Sabrina, her shirt torn.

He fucking touched her.

I dragged my hand down the back of my neck. "I got back one day and Lock was bloody, my stepdad at his feet."

"You said *you* killed someone."

"He was still alive when I got there," I said.

The next parts of the memory were blurry. Raze and

Wraith going to Sabrina, taking her out of the room. Pushing Lock off.

Slamming my boot into my stepdad's head.

Again.

And again.

"Then we heard sirens," I said. "My biological father must have been waiting. Watching. Shit, he probably called the police. Because as the sirens started, he appeared in the doorway and offered a deal."

He wore the same long, dark wool peacoat. His hands were in the pockets, shoulders relaxed, uncaring of the body or the sirens.

I can make this go away, just say the word, Santos.

"I needed his help. And he knew it." I rubbed my brow. "The rest is history. He covered up the murder, in exchange for our servitude. The contract was for five years. Five years doing whatever he asked, no questions. I think he was hoping by the end I'd have either wanted to join him, or he'd have something else to use against me, but it was nearing the end of our contract, and he hadn't succeeded."

"Then I happened," I whispered.

The whisper in her voice pissed me off. I whipped my eyes off the floor, locking with hers.

"You didn't force me into this. I forced you."

Her lips pursed. "I don't understand. Why? Why didn't you just let me drown? Why did you come *back*? You could have walked away—"

Because I couldn't let you go.

I *still* couldn't let go.

"You would have done it again," I said. "But if I took your contract, if I agreed to kill you, you would never do it yourself. And I could keep you." *For a time* lingered stale in the morning air.

Gemma stood off the bed, walking to the other side of the room. She paused, staring at the door for a good minute, then quickly turned around and closed the distance, stopping at my feet.

"Why didn't you just not tell him? It's not like I would have told anyone."

The day after I saved Gemma, we were scheduled to meet. He was smiling when we came in. I didn't know how he knew, but he did.

For as long as you wear that mark, you're mine.

"I could lie and say I didn't have a choice, but...I did. I chose to keep you." Her lips parted, eyes wide. "He extended our servitude until I finished our contract."

And every day Gemma's contract went unfinished was another she was stuck with me.

"So tell him it's finished," she said.

I laughed. "Kinda hard when you're walking around breathing."

Gemma's expression froze mid-movement, breath stalling in her chest.

"Breathe," I said.

She blinked and released the breath she was holding. "So he knows? He knows what I asked you?"

I had so many opportunities to get out of it. I could have lied about what the ink meant, could have crossed it off my chest and pushed Gemma out of my life.

But the ugly, fucked truth was as long as I was tied to my father, Gemma was tied to me.

"If you'd let me die, you would be free." My eyes flashed to hers in warning, but she continued. "If I died, everything would go away. Your dad wouldn't be able to force you into working for him. You wouldn't be on magazines. People wouldn't be trying to attack you. Your life wouldn't be falling apart—"

I reached up, gripping her face between my palms. "You are the *only* reason I'm living."

Her lush pink lips parted. For a moment it was just this, her face in my hands, sweet puffs of air leaving her lips. When she spoke, it was with the same velvety softness now coating the air.

"Are you going to die? Everything you've built will crumble."

"Why do you care?" I bruised my grip against her cheeks, pulling her closer.

Do you love me or something?

She'd said nothing when I asked her, and the silence had grown into thick, spiky barbs in my chest. I never thought I'd be like this. I never thought I *could* be like this, my sanity hanging by a thread over what a girl felt for me. I was pathetic with my need.

I searched her eyes. "Why does this bother you?"

"You want me to say I love you?" She tried to push me off and I stood up, towering over her, sliding one hand to grip the back of her neck. "You already own everything. Have already *taken* everything. Do you really need that too?"

I dug my grip into her flesh, the sound that left me not quite human. "Yes."

She dragged her bottom lip between her teeth, brow cinched. "If I tell you that, you'll keep it like you've kept everything else. You won't ever say it back."

"You're right, I won't." Hurt collapsed her features, but I continued. "Because I don't just love you, Gemma. You live in my bones, in my marrow." I dragged her down with me into the chair. "A thousand years from now when my bones have dissolved into the soil, when I'm nothing but dust and ashes, the earth will still feed on my love for you."

Her lips parted, no sound came out.

I traced my fingers along the mark at her neck. "You've only been inked on my flesh for five years. You've been inked on my heart since the day I met you." Before she could second-guess me, I crushed my lips against her mouth.

"But—" She tore her lips from mine on a gasp. "—your father. What are we going to do?"

"I'll give him what he wants." I went to her neck, sucking and biting.

"But...but he wants *you*—"

"Gemma." I tangled my hand in her hair, holding her head still, waiting for her thoughts to quiet and her cheeks to flush. "Get to your knees."

She dropped without a second thought, sliding between my open thighs. Her simple, easy obedience shot straight to my cock. *Fuck*. She was fucking made for me. I massaged my grip in her hair, moving her skull around until soft little sighs left her mouth. Then I dragged her head back so our eyes met.

"You don't worry about this. *I* take care of *you*." A cute wrinkle formed between her brows. I tugged at her hair, quieting those thoughts. "Say it."

"You take care of me, Grim."

FORTY-EIGHT

GEMMA

I take care of you.

I tossed in bed, rolling from one side to the other, sheets getting annoyingly tangled between my ankles. He'd left to go tell the Horsemen the plan. His *stupid* plan. When Grim kissed me, it felt like a funeral.

A thousand years from now when my bones have dissolved into the soil—

With a frustrated sigh, I sat up, throwing the covers off. The night air was chilly with winter, and goose bumps pricked my bare legs. The kind of cold that lives in the cracks and secrets of antique houses. No furnace could ever compete.

When I'm nothing but dust and ashes, the earth will still feed on my love for you.

Death.

That was the one consistency between Grim and me. When we first collided, in tears and blood. When I tried to kill myself and he became my reaper. The bodies piled like fucked-up bouquets between us.

A cold, blue morning shone through the window, bright yet dewy with night. I didn't want that to be the only thing we shared.

I wanted a future.

Life.

I hopped out of bed, not bothering to change, and went downstairs. The hardwood floor was gelid beneath my bare feet. This couldn't happen. I wouldn't *let* it happen. We couldn't have gotten this close. That was—

"Bullshit!" I came to a stuttering halt just outside the kitchen. That sounded like Lock. I pressed a palm against the scratchy, antique wallpaper, listening.

"We didn't go through all this just for you to play fucking martyr at the end," Lock continued.

"You act like you forced us into this," Raze said. "We're just as invested in this as you. The beginning might be fucked, but we built this together. People depend on us."

"That's what I'm trying to help," Grim said.

"Feels lazy," Wraith said, apathetic.

"We don't have a fucking choice," Grim said, voice sandpaper. "He's not going to leave us alone. If we don't give him what he wants, he'll force it. He'll come for Gemma. Or Zabby."

Silence.

The sound of a chair squeaking on the marble, like someone getting up.

"It's the only way—"

I walked into the kitchen, cutting Grim off. "Let's fucking kill him." I was going on zero sleep, my hair needed a comb, and I wore an old shirt of Grim's. I must have seemed unhinged, but this was the most certain I'd been of anything.

Lock blinked. "Damn, princess."

I met Grim's stare across the kitchen. He leaned against the wall, a mixture of emotions shadowing his features as he studied me. Surprise in his parted lips, concern in his cinched brow. Raze sat at the kitchen table next to Wraith, who ate cereal with a book open. A single chair was shoved away from the table. Lock leaned against the fridge.

"I mean, it's kind of what you guys *do*," I said. "I don't know why—"

"You don't think we've thought of that?" Grim closed the distance between us until I had to crane my neck to meet his gaze. "He's never alone, always surrounded by ten to twenty plainclothes guards. He's always one step ahead." He stroked his hand down my cheek.

I ached with the softness of his touch, leaning into it.

"This is the only way," he said.

Always surrounded. Never alone.

Except...an idea began to form.

"The party tomorrow," I said, stepping back from his touch. His hand lingered a moment in the air, before dropping to his side. "The big Crowne anniversary party culminates in the hedge maze. My mom will make everyone go through, but he can't take ten people into a maze."

They shared a look.

"We can isolate him," I said, telling myself their silence meant interest. "He won't expect it. You can pretend that you're giving in. He'll think he's won."

I found Grim, pleading with my eyes.

Grim stared back at me, brows drawn, features unreadable.

"If so many people are in the maze, won't a murder be obvious?" Raze drawled.

"The maze is bigger than a football field. My mom will outline the quickest way to the center, so that no one *actually* has to use their brain. Grim, while you make him think he's won, you can lead him in a different direction. I know that maze by heart. This time, *we'll* be one step ahead of him."

The room fell silent. Nerves twitched up and down my spine. They *had* to listen.

Lock quirked a brow. "Us at your pretty little ball?"

Raze rubbed his jaw. "It's not a bad idea."

I exhaled a breath I didn't realize I was holding. They were going to do it. There was *hope*.

"Better than your bullshit idea," Lock said, looking at Grim.

Grim stepped back to me. He slid his hands to me, fingers digging the back of my neck, thumbs at my jaw. "I won't risk you."

The kitchen dissolved until it was just me and Grim, that ache in his eyes, and the deep piercing fear in my heart.

"We have to try." I gripped his wrists. "We're too close."

His eyes searched mine, back and forth, looking for something that I hoped he found.

After an agonizingly long minute, Grim spoke. "You won't be part of it. You tell us the way and then you stay the fuck away. Deal?"

I smiled. "Deal."

FORTY-NINE

GEMMA

Grim and I stayed awake through the night and into the next day. Thick, tumorous clouds now blanketed the horizon, so nothing changed as day faded into night. The sky was eerily black.

Grim held me against his chest, our bodies facing the black sky. All day we hadn't left the bed.

He touched me lazily, tracing paths along my flesh. A line from my hip to my lower stomach, from my belly button to the space between my breasts. If I fell asleep, I woke up to him inside me, whispering hot, Spanish words against my flesh.

I almost forgot what we had to do, pretend we were normal. We could be a couple who argued about who ate the last Pringle or something. Not what we *were*.

As we lay in bed all day, I learned about him, asking a thousand and one questions, desperate to know everything about him. He was allergic to cinnamon, which made enjoying mole difficult. His favorite junk food was vanilla Oreos. And deeper things, too, like how he missed his mom, even though he still resented her for making his life what it was. That he used to wish he knew his father, until Vander showed up.

I felt the proverbial strike of midnight inside me, the illicit sanctuary we'd built crumbling. Soon we'd have to go back to my world. But Grim stroked up and down my arm, along the curve of my hip. No urgency in his movements.

"Tell me the plan for tonight again," he said.

"We start by pretending like everything is normal," I said. "But you'll be with me, he'll see you at the party, and—"

"No," he interrupted. "What happens if something goes wrong?"

At my silence, his hand paused on my stomach. I knew what I was supposed to say. If things went wrong, I would run. But I couldn't, I *wouldn't* run. After another moment, Grim disentangled himself, and I felt the bed dip with his movement.

He came around the bed, and even in the darkness he was deliciously, distractingly naked. The shadows clung to the ridged parts of him, delineating brutally cut muscles.

"I'm not running," I said.

Emotions battled in his eyes as he stared down at me, the angle sharpening his jaw. Then he bent over and kissed my forehead, mouth moving against my flesh. "I got you something. It's in the closet."

His lips lingered on my skin, hand curling around my neck, before stepping off. I watched him throw on a pair of black pajama pants and leave the room. After a moment, I went to the closet to see what he could have possibly gotten me.

Grim never struck me as a physical gift kind of person. His gifts were action and blood. But sitting atop the island counter was a rectangular black box. It was surprisingly heavy, wrapped in a leather box with texture like snakeskin.

Inside sat a simple teardrop pendant among the sea of black velvet, a small handwritten note underneath. The diamond was a unique, smoky red.

I picked up the letter.

This diamond was seeded with my blood, grown just for you. I'd cut my heart out if you asked, but maybe this will work for now. My heart is yours, my blood is yours. Always.

I lifted it back up, smoky red rivulets catching in the light. This was his blood? Goose bumps shuddered on my skin.

The author wore her husband's petrified heart as a necklace.

It meant more to me than all the diamonds and jewels men had gifted me. This was something I'd told Grim once, years ago and never again. Yet he'd remembered.

I gingerly placed it back in the box to get dressed. It still shocked me how prepared he was, how similar this was to my closet at Crowne Hall.

I dragged my fingers through rows of pink, the fabric cascading off my fingertips like a waterfall. This was what Gemma Crowne was supposed to wear.

I pulled out a black dress. The front dripped down to my navel, exposing the sides of my breasts. It fit like snakeskin and shone like black scales. For a finishing touch, I put on the necklace. The red diamond teardrop fell right between my breasts.

I gave myself a final once-over in the mirror.

Sexy. Gothic. Intimidating. Not something *America's Princess* should wear. Something *I* would wear.

Grim and the Horsemen were already downstairs. They talked about something I couldn't hear. Raze shoved Lock and then they laughed. They looked sinful in their black tuxedos. Illicit and expensive. There was something dangerous to it, different from all the black suits and tuxes I'd grown up with. An undercurrent of power rippled, like they were escaped demons and the fabric barely contained their true nature.

My foot hit the steps and Grim spun at the creak, eyes locked on me even as the Horsemen continued their conversation. The look in his eyes could sear the clothes off my body.

The moment my foot touched the bottom floor, Grim snaked his arm around my hip and dragged me into a rough, consuming kiss.

When he pulled back, my body and mind still swirled with him. My hands on his chest, I stared at the silky black fabric, dazed. Dizzy. Couldn't think. He squeezed my hip, as if trying to drag me back into the present. I curled my fingers into the silky black fabric on his chest and he lifted the necklace at my neck. Playing with it.

I think I heard someone say to *get a room*, but I could barely focus.

"Are we doing this shit or are you going to spend the night eye-fucking?" Lock asked.

Grim released the pendant, soothing it against my skin, palm lingering on my chest. Together, we walked down to the garage. Grim held the front door open for me as the others got into the back. I caught their gazes in the rearview, the first time I'd been in the car slamming into me.

Grim grabbed my hand, dragging it into his lap.

We arrived two hours past the party's start time. Spotlights lit up the sky. A red carpet that led around the house to the garden had been draped over the cobblestone. Paparazzi lingered behind velvet ropes.

"Okay," I said as Grim maneuvered past the valet, into a more clandestine area. "Wraith and Raze, you will already be in the maze by the time he enters. Once he enters, Grim and Lock will follow close behind. The way to get to the right location—"

"Left, right, left, left, right," Lock said, yawning. "We know, princess."

I worked my mouth.

It was less that they were ignoring the potential consequences of what we were doing, and more that they were okay with it. Okay with their life crumbling. With dying.

For me.

We sneaked past the paparazzi and stopped just before the garden. Nerves shimmered in my blood, but this time not for our plan. Soft laughter and the clattering sounds of a party drifted around the corner. My cage. The world I'd lived in as an idea, not a person. I glanced down at my black dress. This world was like footprints in the snow. It was not that I wanted to go back, but I knew the steps so easily—

Grim dragged me by the back of my neck into a brutal kiss, interrupting my panic spiral. His other hand knotted in my hair, tongue diving into my mouth.

With the hand in my hair, he tugged my face back, angling me to get deeper access to my mouth. When I opened wider, his growl was my praise. He kissed me until I couldn't think. Until I couldn't remember where I was or anything but him and his teasing, torturous tongue. His hand tugged at my hair just enough to make me gasp as his tongue stroked, gentle and punishing. Pain and pleasure swirled into perfect glissando.

I melted into the intoxicating dichotomy.

I stopped trying to hold myself up and let him keep me steady. I melted. Melted into him, into his grip on my neck, the other in my hair, keeping me possessed. Safe.

"Good girl," he praised against my lips when he felt me slacken into his touch, submitting.

A cough sounded.

Everything came rushing back—where we were, what we were doing. The string quartet and low hum of conversation was like water breaking through a dam.

Can't put it off any longer.

Grim untangled his hand from my hair, still gripping the back of my neck. His inky stare searched mine for an answer. Even though this was our only option and not going through with it was the same as condemning him, I knew he would choose that fate if I said I wasn't ready.

I smiled. "Let's go."

FIFTY

GEMMA

Despite the cold, the party was held in the garden. I think my mom saw it as the ultimate power play—control of the elements. My mother also saw the garden at Versailles and thought she could do better. A deeply manicured lawn, exquisitely mowed into horizontal stripes. A cobblestone path, reminiscent of old England, wove through rows and rows of flowers that would bloom in the summer, but were now just frost-blanketed stalks of green. And beyond the center of everything, where the party continued in full force, was the hedge maze.

Swaths of elegantly dressed partygoers streamed into the maze, disappearing behind green-black leaves.

Heat lamps designed like blown-glass hearts were strategically placed to keep guests from freezing. Crystal chandeliers were suspended from bare winter trees with invisible wire. People mingled around a massive stone

sculpture spelling out 200 *Years*. It appeared to be marble and, knowing my mother, it was.

Portraits from the earliest Crowne members up to now lined the edge, creating a makeshift boundary. I stared at my portrait. It must have been rendered off an old photo, because I still had long hair. I stared at my *America's Princess* smile drawn in oil, feeling like I was looking at a stranger.

"We should get into position," Raze said as silence fell like dominoes, heads turning one by one to see Gemma Crowne with the four Horsemen at her back. Across the party, I studied people whose opinion had once meant so much to me. Blaire and Kennedy watched, brows furrowed. Grayson and Story stared, concern etching their eyes. The glitterati stared with a hunger reserved only for scandal.

I paused at the center, where my mother stared back, ice in her eyes. And in that moment I felt a weight lift from my shoulders.

I didn't care.

I didn't care what she thought. I didn't care what the world would post on social media. It was like I could see the effigy they'd raised of me, the object they used for jealousy or hate. For so long I'd been hostage to another's perception because I didn't know who I was and I definitely didn't have confidence to stand in it. Now I could easily light that effigy on fire.

It had nothing to do with me.

I scanned the crowd, this time ignoring the faces staring back at me. Where was Vander?

"I don't see him," I said.

What if he wasn't here?

Then all of it would be for nothing—

"Gemma."

Before I could think, Grim gripped my face and crushed his lips against mine. In the back of my mind, a small voice reminded me where we were. Everyone was watching. If they'd had doubts before, those were in cinders.

Any thought was quickly burned away by the hunger in his lips. His thumbs dug into my cheekbones, lips hurried, breath fast, all the fear Grim refused to let himself feel bleeding into my lips.

He pulled back too soon, still holding my face. I was dazed, lips buzzing. The space between us filled with some kind of magic.

"Time to go find dear old Dad and let him think he's won," Grim said. "Stay here," he added, voice soothing, rubbing circles with his thumb against my cheek. "I'll find you after."

With that, he and the rest of the Horsemen disappeared from view. I entered the party, trying not to think about where they were, what they were doing. For hopefully the last time, I put on my Gemma Crowne smile, and I pretended.

I grabbed a flute of bubbly gold champagne and I mingled. I laughed at jokes. I asked how *so-and-so* was doing. No one brought up Grim. If our world was good at anything, it was ignoring the elephant in the room.

My gaze drifted toward the hedge maze. Lanterns flickered along the edge of the maze, ending at the leafy maw that disappeared into velvet and shadows. Wraith and Raze would be inside it by now—

"Gemma Antionette Crowne."

My name hissed from my mother's lips. There was still a part of me that clung to her opinion. That felt like her unhappiness wasn't just my fault; it was my burden.

I sucked in a deep breath and turned. "Hey, Mom."

"Do you have any idea what you put me through?" She gripped my hand. "We can still fix this. I've hired crisis PR, the prince still—"

Something in me snapped. Maybe it was the mention of the prince, the man responsible for *all of this*. More likely it was the mention of having PR. A normal mom would be concerned for their daughter. By outward appearances I'd run off with (or been taken by) a criminal.

I tore my hand out of her grip.

"What I put you through?" I asked, voice rising. "The last time you saw me I was dragged across a bloody body, but you're worried about PR?" I paused, needing a breath. "What if I'd died?"

"Not here." She lowered her voice as all around us people turned to look.

Good.

"Who fucking cares?" I yelled, gesturing at the garden. "Why are their opinions more important than my happiness?"

My mother blinked, stunned. But even still, with a wave of disappointment in my gut, I knew that didn't equate to understanding. She was stunned by me standing up for myself, by me being *me* in public, not because the words I'd said affected her.

"I really thought you needed me," I said. "I thought I was saving you. I let that hold me hostage for over a decade. But you're..."

She was fine.

I didn't think that the times I'd found her passed out on the floor were preplanned, that she'd set out to manipulate and control me. But I did think she knew the effect it had on me, and felt a guiltless comfort in the control it gave her.

"It's not about happiness," I continued. "It's not even

about safety. Grayson and Abigail broke your rules and are the happiest of anyone in the family. *Why* are you clinging so hard to this?"

My mother's face dropped. For a split second I saw her. The young girl she was before she was married. Then the expression calcified.

She was smaller than me, closer to Abigail's height, but those lost few inches took nothing away from her steely anger. When she spoke next, she didn't lower her voice, wanting the world to hear.

"You are nothing without this family," she said. "Without us—*without me*—you will deteriorate. You don't *exist* without me."

For the first time, her words don't hurt. I saw it so clearly now. She wasn't talking to me, she was talking to herself. I felt weightless at the realization.

So I laughed.

My mother blinked, features twisting into a hundred different emotions. Then without another word, she spun on her heel and disappeared into the crowd.

I set my empty flute on a passing waiter's tray—

Vander.

I'd found him, far from the hedge maze and across the garden, heading toward the stairs. Fuck. *Fuck. Fuck. Fuck.*

I was walking before I realized, pushing through the crowd to reach him. Grim's voice echoed in my head, telling me to stay put. But I had to do *something*. I couldn't just let him leave.

I got to him as he neared the top step. I reached for his arm from the bottom, stopping him.

"Leaving so soon?"

FIFTY-ONE

GEMMA

"Miss Crowne." His lips curved leonine, eyes on my hand wrapped around his. "I wasn't planning on staying long." As much as I wanted to drop my hold at his lecherous gaze, I knew it was leverage.

So I stepped closer, turning my voice into something sultry. "Without visiting the maze?"

"I got what I wanted. My son will finally accept his role."

So Grim had at least found him then... Something must have gone awry, because he clearly wasn't in the maze.

"You sure? I have questions." I trailed my hand up his arm, adding, "But not here. Somewhere...private."

His voice lowered into a sickening sound. "Lead the way."

Something in his eyes nearly stopped me. My gut screamed a warning. But I couldn't just let him go. Not when we were so close.

So I ignored it, enclosing his arm in mine, leading him away from the party, toward the maze.

"Why did you come into my world?"

"You have what I want." I glanced at him, and he added, "My son."

We were nearing the entrance of the hedge maze. I steered him so he couldn't see Grim and Lock waiting on the periphery. As I turned Vander away, I caught Grim's gaze burning with fear and fury.

"I thought you wanted me," I fake pouted. "You made my mom think you wanted to marry me."

"Can't I kill two birds with one stone?"

We arrived near the hedge's arched, dark leaf entrance. Subtle, glowing orbs floated fae-like inside. I felt my ability to pretend slipping.

"I know your type," I said. "You need to collect and own. You wanted to collect a shiny Gemma Crowne. You don't care about Grim."

He laughed. "I never said I did. This is his birthright."

"Why won't you just let them go?"

"I let them go. *You're* the reason they stayed. Why won't *you* let them go?"

Anger bubbled up, and I unraveled my arm from his. I could practically picture my mother saying the exact same thing. It was my birthright to be a Crowne, nothing else mattered.

"You're disgusting," I said.

Another laugh. "Couldn't even keep the mask up long enough to get me in the maze? You *have* changed."

Dread drenched my veins cold. Everything blurred with adrenaline. My heartbeat pounded painfully in my head. *No.* I refused to believe it.

"What?" I said. "What do you mean—"

Pop.

The first pop came and lingered, and for a moment I thought I'd imagined it.

Then they came rapid-fire.

Pop. Pop. Pop—

I was on my back with a thud that took my breath away before the third *pop*, pressed into the sand—Grim.

Sharp screams shattered around us like broken glass. Glitterati rushed out of the maze, Wraith and Raze not long behind them, shooting behind them at an unseen enemy. The prince looked down at Grim, then at the hedge maze, and without another word, disappeared into the chaos.

No.

No.

I watched him disappear into the glitterati stampede.

"Gemma." Grim snatched my chin. Eyes roaming my body, my neck, looking for any sign of injury. I tried to focus through all the screams and buzzing in my chest to remember his clenched jaw, his flared nostrils, and the deep, aching *fear* and vicious rage in his dark eyes.

His shoulders visibly relaxed when he found me intact.

Grim shouted furious orders, but I couldn't quite catch them. I only *saw* things. Like the way the muscle in his jaw flexed with each order.

Or how his biceps caged my head.

How his eyes kept darting back to me, brow furrowed.

This close I saw the shadow sharpening his jaw, the softness on his lips, the scar on his upper lip.

The *pops* became few and far between, ending with one that sounded far away.

Grim still pressed me deep into the sand, and I felt warm. Safe. He lifted up a little bit, giving me air, and I saw his shoulder had darkened with something wet.

I touched his shoulder and he grimaced. My hand came away painted red.

"You're hurt," I said.

"Wraith!" Grim yelled, ignoring me, and the smoke in his voice choked. Footsteps muted by the sand landed next to my head.

"We got most of them," Wraith said, eyes on the horizon.

"He's hurt," I said. Desperation clawed at my throat.

"Did you go and get yourself shot?" Wraith bent down, his brow furrowing.

"It's nothing. Who the fuck was it?"

I thought to what Vander had said.

"He knew," I said, despair twisting my voice into something foreign. "He figured it out."

"Gemma?" Grayson's frantic voice cut through the air. "Gemma, where are you?" Moments later, he landed next to the Horsemen. "Gemma, are you okay? Is she okay?"

"I'm fine. Grim is the one who is hurt." I pushed gently at Grim, trying to free myself. "He needs a doctor."

Grim seemed reluctant to let me go, still holding me in that fierce, protective grip. But as I pushed, he slowly released. He climbed off me and held out a hand, still scanning the horizon, his entire body tense, as if waiting for a threat.

I took his hand and hopped to my feet.

Wraith, Lock, and Raze made a wall blocking the hedge's entrance. My brother stood to the side, worry storming in his blue eyes. They all seemed fine. Tense, but not hurt.

I waited for Grayson to yell, to be (rightfully) mad at the danger I'd put his family in, to demand I move back in.

"How many bodies are back there?" Grayson asked, turning his attention to the Horsemen.

Lock rubbed the back of his neck. "I got two."

"I got three," Raze said.

"Bullshit—" Lock started.

"Five," Wraith said, cutting them off.

Grayson nodded slowly, thinking. "I can't stop anyone at the party from calling the police."

"Buy us an hour and it won't be a problem," Wraith said. "We'll clean up and you can say it was fireworks gone bad."

Grayson nodded. "I can do that."

"Grim needs to see a doctor!" I blurted. The urgency bubbled up inside me. Grim was *shot*. How could they sit and discuss cleanup like trying to coordinate a carpool?

Everyone turned to him, and Grim shook his head. "It was through and through."

"Okay, well, I'll leave you to it..." Grayson's gaze lingered on mine.

"Why are you doing this?" I asked as he was about to leave. "Why are you helping them?"

"I'm not doing this for him. I'm doing it for *you*, Gemma." He paused. "Story wanted me to tell you that you still have to be Sonnet's godmother. Whatever happens."

With that, Grayson left.

Realization settled heavy in my blood. This was our last chance, and we *blew* it.

"We can still go and catch him," I said.

Grim turned to the Horsemen. "One hour."

"Stop fucking ignoring me!" My scream pierced the night. "We can't just let him go!"

In response, Grim dragged me to him, pinning me against his chest even with a bullet wound.

"We have to go," I insisted. "We have to find him."

Grim massaged his hand in my hair, rubbing my scalp, soothing me. He ever so softly pressed at my skull, fingering for bruises. I knew he was trying to calm me, take my mind off the very real fact that we had *lost*. Even still, I melted.

Grim looked over my head at the Horsemen, exchanging a silent conversation, and then they left.

We were alone on the beach.

Grim rubbed my back. Gentle. Soothing *me*, even though I wasn't the one with a gunshot.

We have to go.

We have to go.

"You need a doctor," I mumbled against his chest.

Grim pulled back just enough so I could see his eyes, which were a heady mix of fire and ash, like a phoenix rising. Burning. Smoldering. Finality in the dark depths.

This was not Grim, this was the Reaper.

Now I had goose bumps.

Now I couldn't breathe.

When strangers had tried to kill me, I was bored. With that look in Grim's eyes?

Fucking terrified.

Grim gripped the back of my neck, dragging me to him. "I need *you*."

FIFTY-TWO

GEMMA

Grim kissed me rough, desperate, edged. The world narrowed to the reckless space between our mouths, breath stuttering, teeth knocking. He gripped my face like he needed to feel my pulse under his palms.

"You need a doctor," I said as he broke to trail kisses down my neck. "You need—"

His lips found mine again, stifling my protests.

"Please," I gasped against his mouth. "I can't lose you."

Grim pulled back, our foreheads touching. The silence between us throbbed.

"I'm going to fuck you, Gemma," he said. The authority choking his words slid into my veins, every atom of me zinging with the need to let him. But...

"You're hurt."

He dragged my hand to his bicep, pressing my fingers into the wound. "The pain lets me know you're still here." I had a second for that to settle like broken glass in my chest, when his lips found mine again.

He dragged my bottom lip out in a bite, and said against the flesh, "Get on your knees." His hands gripped my shoulder, but he didn't push me down.

He didn't need to.

I dropped to my knees without thought.

Grim exhaled, deep and slow, a quiet rumble of approval vibrating through him. His thumbs circled my shoulders, unhurried. He turned and faced the ocean, ripped off his bloody shirt, throwing it to the sand.

I had a sudden, stark flashback to the very first time.

Grim spun around. "Lie down."

"Wait—"

I broke off at the raw dominance in his features. Grim's expression had settled into something calm and unyielding. He was done playing around. But...I wasn't playing. I grabbed his hand, trying to tug him down.

He stilled.

"At least let me do the work," I said.

Another split second passed, Grim's grip firming just enough to remind me who was actually in charge. Then he let me pull him to his knees. On the sand, I pressed a palm into his chest. He wrapped his hand tight around mine, pulling me with him as he fell to his back.

Wordlessly, I climbed on top of Grim. I hiked my dress up past my hips, spreading my naked thighs on either side of him.

Grim slid his hands up my bare thighs, lids heavy.

"Now this is a fucking sight," he said, voice raspy. He pressed his palm between my thighs, landing hot on my pussy. I inhaled a sharp breath as something between a groan and growl slipped out of him.

I craned my arm, reaching behind to unzip him. His cock sprang free, hot and throbbing on my inner thigh. We didn't need to talk. A spell had been cast. It glittered between us, made the air heavy and hazy.

Silently, Grim took my hand to his bicep again.

The pain lets me know you're still here.

I let him press my hand to the bullet wound, grabbing his cock with the other. He hissed at the combined contact. The oxygen between us ignited in his hungry eyes and set jaw.

The waves shattered at our back. The sand cushioned my knees. Memories collided with the present, crashing into one another like atoms unstable and incandescent, until something new caught fire between us. The blood dripping from his shoulder and pooling black into the sand merged with the first time he stole my life for safekeeping.

With the memory throbbing between us, I slid Grim inside me. Grim's head fell back on a low groan, throat bared. His eyes never left mine, heavy lidded, catching me even from that impossible angle.

I started to move. Testing him inside me. He felt even fuller at this angle. I could barely breathe from it, but it was a good breathlessness. The kind that happened when you laughed too hard or ran too fast. Everything faded. There was no failed plan; there were no bodies to clean up. It all disappeared into the pull of being totally fucking consumed.

I felt his stare all the way in my throat as I dug my hands into his chest, rolling my hips.

The past crashed around us with each thrust. His dark eyes, our hot breaths, the groans, the strain in his body built a melody. Notes I'd heard before, rearranged but unchanged.

Could he feel it too? The way this moment shattered into five years ago. How it was always going to be this. Inevitable.

"It was always you," he said, voice raspy and hoarse. "It could never be anyone *but* you." He gripped my hips, and I was no longer riding him. I might be on top, but he was in control. Thrusting into me deep and frenzied.

"I will always find you," he grunted. "I will follow you into the afterlife. I won't drink from the river so I never forget you."

Something wild overcame me. Spurred by the frantic way he plundered me, and his deep, aching words. By his cock spearing me with each confession, like he was trying to bury the truth inside me.

I bent over his arm, licking the blood off him. No sooner had my tongue hit his flesh than Grim knotted his hand in my hair, pulling me into a rough kiss. Our lips collided, bloody.

He kissed me as I rode him, thrust his tongue into my mouth. Breaking only to drag his tongue along my flesh. Licking from the hollow between my collarbones, up my neck, swirling around my ear before biting the lobe. He whispered hot words I barely caught, consumed by the fire burning between us.

My abdomen contracted with unreleased rapture. My thighs shook, my fingers dug into his chest. I was going to come. It was building inside me, as inevitable as this night. Grim anchored me against him, gripping my hips.

Grim's grip flexed, fingers bruising my hip bone. "Not yet."

"Please," I begged. The soft, dulcet edges of pleasure were transforming into something sharp and broken. The heat of the flames no longer licked my skin, they threatened to consume.

"No," he said, simple but firm. I let out a choked sound, somewhere between a groan and scream. I sawed my nails into his chest, mindless with need. His hand came to my back, dragging up and down my spine. The soothing motion only added to the ache.

"I love you," I said, but my voice came out a broken, strangled plea.

"Fuck." His voice deepened into something jagged. "Say it again and you can come."

"I love you," I said, coming apart. "I love you. *I love you.*"

My words came out rushed and breathless, sounding more like *thank you* and *please*. I repeated them like a prayer, like they would anchor me while jagged pleasure cut and tore me apart, limb by limb.

I felt Grim come before I heard his strangled groan. The fullness and throbbing of his cock stretched my pleasure into something rough and barbed. I went blind with it. The stars above blended with the sand below, until there was nothing but Grim and this perfect, beautiful feeling.

"In case it wasn't obvious," Grim said, knotting his hand in my hair, yanking me up against his lips. "I love you." He kissed me, vicious and hurried, biting lips and knocking teeth. "I will only ever love you."

He released me and I fell to his chest, breathing hot into his skin, legs jelly—spent.

Time passed in the crashing of the waves, the moon changing positions in the sky. The blood on his arm still messy, but somewhat dried. Eventually I climbed off him, and lay next to the Reaper in the sand, my flesh hot against his, one leg wrapped across his thigh. Hot and sweaty but for the chilly, salty beach whispering on my bare flesh.

Waves continued to count time, crashing at our feet like they had five years ago, the same ocean, now totally different water. That felt right. Because that was me and Grim. Immutable and ephemeral.

"What now?" I whispered.

"Hmm?" He stroked my hair like we had all the time in the world.

I lifted my head on his chest, catching his eyes. "What do we do now? Our plan failed."

I felt his shrug. "I'll figure it out. If I have to work for him, I will. Until I can find a way to get out."

His past had already foreseen that future. Vander had blackmailed him into this, and whatever he made Grim do under this new tenure would mean Grim would be stuck. Forever.

"I can't be the one who ruins your life," I said. "I can't do it."

"I will gladly stand in the ashes of my world for you. I'm not losing you, Gemma," he growled. "It took me ten years to get you."

He'd never let me go. He never *would* let me go. But it was destroying him. I sat up next to him, looking out at the ocean. A finality slid calm and cool into my veins. I started this one way, I could end it the same.

"Maybe you don't have to," I said. "Maybe there's another way."

Five years ago, Grim saved me in exchange for his freedom. That contract bound our lives, but it could also mean freedom. He arched a brow, waiting for me to explain.

The prince wasn't supposed to kill the princess, and the

princess wasn't supposed to wait for his knife. Maybe that was why our story got so twisted.

We were never meant to be a happily ever after. We were always a tragedy.

Resolved, I turned back to him. "Kill me."

FIFTY-THREE

AMERICA'S PRINCESS *FOUND DEAD*

Heiress Gemma Crowne Dead Hours After Mysterious Shoot-Out

By Maren Hollis, Senior Staff Writer

Crowne Point's elite were left stunned this Valentine's Day by the sudden death of Gemma Crowne, the eldest daughter of the influential Crowne family, also known as America's Princess.

At approximately 9:47 p.m., fireworks the Crowne family had purchased for their party went off unexpectedly. Witnesses describe the experience as "harrowing" with another saying "I thought I was going to die." By the time the dust had settled, Gemma Crowne was found dead.

Sources close to the household describe "shock" and "confusion" after the heiress allegedly disappeared for several hours before being found. Officials have not released a cause of death, but overdose is suspected.

Grayson Crowne, CEO of Crowne Industries and Gemma's brother, had this to say.

"There is no scandal or conspiracy here, just simply a truth that my family has long tried to hide. My sister was always troubled. She was addicted to drugs and dangerous men. I think it's clear by the company she kept toward the end of her life that she was spiraling somewhere we couldn't bring her back from. She ended her life, but for us, it had been over for years. The only person responsible for Gemma's death is Gemma. We ask for privacy and respect during this time."

The beloved socialite had largely withdrawn from public view in recent weeks. Rumors of a secret relationship had surfaced, though sources close to the family insist such claims are "unfounded" and "deeply inappropriate at a time like this."

A private memorial will be held later this month at the historic Crowne Estate Chapel. Attendance is by invitation only.

The Crowne Point Times *will continue to follow the story.*

FIFTY-FOUR

GRIM

The Crowne family graveyard was designed to reflect status even in death. Moss carpeted stone mausoleums and leaves dripped from overgrown trees, blanketing the cemetery in shadow. The ground was a mix of sand and flora—creeping thyme, mossy clover. The weathered stone and trees made it appear from another time. It was easy to fade into the background.

Yards away, a black casket suspended over an open grave. More than family were in attendance for Gemma Crowne's funeral. All the world's rich and privileged had come to mourn, dressed for tabloids that would print their solemn faces.

A body slipped next to me. I knew who it was before he spoke.

"Tragic," Vander said.

I glanced at him out of the corner of my eye, his hands tucked into a wool peacoat, looking at the funeral.

"Tragic," he repeated, "and convenient."

"Not so convenient for her, or her family," I said, focusing back on the funeral. Grayson threw dirt on the casket. Solemn silence shifted as attendees started to whisper about things like valet and brunch.

"Seems so to me. Right after you tried to kill me—I know that was the plan, and it failed, and right after it failed, she's dead."

I rubbed my jaw, working out the muscle.

"You're also remarkably well composed," he continued. "The girl you threw your life away for is dead, and yet...you seem fine."

"Gemma Crowne is dead," I said, not giving in to the bait. "That was the deal. You can't weasel your way out of it with conspiracy."

He laughed. "If you think you'll get to walk away so easily, you're forgetting you have other family—"

I spun, cutting him off. "Yeah, I know. You've kept me hostage for a decade with that threat. So let me give you one. If you ever go through with it, know your life is over."

His lips twisted in amusement. "You tried killing me once. You failed."

I shook my head, taking another step closer, until he could feel the truth of what I said.

"I don't want you dead," I said. "I want you alive and watching as I dismantle everything you've ever built, brick by brick. If I have to live in the world you forced on me, know I will rip your existence out of it. I will follow you from town to town, from this life into the next. As long as I live, you'll never know peace. I might not be able to kill you, but I won't stop until you're forgotten. Powerless."

Vander's eyes narrowed, as if trying to read the lie in mine. He wouldn't find it. I had a feeling he wouldn't let me go so easily, so I'd thought about it all week. I'd played out certain scenarios and consequences in my mind.

I couldn't control Vander. I didn't have enough power yet to kill him. But I could strap dynamite to my chest and take him down with me.

"Walk one step into my town and I'll assume I have my answer," I said, echoing the threat he'd given me before Valentine's Day.

Vander responded with a tight smile that didn't meet his eyes. Without another word, he left. I watched him disappear through curtains of weeping foliage.

I knew this wasn't over. At some point in time Vander would come back. But for now, we were safe.

Still, my back was tight with nerves as I turned again to the funeral. The crowd had nearly cleared. The only people who remained were immediate family. I couldn't shake the tension.

Uncharacteristically, I pulled out a cigarette and lit it, just as it was yanked out of my hand.

"Don't smoke." Gemma smiled at me, taking a drag from the cigarette. "You taste better."

FIFTY-FIVE

GEMMA
One Week Before

"Kill me," I said.

Grim stared back at me, the look in his eyes a mix of anger and irritation. An insanely inappropriately timed thought came to mind. His face reminded me of that one *SpongeBob* episode.

How many times do we have to teach you this lesson, old man?

I nearly laughed, but instead put a hand to his heart, calming him. "*Gemma Crowne* has to die. My family is at risk. *Your* family is at risk. And as long as I live, you'll never be free."

"Gemma—"

"But," I interrupted. "Just because Gemma *Crowne* has to die doesn't mean I do."

Suspicion narrowed his eyes, but something else glimmered in the dark depths—hope. He rose up next to me, hands planted in sand silver with moonlight.

"What are you thinking, Rich Girl?" He gripped my chin between his thumb and forefinger. "Say it clearly."

"We fake my death."

He rubbed circles in my chin with his thumbs, eyes unreadable. Our breathing created wispy tendrils of hot-white smoke in the cold. Beyond Grim, the hedge maze towered, golden lanterns flickering against the black-green leaves.

After a moment he released my chin. "You can't go back from this."

"I don't *want* to go back," I said, grabbing his hand. "I want to go forward."

The pure, concentrated devotion in his eyes nearly floored me. He shook his head, exhaling, and turned toward the ocean.

"If I were a better man, I'd try to talk you out of this," he said, rubbing his forehead, eyes still on the ocean, moon reflecting broken shards.

I grabbed his face between my palms, turning him back to me. I leaned forward on a smile I couldn't contain, and kissed him.

"Good thing you're not a better man," I said against his lips.

When I pulled back, some of the heaviness cloaking Grim had dissipated. A soft smile curved uneven on his lips.

"It's too cold for you," he said, rubbing the goose bumps off my arms. "And we have a death to fake." He reached for his shirt, discarded in the sand.

"You're the one who's shirtless," I said, but let him drape the black fabric over my arms.

Grim stood and held his hand out for me. I clasped it

and he dragged me up off the sand, into his arms. He wrapped one arm around my back, the other caressing my cheek before sliding into my hair.

I felt safe. Protected.

He inhaled, eyes searching my face for something. Then he crushed his lips against mine. His palm cradling my face, his hand on my back pushing me closer. He kissed me with a devotion I felt in my bones.

When he pulled back, I was dizzy. Our breaths heated the small space between our heads.

"I don't actually know *how* to fake a death," I admitted.

He dragged his thumb across my lips, a knowing smile on his face, as if he knew something I didn't.

"It's been almost an hour," he said, and stepped back, but not before encircling my hand in his. "The guys should be finished cleaning."

Still, we went into the maze to double-check. Grim's hand in mine was a welcome heat in the cold. The maze was spotless, the only sign that something might have gone awry the occasional protruding leaf.

"Is it done?" Grayson's voice carried into the hedge maze. My hand still in Grim's, we walked back out to find my brother.

My brother raked his hands through his rose gold hair, his dress shirt unbuttoned at the top. When he saw us, he continued.

"I can't hold them off any longer. Story is distracting them long enough for me to warn you."

"The place is clean," Grim said. "No one will ever know."

Grayson visibly relaxed. "Okay." He exhaled. "Good. Well..." He glanced between Grim and me warily, before landing back on Grim. "You should still get going."

"We will," he said. "But first, I'm calling in your debt, Crowne."

Grayson turned his attention to me, brows pinched. My lips parted, because I didn't know what Grim was thinking either.

"Gemma wants to die," Grim continued. "We need your help."

Too many emotions flashed through my brother's face—anger, despair, anger again. He opened and closed his fists. Grim knew what he was doing by saying it that way, and he probably did it to get back at me for the way I told him earlier.

I elbowed Grim. "That sounded so fucking dramatic. I don't want to die for real. I want to fake my death. I want to be free, Gray."

Grayson stared at me for a long time, and I could see the words in his eyes. We'd never had a chance to be siblings. We lived in a home where emotions were considered uncouth. The way we bonded had been backstabbing. Abigail and Grayson had got out, and they'd hoped the same for me. Maybe then we could be a real family.

But I was asking for an out.

That future dissolving as quickly as the hope for it came.

On a deep exhale, Grayson turned to Grim. "I don't see what I can do."

"The press," I said, sensing what Grim had in mind. "Tell them I overdosed. Tell them I was troubled. Make them believe it. Give them something juicy—*and believable* —enough that they don't look deeper into my death."

His brow cinched, mouth twisted in a grimace. "I'm not going to say that about you."

I grabbed his hands in mine. "Please. You dissolved my

engagement because you wanted me to be free. Now let me."

The groove in his brow deepened. "This is what you want? Truly?"

For the first time in my life, I knew who I was. I knew what I wanted. I could answer the question that had plagued me ever since Abigail asked it. *What do I want?*

"Yes," I said. "I want this."

He searched my eyes, looking for the lie. When he didn't find it, he released another exhale. "Fine. I'll handle the press. I'll get you out of this world in print, but I don't see how any of this matters if we have nothing to put in a casket."

I released Grayson's hands, stepping back. *Right, that's kind of an important piece of the puzzle.*

"We have a guy that can fake an autopsy," Grim said.

Grayson laughed bitterly. "Of course you do."

After a bit of back-and-forth on what else was expected and what needed to be done in order to kill Gemma Crowne, Grayson left. But before he did, he dragged me into a deep, brotherly hug. The type of sibling affection we'd heretofore never exchanged.

"So what now?" I asked when Grayson was gone, turning to Grim.

Grim grinned. "You finally get your wish, Rich Girl."

FIFTY-SIX

GEMMA
One Week Before

Grim and I returned to the Wharf. He held my hand, taking me upstairs, and to his room. He put me into bed, and I protested about his arm again, but he just lifted the sheets to my chin.

"Sleep," he commanded.

So I did. When I woke, the sun was setting again. I rubbed my forehead, limbs heavy with sleep. I'd slept through an entire day. Was I already dead?

"You're late."

I turned at the voice, finding Lock leaning against the doorjamb. He wore a black three-piece suit with a silver chain hanging from lapel to pocket.

"Not this game again," I said, sitting up in bed. The last time Lock had appeared in this room saying something cryptic, I'd ended up in the real Underworld. "What am I late for?"

He grinned, his teeth white and sharp, the piercing in his lip glinting in the dying sun.

"You'll find what you need in the closet." He nodded in the direction, then shut the door.

I stared at the door for a minute. *Wedding?*

I pushed the silky black sheets from my body, feet hitting cold hardwood. Inside the closet hung the most gorgeous, black lace dress, backlit by pale, white gold light.

I slid my touch across the fabric. I was no stranger to expensive dresses, had worn everything from vintage Chanel to Iris van Herpen, so it wasn't its perceived value that had my heart pounding. Those dresses weren't made for me, they'd been draped on me like I was an expensive mannequin.

This dress clung to me like a secret. Black as the ocean the first time Grim took me, it bared my collarbones and shoulders in a soft, deliberate drape. The fabric pooled low across my chest as if gravity itself were complicit. Lace traced my body in sheer, suggestive panels. Lightweight chiffon fell dark and weightless, and a sharp slit opened on the side from ankle to thigh.

I swayed back and forth in the mirror, watching the fabric ripple in the air. I'd never worn a dress like this, one that reflected my soul. This wasn't just a dress, it was what Persephone would have worn when she reigned in the underworld, what Psyche did wear to her wedding.

Once again, I was shaken by just how much Grim knew me.

The necklace Grim had given me glinted smoky red between my collarbones, the only color on my body. With a deep inhale, I headed downstairs.

Lock and Raze were waiting for me. Raze was dressed

similarly to Lock, in a dark black suit, but his tie was textured, like velvet and lace.

"All right..." I said, hitting the floor. "What now?"

They exchanged a look, then wordlessly held out their arms. Nonplussed, I encircled my arms in theirs. They led me out the back of the house, across the abandoned pier, and onto the beach.

The sand was silvery under the moonlight. The midnight blue sky was painfully clear, stars sharp and over-bright with winter. Rows of tea lights glimmered, casting a flickering orange glow against the sand. The lights were arranged parallel, leading from where I stood down to... Grim.

Where the tide met the earth, Grim stood, water splashing at the hem of his black pants. He wore a black dress shirt, unbuttoned and folded up to his forearms. Grim was already looking at me, smiling, before I'd realized he was there.

"What is this?" I asked, too nervous to say aloud my hope.

They didn't answer.

I swallowed, because I already knew. This was an aisle for a wedding. That was what the tea lights were for. I tried to imagine four scary, reckless criminals spending time lighting hundreds of candles. It did not compute.

"Traditionally the father gives the bride away," I said, trying to ease the nerves glittering inside me.

"But we're not traditional," Raze continued.

"We're not giving you away," Lock said. "We're walking you down this aisle and into the family. You're stuck with us."

Their hands landed on my arm, securing my place inter-locked with them. Then we walked down the makeshift aisle. My breath came shaky, not from nerves, but hope. I'd forced myself into their world with a tattoo. Now they were saying they wanted me here, for real.

A warmth slid into my heart, down into my bones.

Safe.

Beyond the danger that I knew would lurk in this world, I—*my soul*—was safe. These men knew who I was. They had seen all the skeletons in my closet (and had even put a few there) and they still welcomed me.

The sound of the ocean and soft crunch of sand was my wedding march. I thought back to Psyche, arrayed in funeral attire for her wedding. Escorted to fate, finding freedom in death.

Gemma Crowne was dead, but I was just getting started.

I stopped before Grim. Wraith stood next to him, in the middle of us both. Was he officiating? I tried picturing his tattooed, monstrous face asking me to take my husband. Lock released me and stepped to Grim's side. Raze joined him.

"Hey, Rich Girl," he said softly.

"Hi," I said. I bit my lip, looking at the makeshift wedding. "What does it mean to marry the king of the damned?"

"Marry?" he asked. He arched a brow, slightly tilting his head in a way that accented the sharp shadow of his jaw.

"This isn't a wedding?" I said, throwing my arms out and gesturing to, well, everything. The dress, the aisle, the fucking officiant.

"You can leave a marriage," Grim clarified.

I sucked in a breath just as Wraith started talking. His speech was different from the usual wedding fare. Darker. Wraith spoke of death and eternity. Of soulmates and things only fate could know. I tried to focus on it, but my attention kept slipping to Grim. He stared at me relentlessly, like a sailor finding land, like a wolf worshipping the moon.

His black shirt was undone, showing our first tattoo.

Wraith stopped speaking and Grim took my hand in his.

"Gemma—"

"I didn't prepare vows," I said, cutting him off. "I didn't know."

A secret smile speared his lips. He released my hands and wrapped his hand around my neck.

"You already said your vows," he said, thumbing my tattoo for emphasis. "Now it's my turn."

I don't remember if I responded. I was stuck in the soft way his voice caught, but still hinted at something dangerous. In his gentle, possessive stroke on my neck paralleled by the hot gleam in his eyes.

I swallowed and simply nodded.

"This tattoo doesn't mean I own you, it means you *own me.* Your safety, your well-being, your *life,* are all mine to keep safe. If you want something, I'll give it to you before you have to ask. You will always have a home here. The Horsemen are your family. They will protect you from anything, even me. You will never be alone."

Grim thumbed my cheek, swiping fugitive tears away. His palm lingered on my face, cradling.

"I was dead until you." With his free hand, Grim took my own and pressed it to his bare chest, against the tattoo. "Now my heart beats inside your chest. I will always be in your debt."

Before I could think, he dragged me in for a devouring kiss. It wasn't hunger fusing our lips together, so much as inevitability, like gravity finally giving in. His mouth claimed mine with the weight of his vows. I felt it everywhere: in my ribs, in the ache behind my eyes, in the place where fear used to live. The world narrowed to breath and heat and the quiet violence of being chosen completely.

Someone coughed.

"I think you're supposed to wait until the end for that," Lock said wryly.

Reluctantly, Grim pulled back, our faces still close.

"Wraith has something to ask you, Barbie," Raze said.

I waited, expecting him to ask if I took Grim as my lawful husband until death do us part—you know, the usual.

"Will you take Grim in death and let life never part you?"

I swallowed. That was so much more intense. My eyes returned to Grim's and his stare caught me like a hook, stripped of everything but me. No command. No demand. Just a depth that made my chest ache.

You have three lives. Your past, your present, and your future. Grim owned my heart in all of them.

I sold my soul to him in my past life.

Died for him in my present.

Hoped to make a life together with him in my future.

Our past swirled between us in watercolor memories. That empty high school room, where we first collided in pain and blood. The warm, July night when I tried to kill myself and Grim stole my life for safekeeping. And now here, alive only in death.

Death had always been a dark root twisted at our ankles, weaving our stories together.

I smiled. "There was never another ending for us."

We kissed, sealing our vows in this life and the next.

FIFTY-SEVEN

GEMMA

Present

"Don't smoke," I said, taking the cigarette from Grim and repeating the words he'd said so many times before. "You taste better."

Grim glanced at me as I took a drag from the cigarette. "I told you to stay home."

"And miss my own funeral?" I batted my lashes at him.

He wasn't amused. "You could have been seen."

"I waited until Vander left. No one is looking anywhere but my casket."

I'd been staying with the Horsemen since my "death." Grim said it wasn't *his* home; it was ours. Zabby had returned. There were no more threats on my life or my family's. The Horsemen were safe and free from HSOG. They didn't have to take any more contracts for him. They could do what they'd always wanted, keep the neighborhood safe.

Grim stared toward the funeral. Only my family were allowed at the end, when my casket would descend into the grave.

"You don't listen, Rich Girl," Grim continued, an unspoken promise of punishment edging his voice and sending a shiver racing down my spine.

I worked my mouth. "I don't know if you can call me that anymore. Maybe dead girl."

"Nah." He wrapped his arm around my waist and dragged me in front of him. "Good girl, maybe, when you behave." His head dropped to my shoulder, cheek to cheek. I sucked in a chilly winter breath. Would I ever get used to having him?

"Your girl?" I asked.

I felt his cheek stretch against mine with a grin. "Yeah. My girl."

A broad hand swallowed my lower stomach, lips landing at my neck. Grim kissed slow, languid, punctuating with a bite or a deep, hollow suck beneath my ear.

My eyelids fluttered, trying to focus as the casket descended.

A hand brushed against my spine and Grim tugged his zipper down. He bunched my dress around my hips.

"What did I say about wearing underwear?" he growled, palming the lace at my pussy. Before I could respond, he stretched them to the side, and I felt the heat of his thick head edging me open.

I swallowed air, grasping the headstone of some old, deceased ancestor. It smelled like damp earth and sweetly rotting leaves.

"You get your wish." Grim slid an inch deeper,

stretching me wide in a delirious ache. "I'll fuck you until you die."

Should I fuck you until you die? Feel your cunt squeeze me until your life drains around my cock?

His words spun me back to the body at my feet, to the night that changed everything.

This was why Grim was so addicting. Death wasn't necessarily what I craved, but total surrender. Letting him do anything he wanted with me, and knowing he would only do what *I* needed.

He slammed his cock the rest of the way inside me. It was thick and hard and I couldn't breathe from the fullness. The pain of it melted into a jagged, cutting pleasure.

"Didn't know a dead girl could have such a perfect pussy." He thrust hard and rough, words scraping against my flesh.

"It would be so easy to kill you." Grim's hand closed around my throat, slightly bruising. "*Fuck.* You're so fucking wet. This get you off? You want me to kill you?" His lips were hot on my cheek, moving jagged against mine with each thrust.

I lost myself to the feeling of being completely vulnerable, split on his cock, while he drove into me, punishing and deep. Suicide had been a way to control the uncontrollable. This? This was surrendering control, letting Grim have it.

"Kill me," I breathed. "Fuck me. Whatever you want."

His head fell to my neck on a groan, licking and biting his mark. "So fucked up. So perfect. Fucking made for me."

His pace picked up, driving hard and cruel. I shook with the force of him, gripping the headstone for dear life. The stone was rough beneath my fingertips, stabilizing me as Grim punished me with his cock. I was totally at his mercy. And that realization had my eyes rolling back.

No sooner had my eyes closed than Grim barked, "Open them. Watch your funeral."

My eyes popped open, my casket nearly in the ground. Grim hammered into me as *Gemma Crowne, America's Princess* was laid to rest. He whispered hot things. Unholy things.

Such a good girl, letting me kill her.

Even when you're dead, this pussy is mine.

Die on my cock.

It was so fucked up. So wrong. Something about the unholy marriage of sex and death had me panting. I scraped at the headstone, fingers abrading.

"Be quiet when you come." Grim slid the hand at my neck up, spanning my jaw and mouth. "Dead girls don't speak."

His other hand gripped my neck while he pressed his thumb between my teeth, holding my tongue down. Split on his cock, my neck in his hand, hand in my mouth, I was completely filled up. I couldn't move, at Grim's mercy as he slammed into me and my orgasm built to painful heights.

He bit my neck and I fell apart.

I came as the casket disappeared into the ground. Sharp, jagged pleasure rolled through my body in waves. I felt it everywhere. From the tips of my fingers, to tingling between my teeth, to the muscles stretched thin in my calves.

Grim held me through it all, whispering coaxing, dirty words against my flesh. When it was over, when I was nothing but a spent, panting mess, he still held me. He kissed my neck, slow and gentle. Pulled my head back to lick away the tears.

Bringing me back to earth.

Grim slowly disentangled. Slid out of all parts of me—my mouth, my neck, my pussy. He held me against his body so I didn't fall to a puddle on the earth. His palm came between my thighs, and I jolted at the sensation. *Too sensitive.*

His free arm bolted around my waist, keeping me pinned as he massaged my pussy, pushing the come back up inside me.

He removed his hand and spun me around, back pressed against the headstone. He fucked his finger into my mouth, bruising the back of my throat, letting me taste him and me together.

"Good girl," he said, voice warm and pleased.

He slowly removed his finger, dragging it along my tongue. A little bit of spit or come or maybe both dripped down the corner of my mouth. Grim licked it up, tongue slow and hot.

My thighs clenched.

He pulled back, caging my head in his hands, and took a deep, unsteady breath.

"*Mi locura.*"

He crushed his lips against mine. No tongue, just pure pressure, and over too quickly. Then he righted my dress, tugged the fabric down. When he finished, I was still reeling. My brain short-circuiting.

Grim held one hand on my lower back, keeping me upright. A small smile quirking his lips, like he knew.

He dragged his knuckles gently along my jaw. "Ready to go home?"

Home.

I glanced over his shoulder, taking a last look at the place I'd called home for the first two decades of my life. Cobblestone paths, wrought iron gate, black shingles at odds with the rest of Crowne Point's nautical blue. A castle built for a princess, not a daughter.

This was where America's Princess was conceived, every piece of her carefully crafted to be perfect for her prince. Where my friends dreamed about Prince Charming, where my mother put all her hopes and dreams on finding him.

Prince Charming showed up at the end of the princess's story, taking glory for her salvation. Grim wasn't and would never be my prince; he was my reaper. He walked with me through hell and carried me out of the darkness.

I nodded at Grim, and he wrapped my hand in his, dragging me out of the cemetery to my real home. His tattooed hand dwarfed mine, strength that he used to break me and put me back together.

I rubbed my thumb along the tattoos on his knuckles. He shot me a look, dragging me closer to him as we walked toward home.

I was never meant to fall in love with Prince Charming.

My soul always belonged to the Reaper.

EPILOGUE

GEMMA

Crowne Point whizzed by in a watercolor of blue and white as we headed to my goddaughter's christening in New York. Winter had given way to a bright, blustery spring with cold blue skies.

I bit my nail, trying to expunge the feeling I'd woken up with this morning. Like the blood in my body was too heavy for my heart. Like a fog had fallen, dulling the world's colors. Like living was too much effort—

Grim grabbed my hand, pulling it into his lap as he drove with the other hand.

"Give it to me, *mi locura*," he said. "Let me feel it."

Like I'd said before, Grim's perfect dick didn't heal my broken soul. Even in my happily ever after, there were still days when gravity felt too heavy.

The difference now was Grim.

I scythed my nails into his skin.

He hissed, nostrils flaring. "Good girl."

By the time we got to the church, most of the heaviness had dissipated. Grim parked next to the Gothic cathedral, and I rubbed my thumb over his wrist, where crescent-shaped marks had reddened. Bloody. I still felt bad, even if he said he wanted it. This was my pain. I was supposed to deal with it. Not force it on him.

As if seeing the words in my head, Grim snaked his hand around my neck, yanking me into a brutal kiss.

"Thank you," he said, words heating my lips.

Grim got out of the car and opened my door. Together we stepped out into a cloudless cornflower blue sky. My family was waiting on the church steps. When they saw us, conversation stopped dead in the tracks.

"Gemma!" Story spotted me and waved me over.

Story wore a satin, bottle green cocktail dress that complemented her brown sugar skin, her curly hair glowing in the sun. My brother held their child as the steepled roof behind them seemed to jut miles into the clouds. Their daughter, Sonnet, donned the white christening gown that had been in our family for generations. Hand-sewn Chantilly lace cascaded all the way down to the steps, and a little bonnet covered her carob-colored hair.

Hand in hand, Grim and I headed up the steps.

"I hear you're the newest Crowne to bring shame upon the family," my sister, Abby, said as we arrived. Her red-brown eyes glimmered with humor.

"Is that off the rack?" I asked, egging her on.

Abigail smiled. "I got it on sale."

"Ew," I said. "You would."

But we smiled.

Even her husband, Theo, looked good. I was so used to him with bloody knuckles and dark, angry eyes. With an air like he was a second away from snapping and breaking your nose. And yeah, he still had that air, but his red lips tilted up as he held their son in his arms.

His tie was a little askew over his white shirt, but it worked.

"For real, sister, I'm happy for you," Abby said. "Mom is happy, too, in her own way." Over Abigail's shoulder, I found my mother standing with folded arms. She was dressed for a funeral, not a christening. A black, wide-brimmed hat on her head and black sunglasses.

"Maybe," I said.

She *had* kept my secret.

"Ready?" Story asked, holding Sonnet out to me. Sonnet peered up at me with big doe eyes, a mix of Story's mossy green and my brother's deep Atlantic blue.

"How are you going to explain to her that her godmother is dead?" I asked, eyes still on Sonnet.

"You can explain it," Gray said. "When you come to visit every month."

The ceremony was short and quick. Afterward, I exchanged hugs with my family—well, everyone but Mom—and promised to visit soon. As Grim and I walked to the car, I glanced back at them, and something warm and surreal overcame me. Everyone got a happily ever after. Even me, in my own way.

On the drive back we didn't talk much. Grim held my hand in his, stroking the bare skin. I was excited to get home. It was Tuesday night, and Raze always made tacos while Lock insisted on playing board games.

Zabby had since adopted me as her sister. She'd said she was so excited to have one, since she'd grown up with boys. She couldn't wait to paint each other's nails and gossip and watch rom-coms—things that sisters did.

I thought of my own sordid relationship with Abigail. Cutting each other's hair, finding fresh skin to stab.

Yeah, I'd told her. Because that *was* the kind of sister I was going to be.

When we got back to the compound, there was no smell of tacos, and we could hear yelling from the garage. Grim exchanged a look with me and gently pushed me behind him. As we rose up the steps, the shouting became clearer.

"Do you know who I am!" I stopped short at the voice. Because that was a woman's voice, and it didn't sound like Zabby.

Ignoring Grim's obvious attempt to shield me, I ran past him and pushed through the door.

"Blaire?" I said, stunned.

Blaire was in the living room, tied to a chair, glaring up at Raze, who towered over her. Wraith sat on the couch, reading as always. Lock tried to defuse the situation, a hand on Raze's shoulder.

"Gemma?" Blaire's gaze found mine. "I thought you fucking died. I went to your funeral."

"I know," I said wryly. "I saw the selfies."

"But you've, what, been here? Getting gangbanged by the Horsemen?"

"My Horseman doesn't share," I said. As if to emphasize, Grim appeared, wrapping a hand around my waist, tugging me closer.

Her mouth fell open. *"Your* Horseman?"

"What's going on?" I turned to Raze. "Why is she here?"

"She knows," he growled, not looking at me.

Blaire glared at him with familiarity.

"Seriously?" I said. "First Wraith and now you? Does every Horseman have a hard-on for my friends?"

"Wraith?" Lock asked. "What do you mean *Wraith*?"

Wraith looked up from reading, shooting me a death glare.

"Uh... How long is she going to be here?" I asked, changing the subject.

"Who knows." Lock rubbed his forehead. "This is what we do now, apparently. Kidnap socialites."

Grim went and dragged Raze away from Blaire. They exchanged muted whispers by the window. Raze seemed about ready to punch a wall. Then Grim exhaled, coming back to me.

"I need to know if she's staying for dinner," Lock said. "Raze was too busy kidnapping another famous girl to buy shells. Oh, do you play Settlers of Catan?" He turned the question to Blaire.

"She's staying," Raze gritted. "She doesn't need dinner."

In response, Blaire spat at Raze's feet.

Grim came back to me, ushering me toward the stairs. "What's going on? I can't just leave her."

"He won't hurt her."

I wasn't concerned about that. I knew them well enough to know they didn't hurt people indiscriminately, and never women. Blaire had a mean streak. Her dad was a card-carrying Republican—she knew how to use a gun.

"She stole something of his. He won't tell me what."

I looked over my shoulder at Blaire. What could she have possibly stolen? And how did she get access? Lock held up a different board game, asking if she preferred this more. Blaire glared.

"He's not letting her go until she returns it—and until he can be certain she won't spill the beans about you," he added with bitterness. He continued talking as we went up the stairs and back to our room. "It was fucking stupid bringing her. He wasn't thinking. Can't exactly get mad at it, though... You know, pot and kettle."

Grim shut the door.

His features softened and he stepped to me, cradling my face with his palms. I'll never get over his touch, like he couldn't decide between breaking me and putting me back together. People always wanted me because I was *Gemma Crowne*. Once the novelty wore off, so did their affection.

Every day Grim looked at me like he couldn't believe I was still here.

"So she's, what...staying here?" I asked.

Grim gestured for me to turn around. When I did, his fingers found the buttons of my dress, undoing them slowly, one by one, as he spoke.

"Maybe you'll get a friend from your world." Grim slid his palm along the now open dress, hand brushing bare flesh.

"*This* is my world," I said, spinning around to find a small smile tugging one side of Grim's lips. He said it to rile me up.

Well...it worked.

His palms cradled my face. "Yeah, Rich Girl, it is." He crushed his mouth against mine, kissing me into our forever.

THE END

AUTHOR NOTE

I have so many people to thank for this story. If you subbed to my newsletter, you may already know a bit about why it took me so long to finish *Savage Sanctuary* (six years!).

I never liked to talk about how sick I was, because writing was where I could pretend I was normal. When I was thirteen, I was diagnosed with POTS (Postural Orthostatic Tachycardia Syndrome). At fifteen, epilepsy. At nineteen, Chronic Fatigue Syndrome and Fibromyalgia. Over the years I've also added endometriosis and some fun mental illnesses, like Bipolar, Borderline, and ADHD.

Savage Sanctuary took a long time to finish because for the first time in my life, I focused entirely on healing. I started writing it when I was deeply suicidal. As I started to heal, going back into the world was deeply triggering.

For the last five years (I can't believe it's been so long) all of my focus has gone into healing. I am now off all of my medicine, my resting heart rate is lower than 80 for the first time in like...ever, I'm seizure free without medicine, and stable.

And *so* excited to bring you more stories.

So...what's next for Crowne Point?

As you can probably tell by the ending, I have much more I plan to do in Crowne Point, but I need a little break. I've spent been almost a decade in this world! I'm looking forward to bringing you something new, and will definitely *not* take another six years.

ACKNOWLEDGMENTS

I have so many people to thank for this story. It has been six years, so much has changed with the Bookworld! And still, it feels beautifully full circle to finish Gremma as I step into a happier and healthy phase.

Thank you to the readers who stuck by me for the six years I was gone, the ones who reached out asking for Grim and Gemma's story, those wondering if I was alright. You will never know how much those messages meant to me. How they anchored me.

Thank you to all the new readers taking a chance on me. I can't wait to bring you more stories!

Thank you Becca, for being the constant reminder that my writing was worth something and for being the best friend I could ever want.

Thank you to my editor James, for being there six years later, and for humoring my constant deadline changes. And, in the same vein, thank you Rumi, for proofing this book beautifully, and also dealing with my deadline changes.

Thank you House of Hearts and The Smuthood for helping me navigate the new bookish world!

Thank you authors who responded when I reached out, and those who gave me advice.

And of course thank you to my family, who are a constant support and rock.

Also very grateful to Ali Hazelwood, Jacob Tierney, and

Rachel Reid who, despite having never met me, still saved me with their stories.

I was so tempted to paste every blogger into this, but I feel like that's doxing, so please just know if you messaged me, if you liked a post, if you DM me, I know your name. I'm so grateful.

Thank you, thank you, *thank you*.

I'm eternally grateful for your support. Seriously, see you in the next life where I will still be showering you with gratitude.

BOOKS BY MARY CATHERINE GEBHARD

NEW ADULT

Crowne Point Universe

Crowne Point Box Set (Books 1-4)

Heartless Hero (Abigail + Theo)

Stolen Soulmate (Grayson + Story)

Forbidden Fate (Grayson + Story)

Destroyed Destiny (Grayson + Story)

Savage Sanctuary (Gemma + Grim)

DARK ROMANCE

The Hate Story Duet

Beast: A Hate Story, The Beginning

Beauty: A Hate Story, The End

YOUNG ADULT

Patchwork House

Skater Boy (Patchwork House #1)

www.ingramcontent.com/pod-product-compliance
Lightning Source LLC
Chambersburg PA
CBHW061308170626
46817CB00001B/109